THE HIGH-HEELED GARDENER

Debbie Bourne

Eco Romance Series Book 1

MALCHIK
MEDIA

Published by
Malchik Media
www.richardlynttonbooks.com

Print ISBN: 979-8-9860794-9-3

Cover design and illustrations by Elisabetta Giordana
Illustrations by Deborah Jackson-Brown

For further adventures in the Eco Romance Series:
Book 2: *The High-Heeled Eco-Worrier*
www.amazon.com/gp/product/B0C2XL2V41?

For USA and UK book enquires:
richard@richardlynttonbooks.com

The High-Heeled Gardener
A year of digging dangerously…

'LOTTIE'

POT LUCK MAYPOLE
GIVE PEAS A CHANCE!
JACK N' THE BEANSTALK
MISSING A...
Strawberries
mint
cucumber
Pimms Patch
LAVENDER
LEMON THYME
BATH TIME
DORA'S PARSLEY TEA
Chin Chin...
DANGLING A...
CARROTS & CHIVES
GREAT PALS
THE GREEN ROOM
THE CHIPPIE
POTATOES
TOMATOES
MUSHY PEAS
ONIONS
grow bag
FENDI
TOBY'S
JUICY PLUMS
SPUD U LIKE
Adam's "OTHER" APPLE
HEDGEHOG HILTON

Contents

July

August

AUTUMN

September

October

Pro-log
The plot thickens ...

Well, let's face it, the plot couldn't get any thicker, I think, staring out of my window at the derelict field beyond my patio garden. It's a no-man's land that separates my home from the housing estate beyond. I've ventured out into the tangled thicket just once and was horrified to stumble upon old gents' trousers buckled with barbed wire, along with a rusted bathtub, corroded saucepans and all manner of discarded 'used' plastic items. As creatures I hardly dared imagine scampered beneath my Jimmy Choo-encased feet, I quickly retreated indoors.

So now I'm surveying a physical mess that somehow reflects my emotional woes. Suddenly there's a knock on my front door. I shake off my reverie and head for it.

'Hi. The name's Knight. Toby Knight.'

My caller goes on to explain how he's our local councillor and 'sustainability lead' for Camden Council. But at first, I can hardly take it in. He's movie-star gorgeous. He smiles and brushes a hand through his golden hair. 'I'm here to talk to the residents on your block, and the housing estate opposite, about turning the unused land that connects your two properties into a community allotment. 'Are you a keen food grower?'

'Er, well, I'm a fashion designer, really. Although I'm in between jobs at the mo.' I realise I'm stumbling over my words as I take in the low-slung jeans clinging to his long legs, not to mention the black boxer shorts cheekily peeping out over the top. The look is more Brad Pitt than mud pit.

#NTS: Did he really say he was a council officer? Must sign up for council newsletter.

'Do come in and have a cuppa,' I stutter. 'Green tea, of course. Funnily enough, I was only just thinking about that space, and er … imagining its potential. A community allotment sounds very interesting.'

I fail to add how the only time I had green fingers was when painting my nails this season's shade of teal.

'Great, I'm looking forwards to taking this further,' he smiles.

I blush when I note how his hazel eyes are scanning my body. How stupid of me to have bundled it into my son's old, school hoodie. Far too tight!

Councillor Knight offers me his strong hand, and I lead the way indoors.

THE CHARACTERS ...

Deborah - The High-Heeled Gardener.
Nat - Deborah's NBF.
Pete - Nat's hubby
Toby - our hero, or is he? Camden Councillor.
Grace - Toby's long-suffering girlfriend. Or is she?
Hen - actor. Legs as long as string beans.
Mr Parkeeper - Ill-tempered neighbour.
Ben-G-bard -15-year-old Shakespearean exponent.
Pot laureate.
Delia Arundel - RHS Benefactor.
Bernie - Camden Transitioner.
Dougie - National Association of Allotment Gardeners.
Dora the Explorer - Septuagenarian Zimmer digger.
Poor little Sammi (PLS) - Nat's grandson.
Dora's fellow explorer
Gaia - Dire Gire (DG) Astronomical gardener.
Jasper - DG's freegan boyfriend.
Phoebe, Genevieve, Fliff, Percy -
Deborah's b.f.s. and dog.
Cathal - Irish forager – Delicious autumnal delight!
Di - Opera singer from no.11.
Lady Olivia - Iconic '60s actress/thespian
poultry collector.
Hennesse & Williams - Lady's Olly's show birds.

John Innes - Not the actor from *Are You Being Served?*
Albert Camus - Philosopher/founder member
of Absurdists.
Robert Plant - Rock star.
Hilary Benn - Cabinet maker (or is it member?)
The Great Tit - Alan Titchmarsh.
Tikka & Marsala - Canine gardeners.
Tom Cat Soya - DG's new cat.
Che Guevara and Southwark's guerrilla gardeners.
Crotch-grabbing Colin & wassailers.
Hampstead scouts including tight-shorted
16-year-old Nick.
Syd and his moustache. Beekeeper.
Sweet Cicely and Chelsea flower show ladies.
Sex-sax angel Alexandre - Parisian sax player.
Harry, Dixon (of dock leaf green)
and fellow foragers.
Stan and his finest, Buzzy bee Aldrin
and other beekeepers.
The Minge petals.

Not forgetting, James and Stu –
Deborah's son and husbondage.
A host of annual and perennial veg
and self-seeders, wood nymphos, sheogs
and unseen creatures of the night.

WINTER
(or is this season autumn?)
November

Chapter 1
Need your roots doing?

One month, sixty-seven cups of green tea later …

The big dig. It's the day of our hoedown. I'm knee-deep in mud with Toby and other local do-gooders from a local eco group, who've come to help clear our site.

It's been four hours of hacking at brambles, getting stung by nettles, and tugging at roots which clearly had no intention of shifting, unlike the length of rusty barbed wire which has tangled itself around my ankles. We've dug up stony, claggy, waterlogged soil, untouched since WW2 - our every endeavour scrutinized by a plump, bemused wood pigeon.

'It's gonna be great to have an allotment,' says Natalie, my new friend, a tenant from the estate.

'Yes, an eco garden is so on message,' I reply, trying to pull my stiletto heel out of the mire. Finally, Toby announces it's time for lunch. We retire to my kitchen to share the repast (vegetarian, of course) which I have proudly prepared.

'How deep do roots go?' I pour myself a large glass of Pinot Noir and address my question around the kitchen where all fifteen of us are sitting eating.

'Ah, the positive power of gravitropism,' Dougie, an older gentleman with a broad Scottish accent deliberates as he chomps upon a carrot stick. 'It all depends upon the temporal availability of nutrients and the physical properties of the soil.'

'Of course,' I nod in agreement.

#NTS: Gravit what?
I take a large swig and wonder why no one else is drinking wine.

'Whilst the above ground portion of plants is dormant during the winter,' Toby explains, 'roots, particularly when there is no competition from shoots and fruit, are capable of growing all year round.'

Tell me about it, I rifle my hand through my hair. 'Why don't we just spray them with some kind of herbicide,' I suggest, certain to impress him with my newly acquired horticultural knowledge.'

'Herbicide?' Toby's eyes narrow.

'Well, er, an organic one, of course.' I say the first word that comes to mind. Organic always seems to be the right word to extricate oneself from any social faux pas these days. I lift a bottle of balsamic vinegar to sprinkle on my salad.

'Oh, I see, it's a joke, Deborah,' Toby laughs, 'vinegar-organic herbicide, very funny!'

#NTS: Must start writing eco diary 'to-do' list tonight. Buy a nice Smythson green leather notebook to write it in. Call it my little green book. Green is my new black. First topic – research relationship between vinegar and organic herbicide.

'After all, organic only means finding an environmentally friendly way of cultivating the land,' a man called Bernie explains as he pulls off his beanie hat sporting a Greenpeace logo to reveal a bald head save for a little red plait at the back. 'It's about working *with*, rather than *against*, nature.'

'Keeping the garden chemical free will also help attract wildlife,' adds a woman called Henrietta. 'Do call me Hen,' she says as she tells us she's a thespian.

#NTS: Judging from the way Toby is staring at Hen's glorious Helena Bonham Carter-esque mane of wild russet hair, her doleful eyes, and legs as long as green beans, I'd say that's not all the attracting that's going on around here!

'And, of course, you must get compost that is peat-free,' said Toby. His hazel eyes stare disarmingly into mine.

'No, my old man's not yet left me!' Natalie roars with laughter, as she tells the room her hubby is called Pete.

Toby takes my hand. 'After all, a peat bog takes ten thousand years to form, and we must all help save our threatened habitats.'

'Of course.' I lift Toby's bowl and ladle into it another helping of my homemade lentil soup which I was up half the night making. Who knew dried lentils can be soaked in advance?

'Oh, what a shame, it's about to rain. Shall we carry on tomorrow?' I look out of the window at the murky sky, dreaming instead of fading into an afternoon-matineed-red-wine-tinged sunset with the real Brad Pitt.

'Of course not, Deborah.' Toby shakes his angel-like waves of golden hair. 'A kitchen garden is not just about a glut of *strawbs* in summer, but the poetry of winter. Gardening is where we connect with all the seasons, the natural rhythms of nature.'

'Well said,' adds Bernie. 'A garden should have humanity and soul.'

'Top soul you mean!'

Realising that I'm the only one laughing at Natalie's joke, I quickly open my umbrella (why am I the only one using one?) and follow everyone outside.

'Is your wooden handle FSC-approved?' Dougie glares at my brolly with its cute illustrations of wellie boots.

'It was approved in this month's *Vogue*,' I beam. 'Because I'm a fashion designer, I was able to skip the waiting list to get this from Harvey Nics—'

'Attention everyone,' interrupts Bernie, lifting his notepad. 'It's time to set the ground rules.'

The ground certainly does rule. I stretch out my aching back and reluctantly pick up my shovel.

Bernie continues, 'We do have a twenty-metre stretch of land to clear by the end of today.'

'I always say that a garden is never done.' Hen wistfully shakes her perfect mane of apparently root-free auburn hair. 'In gardening, there are no full stops.'

I can't help thinking that at this point, a nice little comma would do.

'It's about being a witness to the world around us.' Toby places his arm around my waist. 'It's about seeing the world with enough detail to notice the smallest changes.'

Talking of depth, I've just dug up an old bath filled with rancid, green water. There are strange-looking insects floating on top, clearly not intent on improving their backstroke.

'Well found, Deborah, this can be our wildlife tank.'

I close my eyes, dreaming of a lavender bath, Toby ladling lashings of bubbles onto my—

'After all, water is the key element in a wildlife garden to attract dragonflies, newts and birds.'

'But remember, never fill it with tap water,' Dougie explains. 'Tap water contains too many additives and chlorine.'

I can't help but wonder how tap water is good enough for me but not my neighbourhood frog.

'We must float leaves in it to provide cover for animals that are mating and buy duckweed, skunk cabbage …'

'Skunk what?' I shudder.

'Then we'll float logs to help small mammals to get in and out, and pile logs to provide shelter for frogs to hibernate. Then a hedgehog home.'

'Ugh,' I scream, my attention drawn away from the five-star Hiltonesque hedgehog hotel. 'Something slimy has just climbed into my boot.'

'It's only a poor darling snail,' declares Hen.

A memory of escargots dripping in garlic butter sampled in Provence last summer suddenly seems less than appealing.

Three hours, thirty sacks piled with bricks and stones, one washing machine, two kettles, a dog lead, TV aerial, ancient pottery, and several of Dougie's wildlife sermons on the mount of rubble later, Toby blessedly calls it a day.

LITTLE GREEN BOOK

11:00 pm. Soaking in third lavender bath of night! Writing first entry in new eco book, which Amazon delivered within an hour. Henceforth to be called: Little Green Book.
#NTS: Must remember to hide packaging. Have researched gardening diaries. Content should be written in weekly 'to-do' sections: Sowing. Cultivation. Propagation. Harvest.

***Sewing** - lining back into Burberry raincoat which barbed wire ripped today.*
***Cultivation** - Researching how to clean mud stains from white settee.*
FSC: Forestry Stewardship Council. Organisation for responsible management of world's forests. In charge of protecting timber from being turned into items like ... my brolly's rainforest wooden handle.
Organic herbicide: Vinegar is one! It's the acetic acid in vinegar which gives it the power to kill weeds.
Peat: About 90% of peat bog habitats have been lost in the UK over the last century ... much of it used in garden compost. Peat bogs absorb and store carbon dioxide from the atmosphere.

Harvest: Half an hour of digging burns up 200 calories.

Hurrah! Scoff down second Lion Bar and submerge myself in bubbles.

Chapter 2
Habitat

Not just a nice furniture store, but a place where creatures live. Gardens provide habitats for all manner of species.

Toby has come over for a meeting to design our site. Natalie has proved a bit of a whiz kid with a drill. She works at a local tool hire shop. *Scrapheap Challenge* is her favourite TV programme. Natalie continues to screw together two builder's palettes she found in a skip to create the fencing for our wildlife centre. In it, we plan to welcome all creatures, both the beautiful and not-so! There will be a shelter for toads and hedgehogs who eat slugs and escargots, species who eat the pests which would otherwise demolish our crop. Plus, there will be a bird feeding centre with bat boxes.

'Just think, Deborah, under your feet lives a whole unknown world of small creatures.' Toby takes my hand and places it on the ground.

"Actually, I'd rather not." I retrieve my hand on the pretence of placing a log on the pile.

'We should also grow a hedge as it can provide a suitable micro-climate for—'
'My Pete's been reading up on those hedge funds.' Natalie turns off her power drill. 'Says he's going to get me one.'

I politely laugh, unsure whether Natalie is telling a joke, and add, 'We could design a hedge in a formal Italianate style with representational forms, which—'

Natalie interjects. 'Well, I like the idea of the garden becoming my new outside living room. I'll bring our old sofas out. We could nail paintings to the fences. Plus, look what I've got us.' She opens up a LIDL carrier bag and lifts out a garden gnome. She places it on a pile of wood. 'Gnome sweet gnome!' She roars with laughter.

I stare at the grotesque gnome with its pointy red hat, rotund cheeks, neon green body. It seems that Natalie and I have *different* creative ideas.

'Anyway ladies,' Toby winks at me, 'shall we walk around and start to plan what else should go where?'

We follow him around the plot. It still looks like a desecrated building site despite the four days of hard labour that we have all put in. Bags of rubble and debris are piled high in one corner. Mounds of barren soil, dead branches, rolls of rusty wire, and bent nails are sticking out of Natalie's makeshift wildlife centre, now piled with old wood. I sigh. A bountiful kitchen garden seems as distant a dream as transporting endless bags of rubble to the local recycling centre, our current nightmare. Unless …

I am suddenly seized by a brilliant idea. 'Why don't we get a TV makeover programme to design and film our site? A friend of mine, Fliff, is a producer for the show *Grand Designs*.'

'Oh God no.' Toby's small but perfectly formed laughter lines crinkle up at my suggestion. 'It would be like creating a horticultural shopping mall. Just add bird song Muzak.' Then Toby whispers in my ear. 'This project should be our own private haven.'

'I really fancy that TV presenter Kevin McCloud,' adds Natalie, as my face turns a brighter shade of scarlet than her tracksuit.

'Hey guys, look at this.' Pete, Natalie's hubby, strolls onto the site. He's carrying a pine dresser. He places it down beside a fence. 'I also found this.' He lifts up a wooden oar.

'They're not the 'oars I'm used to pullin'!' Natalie pinches Pete's bum. 'Only joking babe!'

They roar with laughter.
Oars. Pine dresser. And our very own garden gnome. I'm dreading what will come next. Then Toby takes my arm.

'The first thing you need to decide is what is going to grow where,' he says as we stroll on like two peas in a delectable pod. 'Fruit and veg are traditionally grown in rows, but perhaps tonight you could all sketch out the space available and jot down your ideas. The first thing we can plant is onions and garlic, later this month.'

I excitedly race on. 'I read in *Vanity Fair* that you should plan your menu before starting to plant. How about a Pimms patch laden with cucumber, mint, and strawberries? An asparagus bed for *feuilletes*? Lashings of juicy berries for Eton mess. I'd love lots of edible flowers for salad dishes. They are soo on trend … ' I pause, now podless, to realise that Toby has walked over to the other end of the site. 'It's er … obviously all got to be seasonal.' I rush after him.

#NTS: Must swot up on what's in season and when.

'The only seasons I've ever taken notice of are on a pizza!' chuckles Natalie. 'Get the joke, four seasons pizza? Talking of which, I think one bed should be in the shape of a pizza. We could grow tomatoes, basil, peppers.' She pokes a bamboo stick into the ground and sketches out a large round circular-shaped bed, adding lines for the pizza segments.

'How about growing nettles for homegrown beer?' suggests Pete.

'I think practically you are more likely to have lots of green vegetables for soup,' Toby's impatience is starting to show through his fixed smile. 'Whilst it's good to be ambitious, I think you are best to start off with a simple grid: Potatoes in one patch, root veg in another. An area for peas, beans and the cabbage family, with herbs and salad crops, fruit bushes and trees around the perimeter. Plus a fig tree in a pot.'

I close my eyes. It's as if I am laying under that fig tree with Toby, our ankles tickled by rustling wildflowers, his ruby ripe lips as juicy as the fruit on the tree dangling their promise of—

'Also you must be aware not to sow too much at one time, or you will get a glut,' adds Toby. 'Crops will come to maturity at the same time. Also, consider the summer holidays. The key is to sow little and often ...'

'That's what me and Pete like to do,' winks Natalie.

Toby crouches down and scoops up a handful of soil. 'The beauty of homegrown veg is that by sowing seeds and getting your hands dirty, you are relating to the soil; to plants and nature, whatever the weather.' He pauses to roll the soil around in his hand. 'You are connected to the real production of food as opposed to fruit and veg bought in supermarkets, which lose their nutrients in processing, as well as harming the environment. Homegrown is all about connecting with the real cycle of what we eat. But basically, it comes down to this.'

I'm captivated by his every word as he stands up to take a breath.
He continues. 'We've now cleared and dug over the land. We'll add compost, throw in some seeds ... and hey presto, it will all start to happen.'

I feel ashamed as I listen to Toby. All my pretentious talk of Pimms and *feuilletes*. Perhaps there is something more in all of this. I look up at the sky with its impenetrable sheet of grey. I stare at the grey which on closer reflection is filled with flecks of pink, yellow and silver. A streak of cobalt blue as nighttime approaches. Even Natalie's ghastly gnome seems to wink at me.

I smile and take off my kid gloves. From now on it's heavy-duty rubber ones, all the way.

LITTLE GREEN BOOK

Sewing: *Seeds of ideas for garden layout by flicking through* Harper's Mag.
Cultivation: *Husbondage Stu called. (Have I forgotten to mention I have a husband?) He's having to do another all-nighter at the office. That's the second time this week.*

BF, Fliff, also called to cancel the girls' night out at Momo. Other BF, Phoebe, texted to say she's going to a big fashion party and can't get me on the guest list. The fashion world seems to be moving on without me after my twenty years in the industry. I've only been without a fashion design job for nine months, three days and two hours … not that I'm counting.

Oh well, gardening is my new going out. And garden design could be a new creative passion.

I lift up Harper's Mag. *Flip to the new gardening section at the back. It's very cutting (h) edge. Ha!*

Chapter 3
Keep the home fires burning

It's bonfire night. Have just returned from a spectacular fireworks display on Primrose Hill to find a bonfire burning brightly on our allotment. Natalie and Pete have decided it's taking too long to finish clearing our site so are burning everything in an old metal dustbin.

'But what will Toby say about the pollutants released into the air?' I ask in panic-stricken voice.

'Oh, sit down, Deb, and have a hot dog.' Nat (as she's now told me to call her) pulls me down onto one of our new log round seats which she has built around our brick barbie.

I pour ketchup on the bun Nat hands me and watch the sparks of my new green credentials flare up on the barbie. Tempted as I am to protest, I'm simply more tempted by the delicious smell of sizzling sausages coated in a woody aroma.

'We found a load of wild rosemary growing behind here.' Nat points to a hardy little rosemary bush. Its evergreen spiky leaves are tinged with a silver firelight glow. It's a resilient little survivor amongst all the debris. 'We've placed a clump of rosemary amongst the wood chips and charcoal inside the barbie. Doesn't it smell beautiful?' She smiles.

I close my eyes, breathe in the oakey sweet fragrance, and bite into the delicious hot dog.

Nat races on. 'Talking of chips, Pete wants to create a fish and chips patch, without the fish of course! We will grow peas, toms, onions, potatoes, and parsley for parsley sauce.'

A memory of boarding school dinners congealed in packet parsley sauce as grey as the fish the sauce failed to conceal flashes before me.

'We're gonna call it the chippie!' explains Nat. 'It's going to be designed in four long oblong strips, so from an aerial point of view, the bed look like chips and fries.'

Pete adds, 'My Nat's got such wicked ideas!'

'And listen to this,' Nat continues, 'we're gonna pickle our own onions, make mushy peas, homemade tomato ketchup for our chips. Thought I'd pop by yours tomorrow, Deb, and borrow some of that posh vinegar in your cupboard. We can have a practice run at making the pickled onions …'

My Borgo del Balsamico, Mio Dio community bonhomie is one thing, but procurement of my £50, ten-year-old artisan balsamic from Modena is another. It's so good that Italians sip it as an after-dinner digestif.

And another worrying thought. Just how does Nat know the contents of my kitchen cupboard?

Nat races on. 'If you're around, we could make it together?'

'We're actually going to Oxford for the day.' I quickly change the subject. 'By the way, guys, *grazie tanto* for taking the bags of rubble to the recycling centre. I was planning to help later this week.'

'No need, Deb. Pete dumped them on Primrose Hill late last night, in-between a pile of boxes.' Nat winks at Pete. 'Good bonfire on the hill was it tonight?'

'Yeah, those rockets probably had a bit more bang to them than planned.' Pete leans forward to whisper in my ear. 'Best keep it our little secret, or there's going to be a few more fireworks going off around here!'

Our little secret? I hear how I, fashion designer, urban organic horticulturalist, am now, by implication, turned criminal.

'But isn't there a law against dumping and—?'

Nat shoves another juicy piece of sausage into my mouth.

'Get that down you, Deb,' she laughs. 'Shall I pop by and pick up that vinegar, now?'

Chapter 4
Bill, Ben, and (not so little) Weed

Bill is the ill-tempered man who lives next door to Nat. No one is allowed to call him by his Christian name. It's Mr. Parker.

The kids call him Mr. Parkeeper because if anyone knocks a ball into his garden and dents a plant, he calls the council.

His picture-perfect garden is bordered by wire park fencing and bolted with a padlock and key. It's easier to cross the state lines of New Mexico into the US than it is to get into his garden.

The main problem with Mr. Parkeeper's garden is that no one ever goes in it, apart from him, and that's only to shoo off visiting birds.

Benjamin is the 15-year-old black kid who lives next door to him. 'I'm a rapper. You can call me Ben-G bard.' He tells me about his love of Shakespeare as he stubs his joint out in the onion and garlic plot I've been digging out all afternoon and am just about to plant.

I ignore Ben-G's action on the basis of a) not wanting to dent his enthusiasm; and b) secretly hoping he'll offer me a puff of the next one … clothes and accessory shopping so far having been my only drug of choice.

I continue to read the principles of sowing garlic as explained in my new kitchen garden bible.

'It says here to plant garlic cloves six inches apart,' I explain to Ben-G.

'That reefer was pure organic.' He lifts up a shovel. 'My man Reuben grew it on a bed of rabbit manure mixed with steamed bonemeal.'

'That's, er, great,' I continue. 'Now, we're going to plant a variety of garlic called "Solent Wight." Each week we must push any cloves back into the soil that the birds have pulled up.'

'The earthy flavour makes for great gear.' Ben-G looks up to the sky. 'Blow, blow, thou Winter wind.'

I put all thoughts of blow – in all its incarnations – to one side as Nat strolls out into the garden.

'Bet you didn't know that the slave builders of the pyramids in ancient Egypt received a portion of garlic a day for extra strength,' she laughs. 'I give Pete one each day!'

'Anyway, I'd like to help yon fair maidens with your garden.' Ben-G shoves several garlic cloves into the bed in a wonky line. 'I got some ideas.'

I turn round to face him, proud of how our eco garden is already starting to encourage residents of all ages …

Then Ben-G explains. 'I want to grow some good weed.'

Weeds. According to my bible, every garden has its own weeds. They are part of the character of the place. Ground elder, horsetail, bindweed. Some weeds are welcome. But not in Ben G's case, as Nat and I both agree. We can't see that going down too well with Dougie and the eco group.

Talking of weeds, Toby has told us we are to become weed vigilantes. Weeding will take up about twenty percent of our time tending veg as they rob crops of water and nutrients, and can harbour fungal diseases.

Fungal what?

'Some weeds such as dandelion, sorrel and chicory are edible,' I continue to read out loud. 'Others help control pests, like dandelions, which attract beneficial wasps. Deep-rooted weeds like pigweed and thistles mine the soil to help shallow-rooted plants. Weeds can also help us 'read' the soil, like sorrel which signifies acid soil ...'

'Well, we've got sodding bind weed,' interrupts Nat, ripping open a packet of onion seeds. 'Wonder if that's where the phrase 'get you in a bind' comes from?'

Ben-G reads the packet blurb. 'That's sic. These onion bulbs are called "Shakespeare." They are superb for overwintering and produce darker skin bulbs.'

Nat starts to sow the bulbs. 'It's possible to achieve an all-year-round supply of homegrown—'

'That's what I've been trying to tell you.' I ignore Ben-G's comment and speedily read on. 'The book says we can protect seedlings from weeds by hoeing or laying black plastic in between the rows. We can also use old carpet, which will have the benefit of allowing rainwater to percolate through to the soil.'

'Got any old shag pile you want to get rid of, Deb?' asks Nat. 'What about that nasty beige stuff in your hall?'

'But that's my new ivory worsted carpet from Liberties …' My ponderings on yarn weights are laid threadbare as there's a wet slobbering on my arm. Two dogs have come charging into the garden. One of them starts digging out our newly planted onion bulbs with its paws. The dogs proceed to chomp on them.

'Meet Tikka and Masala.' Nat bends down to stroke them.

'Whose dogs are they?' I wipe my sopping hand with an ivy leaf.

'Our new canine recruits from no.9,' Nat laughs as the dogs start to run riot, chased by Ben-G and Pete, who lift several of the carefully stacked logs from our hedgehog hotel and start to throw them around for the dogs to chase.

'Heel, boys, heel,' a voice of authority calls out, pausing the pandemonium. It's Toby. He strolls into the garden accompanied by a distinguished lady, who is sporting a Barbour raincoat and pearls.
'Meet Delia Arundel,' Toby smiles. 'Delia is from the RHS. She's kindly agreed to look around our garden today.'

Delia turns out to be far from the 'Right Haughty Sloane,' of Nat's far-from-whispered retort, but, in fact, a nice lady from the Royal Horticultural Society. Despite the fact that Tikka has started to sniff up her skirt, and Masala has started to dig up Ben-G bard's joint stub, Delia has come to offer us horticultural advice, and a grant of one thousand pounds

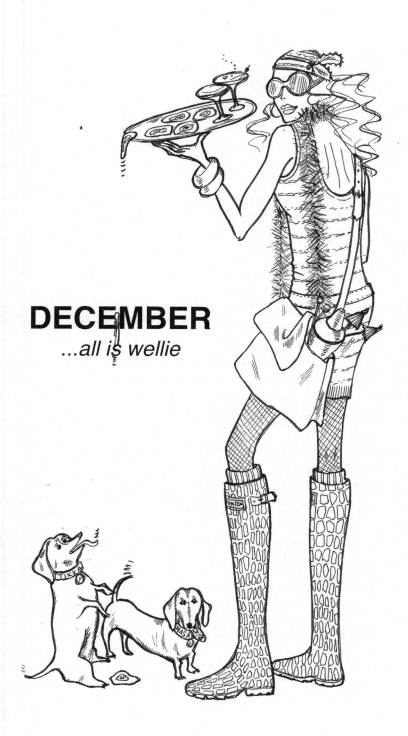

DECEMBER
...all is wellie

Chapter 5
Total rot.

Soil, like my increasingly chapped hands, needs nourishment.

Toby has told us that soil prep will be our most important task at this time of year before the growing season begins. To produce a good crop we need soil that's chock full of well-rotted organic matter, worms, beneficial bacteria and natural nutrients.

He has given us a compost bin to make compost. In six months' time, we will be able to add it to the soil as an improver. We are to put into it raw veg peel (if cooked it will attract rats) fruit, tea bags, coffee granules (fair trade of course). Mix with garden and kitchen paper waste, leave for six months until a rich, dark, crumbly, sweet-smelling substance appears. Bon appetito.

'If we are all here, shall we make a start?' Bernie from the local eco group looks around. He's clearly less than impressed with the small turnout of Nat, me and Pete to hear his lecture on soil. 'Any questions?'

I stare into a set of eyes as dark and foreboding as the sky as they glare at me through his eco warrior camouflage balaclava.

'Yes,' I ask, in an attempt to sound eager ... which couldn't be further from the truth. I point to the set of notes Bernie hands round. 'What is this John Innes no.2?'

'I think he lives at no.12,' says Pete.

'You don't think he was that actor in, "Are you being served?"' shrieks Nat. 'I loved that TV show.'

'John Innes is a range of loam-based composts.' Bernie's sigh of impatience is even audible through the wind which starts to howl around us. 'Loam is the most important ingredient in compost for plant nutrition.'

'You're talking total rot, Bernie!' Nat and Pete roar with laughter.

'Then, there is ericaceous,' Bernie continues.

'Eric who?'

'Ericaceous compost is a sterilised compost that is lime free.'

'I fancy a nice lime soda,' Nat licks her lips. 'Just add vodka.'

'As you know, there are many plants which won't grow in lime-based soil.' Bernie turns round to grimace at Nat. 'You have carried out a ph test haven't you?'

#NTS: pH tests. The only one I've carried out is the 'ph—oar' one in relation to Toby. I keep the thought to myself as I watch him stroll in.

'Oh yes, we did one of those pregnancy test looking things,' says Nat.

'So what phosphorous hydrogen level did you get?'

Bernie sighs. 'Are you alkaline or acid?'

'Neither Arthur nor Martha!' Nat laughs.

'Arthur who?' asks Pete.

'I think she means their soil is neutral, Bernie.' Toby winks at me, as he slowly caresses the mud in his hand. 'But this clearly is clay soil.'
I try to stop staring at his gooey hand and wonder how it would feel over my—

'We will sow green beans as a green manure to improve the soil.' Toby smiles at his hand, and then up at me. It's as if he knows the effect he's having on me. He continues, 'Then there's the question of humus …'

'That's what I had for lunch. I've got a sandwich left, would you like it?' I quickly root around in my new (vegan faux leather) bag for a hummus sarnie, making sure I don't give him the ham one I'm saving for later by mistake.

#NTS: Hummus and plants? I've heard some strange horticultural facts, but this one tops them all.

'Actually Deborah, the humus Bernie is referring to is the dark, organic material that forms in soil when plant and animal matter decay. And no thanks to the sarnie, I've had a rather naughty little lunch with Hen!'

'Anyway back to flocculation.' Bernie races on, allowing for no questions to be asked about humus or Hen.

'Floc what?' Nat roars with laughter.

'I do hope it's a mild winter,' I change the subject in an attempt to show Toby and Bernie how seriously I am taking this lecture, as opposed to dwelling on Toby and Hen's lunch—and how naughty it was.
'On the contrary,' Bernie looks aghast, 'we gardeners need a cold winter to kill off all the bugs and diseases that proliferate in the warmth. Wet warmth is the worst.'

I refrain from adding how a wet warmth with Toby actually sounds rather delectable.

'Warmth in Winter terms means when the night time temperature is above five degrees centigrade. It's a luxury for your average slug or fungal spore.'

My imagination closes down at the mention of fungal spores.

'Anyway, the more of nature we return to itself, the better.' Bernie rolls up his balaclava and strokes his bald head. 'I intend to get buried in a cardboard coffin with climbing beans and peas growing all over my decomposing …'

LITTLE GREEN BOOK

Cultivation: Must increase time spent in bed with Alan Titmarsh and Monty Don. Who says three's a crowd? From now on, bedtime reading is no longer to be Harry Potter, but garden potter.

Homemade compost: A nutritious recipe.

Serves: Lots of soil/plants/armies of microscopic creatures …
Layer cuttings of raw veg, fruit peel, egg shells, coffee granules, tea bags with layers of shredded newspaper, egg cartons, Bernie's red plait.

Mix well. Place lid on. Bake in horrible black plastic box for 9 months.

Dole out to the ground and watch your produce grow …

Testing times: The most basic form of soil measurement, is a pH – phosphorous hydrogen test, to access the soil's acidity or alkalinity.

Soil pH affects the availability of nutrients in soil. Despite Nat's claims to the contrary, we didn't do a test. Have just watched a YouTube on how to do a soil test video with my son James. (Have I mentioned I have a 15-year-old son called James?) We spent a hilarious evening googling gardening websites. Allotment chat was thrilling stuff! More than can be said for 'The Cucumber Club,' a website featuring a naked man holding a large cucumber in front of his …

Let's just say it wasn't the most suitable programme to view with one's teenage son.

Let's also say it was a 'members-only' club. The term self-pollinating comes to mind.

The simplest soil pH test can be bought from any gardening centre. Add a soil sample and testing solution to supplied test tube. Shake and leave for one hour. The muddy solution will change colour. Check colour on chart. Different colours relate to different pH readings on a scale of 1-14. The number 7 indicates pH-neutral soil. Above 7 means the soil is more alkaline. Below indicates acid soil. Most veg like alkaline soil. Nettles are an indicator of neutral soil. Judging by the number of stings on my arms/legs, I'd hazard a guess that our soil is fairly neutral. Unlike the shade of lipstick that Nat often wears!

Wonder what type of soil is used in a beauty mud face pack? I sigh as I recall Toby and his handful of soil. Compost. Loam. Humus. It's total rot. Sexy stuff.

Chapter 6
Nice plums

December is the best month to plant bare-rooted fruit bushes. They are leafless and dormant, therefore establish themselves more easily. We are planting ten fruit bushes around the garden's perimeter. They were purchased by Nat from a reputable local garden centre.

'You've got nice juicy ones.' Nat stares at Toby's crotch as he plants a plum tree in the ground.

'And I like your soft fruit bush,' he raises his eyebrows as she digs a large hole three feet away from his plums. He fills it with water and places a blackcurrant bush into the hole.

Nat and Toby continue flirting with each other, leaving me to feel like the gooseberry I have just planted.
'Haven't I read that gooseberries are one of the rising stars of the soft fruit patch.' I try and draw their attention back to me. 'I've seen this fab gooseberry fool recipe.'

'No Deborah, the uppermost root must be planted at least three inches below soil level,' Toby sighs as he looks at my gooseberry with its root poking out. 'Did you, like Natalie, wet your rootball?'

'Yeah, if you don't plant them right they'll come a cropper!' Nat laughs as she pops a damp redcurrant bush into the ground.

'Talking of prolific croppers,' I shovel more soil around my gooseberry bush, 'I read that tayberries produce a great crop. We could also grow a quince greengage. Even a thornless loganberry?'

'Yes, there's lots of new thornless cultivars around,' says Toby.

'Speaking for myself, I love a bit of good old-fashioned pricking!' Nat winks at Toby.

'And I love sloes, the fruit of the blackthorn bush which grows wild along country lanes,' Toby licks his lips.

'We could make sloe gin,' suggests Nat. 'Pete's mum used to make a lethal one! All you have to do is put sloes in a jar with sugar, fill to rim with gin. Then place the jar in the corner of kitchen for three months and slowly turn it every day.'

'Shaken but not stirred,' Toby drawls, in a convincing Sean Connery impression.

'So how do we look after these fruit bushes?' I ask, my attempts so far today to get Toby's attention proving to be as fruitless as the raspberry bush I dig into the earth.

'Excellent question, Deborah,' Toby beams. 'First, we need to leave keep the soil around each bush weed free. In March, when the soil warms up we will add a potash-rich top dressing. Then in April, it's blossom time: the delight that precedes the fruit.' He looks up at me as he tenderly caresses the bare-rooted redcurrant bush he's about to plant. 'Anyway girls, I have a present for you …'

A present I hear?

'… It's a cutting of an elderflower tree.'

'Elderflower cordial is so in vogue,' I add. 'I can't wait to make you my homemade cordial.'

'And I can't wait to taste your elixir.' He replies, with what I'm sure is an inflection on the word 'your.'

He continues, 'What's also lovely about elderflowers is their transformation throughout the year. Beautiful clusters of white flowers in June turning to glossy black berries in the Autumn. Tradition states that the English summer is here when the elder is in flower. It ends when its berries are ripe.'

'You gotta respect your elders!' Nat adds.

'The elder tree also has great mythical properties.' Toby takes my hand. 'Myth states that the most auspicious time to encounter fairies is under an elder bush on Midsummer's eve when the faerie king and queen can be seen passing ...'

I close my eyes. Imagine Toby and I dressed in (matching) white linen, strolling hand in hand.

'Washing a woman's face in dew gathered from elderflowers is also believed to enhance and preserve a woman's beauty.'

'Talking of beauty...' Nat, a thorn in my fairy tale, hands me a blackberry bush to plant. 'In your Vanity Fair magazine last week there was this article about a homemade blackberry leaf face tonic. Might be good for acne-prone skin like yours. Only joking, Deb!'

LITTLE GREEN BOOK

Gooseberry (but I'm no fool) recipe.

Fill saucepan with 1lb of washed gooseberries. Add 3 tablespoons of elderflower cordial. Cover and boil. Heat 150ml of milk in a pan to the point of boiling. Remove from heat.

Beat 2 egg yolks and 30g of sugar in a bowl. Add to milk mixture to form a custard.

Whip 150ml of double cream. Fold into gooseberry mixture.

Add in 150ml of elderflower cordial and custard mixture.

Mix well. Chill in fridge.

***Harvest:** To activate our grant from Delia from the RHS, we need to set up an official eco-club with a bank account. Nat has nominated herself to be chairman. Pete is treasurer. I am to be secretary. As our illustrious chair, Nat has promised 'transparency.' To this end, she has kept receipts for the £30 laid out for the fruit bushes she purchased from a 'reputable' local garden centre. Just wonder what the £1.99 LIDL labels I saw poking out of her parka were for?????*

Chapter 7
The early bird ...

It's 6:30 am. Have just come downstairs to make a delicious espresso. A lazy couple hours of Sunday newspapers, style magazines, and croissants lay temptingly ahead of me before James and husbondage, Stu, get up. As Stu has been in the USA on business all week, he instructed me not to wake him this morn.

Looking out of the window in the diminutive light, I spy Nat in the garden flapping about in a nightie and wellies. And not just any nightie, but a peach flannel one! Armed with a carrier bag over-spilling with peeled veg, egg cartons, etc., I watch her empty it into our compost bin thingy. I didn't think anyone was actually going to use it.

Talking of early birds and newspapers. *Vermiculture* is not a Sunday supplement, but the rearing of worms for the purpose of making compost. How do I know this? I had to cancel my girlie outing with Phoebe and Fliff to our occidental worship at Selfridges yesterday to attend the installation of our wormery. My reputation with the girls is now as soiled as the horticultural events I am currently attending.

'Making a wormery is a rewarding pastime.' I place my coffee pot on the Aga to heat and chuckle as I recall the scenario when Toby placed our new wormery bin in Nat's kitchen, mine currently out of bounds due to the new energy-saving boiler I am about to install (no really, I am planning it!)

'Worms never sleep, so are composting all the time,' Toby told us as we placed hundreds of worms in a big plastic bin. 'Their "castings" contain five times more nitrogen than—'

'Ugh, I've just cut one in half.'

Toby calmed my yelp of horror with the reassurance that by accidentally cutting a worm in half, only half of it would die. The piece with the pink, fat saddle would survive.

Here are some interesting facts on the little squigglers. No really, they are. Worms don't have legs. Hairs and bristles help them to move. They don't have eyes. They hate light. They can live for ten years. Have existed for 600 million years. There are over thirty thousand different kinds of worms. The largest is twenty-two feet long and found in Africa. Worm composting produces a liquid worm tea called leachate …

Enough said … well, here's the best bit. They are hermaphrodite. Each has male and female reproductive organs.

'Worms improve the structure of the soil. They make burrows in the earth which bring in air and allow water to drain away. Toby had summed up the afternoon by telling us that, 'worms are a gardener's best friend.'

'Pete's mum used to keep them as pets.'

Nat's comment was not one I needed to know. Unlike Hen's revelation that worms excrete their own body weight in castings a day. Their castings are not to be confused with the thrilling castings she goes on as an actor.

'The compost from a wormery should be solid and moist, like a good fruit cake.'

I push the memory of Bernie's comment along with my croissant, to one side, and pour myself a cup of coffee as a delicious aroma permeates the kitchen. I place the empty coffee pot in the sink. Actually, didn't Toby say coffee granules should be added to the compost bin? Oh well, when in Rome. I empty my used coffee granules and peel from oranges I have just juiced into a new food waste bin that mysteriously appeared on my doorstep. I look up. A little robin with a plump redbreast, brown neck, and friendly green eyes, perches outside the window. *Chirp. Chirp.* He has come to say hello. It must be the Christmas Robin as it is the second week of December.

Behind him, a puff of blue appears in the sky as another crisp winter morning stretches its sleepy head. I lift up my Sunday Times Culture mag—the only 'culture,' I currently intend to indulge in and leave the early bird to his …

LITTLE GREEN BOOK

Cultivation: *We created our wormery in a 2x3 foot plastic bin. Having pierced aeration holes in the lid, we added layers of sand, shredded cardboard, newspaper and kitchen raw scraps. We added one pound of red wriggler worms (eisenia foetida), which we bought online. Finally, we covered it with a piece of large, damp cardboard.*

Whilst on subject of cultivation, must admit Nat's nightie looked rather comforting. Can just imagine Fliff & Phoebe, my fashionista friends, catching me wearing a peach flannel nightdress.

That would be opening a can of worms.

Chapter 8
The cultivated green room

Finally a bit of light at the end of the tunnel. The polytunnel that is. Our polytunnel has arrived. Henceforth to be referred to more glamourously as: 'The green room.'

A polytunnel is a plastic greenhouse with its own microclimate. It will allow us to increase the length of our growing season by protecting Winter crops from the elements, and cultivate crops which are hard to grow outdoors. Our ten-foot by fifteen-foot green room will provide an environment in which levels of light, shade, temperature, and moisture can be controlled and monitored.

We are holding an Xmas party in the green room to celebrate its arrival and successful erection (which sadly I was not around to witness today due to work commitments). We have invited all the eco-group who helped clear our site.

'The polytunnel will help protect plants from Jack Frost.' Nat swings her pink, glittery bauble earrings to ping Toby's Santa beard. 'Then, in Summer we can get our kit off and use it as a sauna!' She winks at Toby.

Finally from Nat a suggestion worth sharing.

'Oh cum all ye faithful,' Nat starts to sing, 'Works for me every time!'

'Having a polytunnel is a badge of honour.' Toby's cheeks turn a cute shade of aubergine. 'You could grow cucumbers and melon …'

'Why do melons have fancy weddings?' asks Nat.

'Coz they cant-eloupe!' Pete roars with laughter. 'That joke gets me every time.'

'You could also grow VIPs - very important produce,' says Toby.

#NTS: VIPs. My memories of an all-area pass at the green room at an Alexander McQueen fashion show now replaced by a plastic polytunnel.

Models with string bean legs wearing the new 'must-wear' colour, exchanged for mud, the colour of this season. Accessorised with a scooped-out pumpkin handbag and a corn on the cob raffia necklace. Cleaning instructions: Don't bother!

I open my eyes to see Tikka and Marsala demolishing the tray of canapés that I spent hours lovingly preparing. My stilton tartlets, brie and cranberry filo parcels, smoked salmon and pomegranate blinis now reduced to a soggy pile of mutt crumbs in their salivating mouths.

'So where have you set up your eco club bank account?'

My fears that the evening could get no worse disappear with a large swig of vino, at the sound of Dougie's question.

He continues, 'I hope you have put the money into an ethical bank?'

'Actually, my husband's an investment banker.' I quickly regret my words, somehow doubting that Stu's job at Morgan Stanley in derivatives, or whatever his job is, was the right info to share. 'He would've been here tonight but he's abroad with work.'

Dougie raises his voice. 'Morgan Stanley are the worst ...'

'Ah, here you are Dougie. Have a sausage roll.' Nat walks up to us and stuffs a pastry into Dougie's mouth. 'You're sure to like them, they're recycled!' She links my arm and guides me away.

Time for a top up, I think, as I walk on round the green room. I pass Bernie, wearing a Star Trek hat. He's deep in conversation with my son, James, (who's made it out into the garden for the first time) about eco clingons. Next to them, Ben-G is telling Hen how she looks like that girl Ophelia in Shakespeare's 'Hamlet,' and how he hopes she won't get too pissed and end up floating in our wildlife tank.

I walk on, narrowly avoiding being roped in by Pete and several of his mates to join in dancing to Slade's 'Tiger Feet.'

Lifting a tray of sherries, I hand them out to various other members of the eco-club who I haven't got to know very well yet. I overhear snippets of chat from RHS Delia about the merits of poo-ing in a compost bin. I giggle and walk on. Another very tall man is deep in convo with a fierce-looking woman whom I'm introduced to as Yvette, head of Camden Allotments. Their topic is the principles of water management.

I leave their waterlogged conversation and step outside into the garden to find that Nat has placed a ghastly pink plastic tree in the ground and a wrapped rosemary bush in tinsel. She's even draped the wildlife tank with holly and put a mince pie in our gnome's hand.

There's a small mistletoe bush in a pot … aah, perchance to dream, I look back in through the fogged up green room to see the shadow of Toby who is singing 'Silent Night' with the whole party.

'*Chirp chirp,*' our friendly Robin lands on our bird table made up of a chopped tree trunk to join in with the singing.
I breathe in the cold air; the sweet smell of damp, rotting leaves. I lift my refilled glass of vino to toast my lovely new eco-garden. It's actually been a lot of fun over the last two months, and I realise I'm strangely looking forward to what lies ahead.

'There you are, Deb.' My silent night is broken as Nat rushes out and shoves a cracker in my hand. She tugs at the other end of it. The cracker pops, sending a flurry of shredded gold tissue paper over our onion bed.

'How do gardeners learn?' she reads the joke out loud, 'By trowel and error!'

We burst out into laughter. By Nat's standards, it's actually a rather funny joke.

'Let's go back in.' She lassos my neck with a garland of tinsel. 'Ben-G's going to lead us in a group rap to Boney M.'

LITTLE GREEN BOOK

Must ask Nat where she has actually put the money from our grant. Hope it's not under her bed.
Talk about going undercover: Our green room cost £280. It's 10'x15' - We are going to grow half our produce on one side of the green room in pots, and sow the other half, directly into the ground.

Cultivation: *Feeling a bit guilty about not helping with its construction. Crimble lunch with the girls at the Wolseley followed by vital fashion research in Bond Street is considered a work commitment, isn't it? Promise to do an extra hour of weeding tomorrow as penance.*

JANUARY

Ruffled (s)leaves

Chapter 9
Fancy a bunk-up?

'My New Year's resolution is to propagate more!' Nat chuckles as she places a new table, which she claims she found in a skip, into the green room. She opens a book: 'Veg Growing For Beginners.' It may have been written twenty years ago by Alan Titmarsh, who Nat calls, The Great Tit, and as she really fancies him, it is to become our garden bible.

Nat continues to read out from the book. 'Propagate means to dramatically increase our stock of plants by controlling their breeding.'

'We used to do a lot of propagating here during the war,' says Dora, our new septuagenarian recruit. Dora is Nat's neighbour from no.5. Despite her age, she speedily digs up the stony soil with a special tool, her zimmer frame. 'We had an allotment here during the war. Everyone was at it.'

'I always wondered what went on in those air raid shelters!' adds Nat.

'Digging for victory, that's what Winnie told us to do,' Dora adopts a grave tone. 'Every endeavour must be made to produce the greatest volume of food which this fertile island is capable of ...'

'Winnie who?' asks Nat.

'Winnie, the poo.' A little boy with curly brown hair and a lop-sided choir boy fringe comes running into the green room.

'Ah, here's my angel.' Nat swings him around narrowly avoiding knocking Dora over. 'Everyone, meet our new helper, my grandson … poor little Sammi.'

Grandson, I hear, quickly doing the maths in my head. Just how old is Nat?

'I know you're thinking I don't look old enough to be a nan,' Nat nudges me, 'but I got knocked up when I was eighteen. I'm now forty-two. You're much older than me Deb.'

'I'm not, I'm only …'

'Are you Dora the explorer?' poor little Sammi asks Dora. 'You don't look like her?' How old are you? I'm five.'

'I'm five as well,' Dora replies. 'It's the magic marrows we used to grow. Talking of which, girls, how do we sow these caulie and cabbage seeds?'

Cauliflowers: Dora explains to us that the word means cabbage flowers. They are cabbages' temperamental cousins as they're challenging to grow. Mark Twain called them 'nothing but a cabbage with a college education.'

I flick through our gardening bible. According to the Great Tit, there are two sorts of caulies: Summer and Winter. We are planting a hardy Winter variety, Armado, in pots filled with organic compost. The plan is to grow them in the green room, and when the pots have four leaves in mid-March, we should transplant them outside. They should be ready to eat June/July.

'It says here that caulies are ready when the curds are packed tightly …'

'I like a nicely packed curd.'

No prizes for guessing who shared this comment.

I continue to read out loud, 'the heavy green leaves that surround caulies protect the flower buds from getting sunlight, thus preventing chlorophyll from developing so the head remains white.'

'All I ever hear is talk of white heads,' Ben-G sighs as he strolls into the green room holding a green stripy deckchair.

'Caulies are coming back into vogue,' I swiftly read on. 'I'm going to buy us this fabulous new purple-tinted variety called Roman …'

'Bit like the colour of your hair.' Poor little Sammi runs up to Dora and gives her hair a good tug.

'Romanesco caulie forms a series of pinnacles rather than a smooth flat head.' I look at the picture of the caulie in my book which admittedly does seem to bear more than a passing resemblance to Dora's hair. 'Its florets will be great for eating raw with crudités.'

Nat places our caulie seed-filled pots onto our new potting table. 'Poor little Sammi just loves that Colmans packet cheese sauce, don't you my angel,' she smiles as she watches him grab Dora's zimmer frame, turn it into a machine gun and take aim.

'Did you know that Babe Ruth, the famous baseball player, used to wear a cabbage leaf under his hat during games,' Dora tells us. 'He would swap the leaf at halftime.'

Talk about stewed greens.

Cabbages. I open up a packet of 'Savoy Siberia' cabbage seeds.

'The Great Tit tells us that when their leaves are two inches tall, we should transplant them into bigger pots to allow their roots more room to develop.'

'That's called potting up,' adds Nat.

'I need to go potty.' Poor little Sammi whips down his trousers.

What is 'poor' about Sammi I daren't ask, and 'little' cannot begin to describe the amount of pee I watch him distribute in one corner of our newly dug earth.

'Talking of fertiliser,' Nat pulls up poor little Sammi's trousers and laughs, 'the book says every two weeks we need to feed our pots with liquid fertiliser.'

'In late Spring we'll transplant them outside into the ground,' Dora adds, 'and that's when the real adventure starts -'

'Shall we go on an adventure now?' Sammi seizes Dora's hand. 'I'll be Diego, and you with your black face can be Boots the monkey,' he pokes Ben-G to awaken him from the snooze he's having on the deckchair.

'We'll meet again…' Dora starts to sing. 'Talking of which, you know there's a war bunker under here don't you?'

She stops singing, crouches down and rolls a handful of soil in her palm. A teardrop rolls down her face. 'My poor Freddy's buried down there somewhere -'

Buried? Nat and I stare at each other, our eyes wide with fear. We take in a deep breath.

Dora wipes her eyes and explains to us that Freddy was her cat.

Chapter 10
Feeling fruity?

Talking of pussy! Toby has a girlfriend. She's called Grace. Course she is. She has come to help with the planting of our apple trees. Toby will be joining later.

'I know a little about apple trees.' Grace pulls down the hood of her stylish (Burberry) raincoat to reveal a bob of blonde hair tied back in a perfect neat bunch, and (of course) little pearl ear studs. 'None of that Spanish cider for me.' She pushes away the glass I offer her. 'We have to think of the air miles.'

'Indeed we do.' I lift my glass and gulp down its contents.

#NTS: Air miles. Now that I'm a fledgling eco-warrior, better not admit to collecting them.

Grace explains. My father is a pomologist.'

'You don't sound like you've got an Australian accent to me,' says Nat, walking up to us.

'Perhaps you'd prefer a bottle of San Pellegrino?' I offer. Whilst I have no idea what pom-whatever is, I know it's nothing to do with Oceania.

'God no, Deborah. Surely you know it takes one-third of a litre of oil and seven litres of water just to manufacture a one-litre bottle of water.' Grace's perfect porcelain skin flushes with indignation.

'Come to think of it, I bet you're from New Zealand?' adds Nat.

'Hello, I'm here with your trees.' A man in a Camden Council jacket calls out as he wheels in a big tree in a pot.

Never has a council announcement been more welcome. But not so welcome is the photographer from The Camden New Journal who walks in behind him. Grace straightens out the creases in her trim Burberry coat, whilst I look like a giant yellow buoy, cast adrift in my son Jame's ski jacket, which I borrowed in haste.

'Shall we make a start?' Grace asks as we follow her around the eco-garden. 'By way of background information, an apple tree is made up of two parts, the *rootstock* which controls the size of tree, and *scion* or - *cultivar*, which determines the variety of the tree's fruit. There are over 7,000 varieties of apples grown around the world.'

'Cor! Get it?' chuckles Nat as she calls out the letters 'C.O.R.E.'

'There are three categories of apple rootstock,' Grace continues in a serious voice, ignoring Nat's funny pun. She tenderly runs her hands along a branch. 'The most common rootstocks are the M26 variety ...'

'Yeah, we always forget what motorway junction to come off on when we're visiting Pete's Dad's grave.' Nat shakes her head.

'Oh my, I think we have a serious problem.'—Grace looks with concern at the label on one of the trees—'We have here five M27's which are semi dwarfs.' She turns round to look for Mr Camden Council, who is nowhere to be found. He's popped round to the side of the polytunnel (on my suggestion) for a quick smoke. 'Owing to their size,' Grace explains, 'your site will only be able to accommodate three trees. Their roots will also spread too far under the ground taking nutrition from other plants.'

'Nat, why don't we plant the other two round the front of your block?' The photographer takes photos of me as I make my dazzling suggestion.

We troop round to the front of Nat's block and start digging big holes without the help of Mr Council Council. He's now on his lunch break.

'What gets bigger the more you take away?' calls out Nat. 'A hole! Great joke, eh?'

We all burst out laughing with the exception of Grace.

An hour later, having planted the trees and filled the holes with compost excruciatingly measured to the nearest millimetre by Grace, Toby walks in. His hair is tousled (don't you just love that word) in the gusty wind.

He looks like a veritable Apollo bearing a laurel (actually it's an elderflower bush).

'Hello all,' he gives Grace a rather (I can't help but notice) perfunctory kiss on the cheek and winks at me.

#NTS: Hello all, indeed. I can't help but wonder if all is well in the Garden of Eden.

Grace crouches down and places her palms together in prayer. 'God bless this little apple tree. God grant it silver apples of the moon, and golden ...'

I close my eyes to imagine Grace, myself and Nat three fair goddesses - Hera, Athena, Aphrodite - me clothed in flaxen toga, Grace in a garland of myrtle, and Nat - still in her dayglo-blue velour tracksuit - all waiting to claim the golden apple. Waiting to be chosen by Toby, our Paris ...

'Stop,' a voice yells, interrupting my daydream. 'Where the feck do you think you are putting that tree?' It's Mr. Parkeeper. Cue the start of our Trojan War.

'You have to follow the correct procedure,' Mr. Parkeeper stands in front of us screaming. 'The boundary of your allotment does not stretch to the front of MY block.'

'But it's only a little innocent apple tree,' Grace speaks softly.

The term not upsetting the apple cart comes to mind.

'If you leave it there, it will disappear.' Mr. Parkeeper grabs the tree and starts tugging at it.

'A goodly apple, rotten at the heart,' Laments Ben-G, who has popped out to see what all the racket is about.

'It's God's own tree.' Colour drains from Grace's face.

'Feck God, and his trees.' Mr. Parkeeper lifts the shovel. 'A member of the public or a tramp could come off the street and pick an apple.'

'That's the idea you dirty old perv,' Nat shouts, 'I've seen you out there with your binoculars staring at my tits.'

'There's no choice in rotten apples,' Ben-G nods and walks off.

I watch the fall of paradise - Mr Camden Council smiling as he is now on triple time. The photographer snaps away. Nat tussles with Mr. Parkeeper over the tree, whilst a teardrop falls down Grace's cheek. But most disturbing of all, Toby puts his arm around Grace's waist and slides it down to her bottom. Oh to be that cheek. She slides his hand straight back up.

'Mr. Parkeeper is it? Allow me to introduce myself. I'm Toby Knight, your local councillor.'

'The name's Parker. And I know who the feck you are.'

'Sir, seeing what an avid gardener you are, could I possibly ask you to consider planting a tree in your garden?' asks Toby, née Adam (voice of my temptation).

'No you feckin' can't!' yells Mr. Parkeeper, as he storms off.

An hour later of digging the tree back up, we retire to my kitchen for a restorative cuppa.

'Did you know, millions of people over centuries have seen apples falling, but Newton was the first to ask why?' Dora walks into the kitchen holding poor little Sammi's hand.

'Hello young man, I've got a present for you,' Grace perks up.

'Is it iPhone?' asks Poor Little Sammi.

'Well no.' Grace pulls a plastic milk carton out of her bag.

Stop! Rewind.

#NTS: Grace's bag. I'm sure it's a Marc Jacobs?? Could it be a fake?

'Would you like to make a bird feeder, young man?' she asks.

'No. I want an iPhone with the Minecraft app on it.'

'And look what I've got here.' Grace unzips the bag's front compartment and pulls out some birdseed.

I so recognise a front compartment like that.

'But I want a—'

'Maybe Santa will get you one next year,' persists Grace.

'I don't believe in Santa.'

'Here, borrow mine,' she hands Poor little Sammi her phone.

Grace is a saint. It's official. From now on will call her St. Grace.

'We should now talk about how apple trees need to cross-pollinate.' St. Grace sips her chamomile, as she explains the sex life of an apple tree.

'Nana-nat, does it hurt when the man's seed goes into the lady's fanny?' Poor little Sammi smiles sweetly.

Nat looks at me and I look back at her. 'Ask Grace,' we answer in unison and burst out laughing. I'm sure out of the corner of my eye I see Toby trying to suppress a grin.

Community cross fertilisation. Brings a whole new meaning to the term feeling fruity.

LITTLE GREEN BOOK

Pomology: Branch of horticulture which focuses on cultivation, production, and harvest of tree fruits. Pomologist - someone who studies fruit and nuts. Mr Parkeeper excluded!

Cultivation: Have spent evening researching v. important gardening issue. St Grace's bag. Aha ... found it! It is Marc Jacobs. And it's leather! Wonder if her halo's silver plated?

Chapter 11
Permaculture

I am informed is not a hairdo, but a year-round method of
eco-gardening. Toby has suggested we read up on
permaculture which follows nature's cycles in order to live
in a sustainable way without using up the Earth's
resources.

Talking of cycles, and using up all your neighbours'
resources, Nat's concept of recycling is somewhat
different from mine. Several piles of York paving stone
appeared in the garden today. She and Pete apparently
found them last night 'abandoned' in the driveway of the
large house belonging to a rock star across the road. I
just wonder why they are still encased in plastic
packaging.

'But isn't that the rock star, Robert Plant's, house?' I ask,
watching Pete lay the paving in the entrance to 'Lottie' -
the name Nat has now given to our allotment. He
continues to lay the path up to the edge of our onion and
garlic bed.

'Well, he's got the right name for it!' Nat lifts another slab
and smashes it into bits with a mallet.

'Has he written any good stuff?' asks Ben-G, lugging
several slabs of the broken pieces to the middle of Lottie.

'He wrote "Pathway to heaven." All-time classic, ain't it, babe?' Nat lifts a spade and she and Pete start to play air guitar.

'Might get him to come and jam with me.' Ben-G places several stones on the ground in the shape of a large circle.

'Nice one Ben-G, this can be our pizza patch,' Nat laughs. 'The stones around the edge can be its thick crust!'

I, too, who have my recycling contribution to make - one of a more conventional provenance, walk to the edge of the garden and lift a sheet of plastic to reveal several beams.

'They're from my friend's house. The beams are from the attic she's rebuilding.'

'Beautiful bit of wood, Deb.' Pete places the planks around the garden to form the borders for several differently shaped beds.

'Right team, it's time to talk has beans!' Nat gathers us all together. She hands me The Great Tit's gardening bible.

'*Beans,*' I read out. 'An ancient food crop which dates back to 6000 BC. Broad beans can be planted outside in Jan as they like to rough it ...'

'Bit like me,' interjects Nat. 'Do us a fava, Deb.'

'Yes, Nat …'

'No Deb … F.A.V.A.,' she calls out each letter. 'It's a joke! That's what beans are known as in the USA.'

I slice open a packet of seeds that Nat gives me and read out the label. 'This Aquadulca Claudia variety is best for Winter sowing, as they establish very quickly.'

Bit like our new path. I watch Pete lay the final stone in front of the entrance to the green room.

'Broad beans need a cold temperature to be able to perform,' Natalie chuckles, 'bit like my …'

We empty a bag of organic compost into the bed and sow the seeds into it.

'It says here, we should have an eighteen-inch gap to stagger sowing and allow airflow in order prevent fungal disease,' Nat shakes her head, 'I only yesterday overheard the lady at No.16 talking about how her husband has an infection in his …'

'Bean crops come in two main categories,' I quickly read on. 'Climbers which grow around poles, and bush plants.'

'If you were a bean what type would you be?' asks Nat.

'I'd be a runner bean, the people's favourite, covered with beautiful red flowers.'

'I guess I'm more of a haricot vert - French bean,' I respond, 'upmarket, slim, and très continental.'

'But well stringy and tough!' Nat pokes me in the ribs and laughs. 'Only joking, Deb. You're not tough.' She races on. 'Poor little Sammi would be a dwarf bean; Dora a dried bean; and my Pete, of course, would be the broad bean.' She walks up to Pete and slides her arm down his muscle (less) arms.

'S'pose as usual, I'm the black-eyed bean,' Ben-G nods. 'Soul food.'

'Do you know, my son James is always talking about a band called, "The Black Eyed Beans," I add. 'I hear they're great.'

'Think you mean the Black Eyed Peas, Deb,' Nat roars with laughter. 'Anyone fancy a cuppa?'

LITTLE GREEN BOOK

Sowing the seeds of discontent.
So reads the headline of a feature in today's Camden New Journal about our tree planting ceremony. It's a less-than-flattering story and series of photos showing Nat trying to clobber Mr. Parkeeper with a rootstock. Me - my life of Michelin stars replaced with more Michelin-man look, as I dig away in James's yellow ski jacket. Ben-G laying on the ground, clearly stoned, and St. Grace cradling a tree. All onlooked by a laughing Mr. Camden Council.

Cultivation. *Nat's latest joke: 'How do you make an apple puff? Chase it round the garden!'*

Permaculture: *According to Nat, Toby has now gone away by himself for a week on a permaculture retreat. Wonder why he and St. Grace didn't go together? Wonder if know-it-all Nat has the booking detail.*

Chapter 12
No shit!

We have just had a truckload of pure steaming horse poo tipped outside on the road. Far, far too late I fear to be muttering the term don't shit on your own doorstep.

'This organic compost will make your veg shoot up,' states delivery man, Stan, as he shoots off with the first £160 of our grant.

It's three hours, nay - (every pun intended) fifty wheelbarrow loads later, and Nat and I have transported Stan's finest into Lottie. The term shit falling off a shovel does not come to mind.

'I see you've just completed your rites of passage, Deborah,' Toby smiles as he wanders into the garden accompanied by Hen and Bernie.

#NTS: Certainly was the rites of some animal's passage.

'As a vegan, I must say I don't approve of using a soil improver that is a by-product of animal farming.' Bernie nods his head, his red plait waving from side to side like a disapproving finger.

'Hey Bernie, best put on a brave "feces" about it,' chuckles Nat.

'Just like your gnome.' Pete points to the garden gnome. It's still luminous even with a large splodge of horse shit on his nose.

'Talking of excrement,' Bernie adds, 'we really need to talk about urinating into your compost.'

'What I don't understand is why this, er … compost is just pure poo,' I ask. Never was a change of subject more needed. 'I thought we had purchased the best organic.'

'Doesn't get any fresher than this, Deborah,' Toby looks down at the mound of compost still discharging more steam than the Orient Express.

Somehow Toby can even make shit sound sexy.

Before I can enquire about his permaculture course, Bernie races on. 'The reason I've come here today,' Bernie continues, 'is to talk to you about building you a cob oven.'

'Thanks but I just got a great new hob, Bernie,' I smile graciously.

'No not a hob,' Bernie scowls, 'but a cob. It's built using zero energy emissions.'

'And I've come today to talk to you about whether to dig, or not to dig,' says Hen.

'That is the total question!' Ben-G joins the group.

'Digging the soil disturbs the complex ecosystem.' Hen opens out her arms dramatically. 'To dig is like peeling off the earth's skin,' she projects, in full thespian mode.

#NTS: Peels. It's been a while. Must book one.

Wait a minute - am I hearing Hen right? Is she suggesting we don't dig our garden? I soo love this girl. And her theatrics.

'But this soil is so compacted it will take too long to improve with a no-dig approach.' Toby rolls the soil in his fingers to form the shape of a sausage.
But oh, my Toby, what a large sausage you have. I rap my hand. Christ, I'm even starting to think like Nat.

'Perhaps we should get a pedologist in?' suggests Bernie.

'Yes, I also need to book an appointment with one. My Pete's got such terrible verrucas,' Nat sighs.

'Anyway, shall we press on? Have a feel of this, Deborah.' Toby raises his eyebrows as he hands me the rock-hard soil sausage.

My cheeks turn a shade redder than Bernie's red plait as I try and focus on Bernie's trench-building lecture.

'A compost trench will help prepare the earth for hungry crops such as runner beans and courgettes,' explains

Bernie, as he and Toby start to dig out trench for our Jack and the Beanstalk bed.

'All we have to do is bury green and kitchen waste in the ground a couple of months before start of growing season, and add some brown stuff.' Toby lines the trench with a layer of cardboard.

'Gosh, it's all still a bit bare out here isn't it?' I look around the swathes of bare soil which we cover with the flattened cardboard boxes we have collected, mine from Fresh n wild, Nat's from LIDL.

'Far from it, Deborah, the exposed trees reveal the poetry of Winter.' Toby corrects me as he fills the trench with the contents from brown paper bags full of his raw fruit and veg peelings from yesterday. Never mind five a day, in Toby's case, it looks more like fifty.

'I love the patterns the entwined branches make,' Hen adds poetically. 'They are like lace.'

#NTS: Filigree. Knitted lace. Woven voile. Fashion fabrics.

I sigh. I so miss working with them. So miss watching the thick blades of my tailor's scissors slice through beautiful yarn. I'm beginning to wonder whether I'm no longer in between jobs, but more like out of a job. Out of the fashion industry.

I return my attention to Lottie. I squint my eyes, but no matter how much I try to see the world through Hen and Toby's eyes, the bare branches look just like bare branches.

'The starkness of winter affords uninterrupted views of birds, the smell of soil.' Hen takes in a deep breath. 'One can almost smell narcissi on a freezing winter's morn.'

'I can't smell a bloody thing,' Nat lets out a loud sniff.

'I always find scent so atavistic and primitive,' Poet Laureate Hen continues to espouse. 'It triggers the brain like notes of music, flooded with memories.'

#NTS: Ata what?

'Just breathe in all around as the ground becomes dusted with fresh rain.'

As if on cue, we look up as the rain starts to fall, the sky clearly in collusion with one of Hen's dramatic moments. 'Just imagine future smells. Lavender, blackcurrant, honeysuckle, chamomile.'

'Actually, I've noticed flowers don't seem to smell any more in this country.' I, eco warrior, lay a flattened cardboard box sporting a giant Fairtrade logo on the ground and smile hopefully at Toby.

'That's because most flowers sold in the UK in the winter are imported and travel thousands of miles on refrigerated aircraft or trucks. They're force grown using fertilisers and pesticides.' Toby shovels soil over the exposed compost trench and covers it up.

'Anyway, here's mud in your eye,' Nat inserts one of her more prosaic comments.

'Talking about mud, do you know one of my fantasies is … ' Toby stares at me.

Hen waxes on. 'I always also find there's a special fragrance released as the light starts to fall …'

No! Do pipe down, Hen. Go on Toby. Dear God, I didn't say that out loud, did I?

Toby looks at me, 'A naked woman covered in mud, writhing on a …'

Oh to be that naked, feral woman writhing around in a … No, stop. I cannot go there. Not even in a Toby daydream. Seaweed wrap maybe but …

LITTLE GREEN BOOK

Cultivation: *Midnight. Have turned into a night owl as Stu is away once again in Houston … New York, or wherever he is. I've spent more time with Nat over the past three months than my husbondage!*

Snuck into garden to have a sniff around thus impress (Toby) with future perfumed words. Wonder if the neighbourhood fox who joined me smelt anything other than an overpowering aroma of horse shit vaporising in the foggy night.

Found myself sharing garden with other creatures of the night (Nat excluded!) A wood pigeon trying to uproot our onion sets, a little mouse who darted across my foot practically sending me flying.

1 am: Back indoors. Pedology is nothing to do with feet. It's the science of soil. No doubt Bernie's next lecture.

1:05 am. Wooah. Erase that last mean comment. Bernie is soo my new best friend. He can lecture me, or wee on our heap anytime he likes.

Have just seen in Harpers this month a cob oven. It's the new 'must have' outdoor dining room accessory of the season. A cob is wood fired earth oven built from a mix of natural materials, mud or clay, sand, straw. Can bake bread in it, pizzas, pot ou feu, oh, the endless dinner party possibilities.

February

...the must have bag

Chapter 13
This season's 'must-have' bag

Gro-bags are instant gardens in a bag. Just add plants, water ... et voila. We have decided to grow tomatoes, aubergines, cucumbers and chili peppers in them.

Talking about 'must-have' items, I've just purchased a new pair of designer wellies. They're lilac and decorated with butterflies. Have placed outside on porch for Nat to see and covet.

Have also decided it's time to swap one kind of 'must have' bag for another. I need a couple of days away from horse shit and fresh air. Hello ... retail therapy! And that does not mean going with Nat to Homebase.

I'm off to Harvey Nics. All scrabbling about in soggy mud replaced by the utter joy of strolling up and down over-lit floors: Icy breath on a foggy, dank day transposed to hot desirous gasps at the sight of the luxury good on display. Although the fifth floor, with its aroma of deep and musky wild rosemary, does bear a resemblance to Lottie. But it's the third floor that really makes my heart flutter. Bags and accessories! Coarse rotting twigs replaced by the touch of softest calf leather.

Several glorious hours later, I pause by the Marc Jacob counter. Wait a mo ... there it is—St Grace's bag. Not in brown, but in the most gorgeous sage green. I lean forwards to lift it off the counter, only to have it snatched from my grasp. I turn round to see who is standing next to me, only to find it's St Grace, herself.

'Oh, hello there, Deborah,' she says as we eye each other's handbags up and down. I try and shove down the Big Mac wrapper hanging out of my mine. Oh sweet Jesus no, anything but St Grace catching me eating a Big Mac. What will Toby say?

'I'm here to procure free bags for an auction,' she explains. 'I'm arranging a party next week to raise money for the WWF.'

Course you are, I think less than charitably.

'Funny bumping into you here,' she adds. 'Mind you, I thought you might be the Harvey Nics type.'

Whereas you are pure charity shop aren't you? Not! I refrain from replying, as I eye up her new cashmere jumper. St Grace is a bitch. And a sanctimonious one.

'Mind you this might be a blessing in disguise,' she continues. 'I really could do with some help transporting these on the bus home.' She turns round and lifts up a couple of boxes.

I can't believe it. They are filled with gorgeous bags. So it's true then, there is an auction.

'Er, sure. Just let me nip to the loo,' I reply and quickly rush off to cancel my Uber.

Handbags at dawn replaced by a big smiles, I return.
St Grace and I lift the boxes of 'must have' bags,
and head for the bus stop.

LITTLE GREEN BOOK

Cultivation: WWF: World wide life fund. A non-governmental organisation currently supporting over one thousand environmental projects around the world. Has five million members, so it seems, including St Grace.

Wonder how I can get myself invited to her fundraiser?

Chapter 14
Mine's a shish

Shopping. Part Deux. Am off to Homebase with Nat
to purchase items of a more seedy nature. Cabbage,
parsnips, beetroot, rocket, spinach, courgettes, peas,
runner and French beans, potatoes, chilies, herbs. All of
which can be sowed/planted within the next couple of
months. We have allocated £40 for this shopping
extravaganza.

'What about a budget for pots?' I enquire as we sit in my
kitchen sipping coffee.

'I think we should plant as many as poss in unusual
containers,' Nat bites into a biscuit. 'These are well stale,
Deb.'

'They're biscotti,' I sigh, 'a delicacy from Italy designed to
be brittle.'

'Bit like you today,' Nat races on. 'Anyway, how about
growing parsley in Dora's old teapot, mint in poor little
Sammi's sand bucket, peppers in veg oil cans, and
potatoes in tyres? I even found a sink yesterday, which
we could fill with strawberry plants. What about the box
from that plonk you had delivered to your house last
night?'

What about it indeed! I listen to sommelier Nat pass
verdict on Stu's delivery from his vintage wine club.

There's more premier in its cru than in the whole of Pete's beloved Arsenal football team.

'Natalie,' I down my double espresso in one, 'those bottles of wine include several Chateau Lafite's, Chablis, Mouton Cadet's, far from the plonk of your ascription ...'

'Well it's only mouton dressed up as ... hang on,' Nat leaps up. 'I've got a great idea, why don't we grow grapes and make our own wine?'

Grapes of wrath. Chateau Camden Road. Somehow it doesn't have the same ring to it.

'I can just picture you and Toby trampling up and down on grapes in your bath!' Nat roars with laughter. 'You'd love that wouldn't you?'

'I don't know what you are talking about.' My face turns a deeper shade of rouge than the Rimmel lipstick Nat lifts out of her bag. 'Anyway, how much shall we spend on tools?' I quickly move on, 'I saw a beautiful aluminium spade in a catalogue plus a fork with a solid bronze handle, its shaft made of beech and lime ...'

'Actually, I've already got us some.' Contrary to all expectations, Nat does not respond with a lewd shaft joke but pops outside to quickly return with an old shovel, a fork, and several small trowels. 'I got these free,' she strokes the old wooden handle of a spade. 'I'd like to think that they're from some old bloke who's copped it but had been diggin' with them for years. They've got a history that we are carrying on with.'

I lift a trowel, look at its worn handle, its fissures, the fine lines on its metal blade engrained with many a year of connection with the soil. 'They're really lovely. Thanks for getting them,' I smile, humbled by Nat's thoughtful action and words (bloke who's copped it, aside) I feel ashamed that as normal I'd just tried to turn gardening tools into another Le Creuset, designer something, or other, moment.

'And as for plastic pots,' she grins, 'haven't you ever heard of the three 'R's - re-use, recycle or rob? No, we'll use old flora tubs.'

'But I don't think …'

'And before you tell me you don't eat margarine, only posh French unsalted butter, we can also grow crops in those bio-yoghurt pots you put James' packed lunch in.'

Before I can pass comment on Nat's interpretation of the three 'R's,' or ask how she knows all about the contents of my son's packed lunch, she tells me her next re-cycling idea.

'And of course next month, I'll go to Lidl and swipe all the free seed packets from the front covers of Gardeners World! Now come on Deb, drink up, let's go shop.'

LITTLE GREEN BOOK

Cultivation: *9 pm. James couldn't believe I let him order in pizza again tonight … Double ouch. My head feels like it's going to burst. Stu thinks it's sexy that I'm totally sozzed. Says it's good to see me let my hair down for a change, (thought he liked me wearing my hair up? Or at least he does for the boring bankers dinners I so often have to escort him on)*

Ouch, can't talk. Seem to recall that after three tortuous hours in Homebase, our planned pit stop at the local Greek taverna to procure empty vegetable oil cans, turned into the procurement of several unplanned shots of Raki. Said imbibing followed by Nat flashing the man at Kall Kwik tyre repair shop, a flash of my 'spare tyre.' It was clearly not as well hidden under my jacket.

Brings a whole new meaning to the term belly dancing.

11 pm. What is this dirty car tyre doing on my white sofa?

Chapter 15
Companion wanted

Must not be called Natalie. Must be able to help disguise the smell of a vulnerable crop by planting a stronger-smelling one alongside it.

'Companion gardening is whereby two plants are grown in close proximity in order that they provide mutual benefit to each other.' RHS Delia continues her lecture on companion planting which she started at hideous o' clock, on this freezing morning. 'For example, onions grow better when planted beside carrots. Cabbage next to mint. Garlic protects raspberries from aphids.'

The question is what will protect me from Nat? The raspberry blotches on my cheeks, and mint green mint hue glowing from her face, suggesting no mutual benefit was felt by either of us, the morning after our day out together.

Delia continues, 'Creating companion plant communities is not just about pest control. Combined plants can help each other by providing nutrients in the soil, offering protection, attracting beneficial pests.'

I'd rather like Toby to be my companion. I watch him walk into Lottie. Just don't tell my husband! I give myself a little kick.

'Bit delicate are you today, Deb?' Nat laughs.

'Plants are conscious of the company they keep,' adds Delia.

'You should have seen Deb dancing on the table at this Greek taverna yesterday afternoon, Toby.'

'I certainly was not …'

'Sounds intriguing, Deborah,' Toby winks at me. 'Wish I'd been there.'

'Hello allotmenteers, I've bought my National Society of Allotment and Leisure Gardeners handbook to lend you,' Dougie walks up to us interrupting my Zobra-dancing-with-Toby, daydream moment before I could shout Spanakopita! He continues, 'it contains crucial facts like how to clean your tools and the exact measurements of each bed you should plant.'

Toby yawns. 'Must admit I had a late night, too. Grace organised a fantastic Valentine's charity fundraiser for the WWF.' He turns round to face me. 'How many Valentine's cards did you get?'

'There's some charming companion planting folklore …' shares Hen, as she glides up to us. She spins round, drawing attention to her voluminous purple cape, preventing me from having to admit to Toby that I didn't receive any cards…
Or an invite to St Grace's glam fundraiser.

#NTS: Valentines-less-night. Seemed silly to give Stu the card I'd got for him, when he'd clearly forgotten about it.

'Weaving spiders come not here, long-legg'd spinners hence. Beetles black approach not near; worm nor snail, do not offence' That's a quote from Midsummer's Night Dream,' adds Ben-G who also joins us, as Toby and Hen disappear off behind the Green room. Ben-G pulls up a deckchair, opens up Dougie's book, and starts to read.

I close my eyes, The Midsummer Night's Dream of my recall transported from a warm Summers night in a moonlit forest with Oberon and Titania, King and Queen of the fairies, to a back garden in Camden on a dank February morn where I dream of enchantment with Toby. The romantic pursuit of Helena and Demetrius exchanged for Delia and Dougie, who cozy up to share a companionable chat on micronutrients. The asses head, replaced by excrement from Stan's manure which is still steaming all around. And Puck - our garden gnome (which no matter how often I try and hide, Nat always finds and returns)

'Some man or another must play wall,' Ben-G Bard looks up from his book. 'That's my favourite line in the play.' 'Talking of walls,' continues Delia, 'some tall plants, like corn on the cob, act as a barrier sheltering shorter plants from the wind.'

It's half an hour (feels like two hours) later, of listening to Dougie's lecture on National Society of Allotment and Leisure Gardener health and safety rules.

What's going on here? I look up as Toby and Hen reappear from behind the green room. Hen's face is flushed. Her cape crumpled, covered in mud and twigs.

'In summary,' Delia smiles at Dougie, 'complimentary planting produces happier plants that propagate better.'

LITTLE GREEN BOOK

Bedfellows getting laid
Marigolds with tomatoes
Chives with carrots
Toby with Grace
Sweet corn, beans and squash
Toby with Hen?
Cabbage and nasturtium
Carrots and leeks
Beans and onions

*Bedfellows **not** getting laid*
Beans and onions
Stu and me
Toby and me.

Chapter 16
Perennials

I'm informed, are not end-of-year company reports, due end of next month, causing Stu extended work nights, but plants that grow back year after year. Perennial herbs include chives, mint, sage, thyme, rosemary, lavender, tarragon, and chamomile. Annual herbs are those which need to be re-planted each year: basil, chervil, coriander, and dill. Biennials like parsley take two years to complete their biological cycle.

'Are you going to strawb fair, parsley, sage, rosemary and thyme,' trills Nat in a less than dulcet tone certain to frighten the foxes away. 'That's the kind of hippy rubbish Hen would sing. I find her a real act. Did you see that cape she was wearing the other day, it looked like it was made from a curtain?'

I nod in agreement.

'Any sign of life from the onions and garlic's yet?' I ask as we sit basking in the unseasonable hot sun, planning what herbs to grow where. So far we are in agreement about everything; including our mutual dislike of Hen.

'No, just an empty bed,' Nat shrugs her shoulders.

Unlike Toby's, I keep my sage (less) thought to myself and follow Nat over to the broad bean bed.

'Bloody hot for Feb, isn't it?' Nat unzips her hoodie. 'It's like being abroad. I say bring on climate change!'

'Talking about the Med,' I quickly change the subject seeing Bernie enter Lottie, 'let's have a bed of sage and thyme, orange, cream, and green tri-colour sage. It's soo this season.'

'Bit like my top,' Nat whips off her hoodie to reveal a T-shirt with an orange, white and green Irish flag. 'Talking of good footie seasons, Ireland has just qualified for this Summer's Euro cup. Pete's nan was Irish. I think we should put up a giant screen out here.'

'I've read a wonderful Raymond Blanc recipe for port, sage, and onion stuffing," I shift the goalposts.

'Sounds tasty.' Bernie, in an unseasonably good mood, walks up to us licking his lips to reveal a large stud on his tongue. 'Mediterranean herbs like dry, well-drained soil. A thin layer of gravel added to the bed provides a natural way to conserve moisture and absorb warmth during the day. It then releases it at night. Perhaps you should grow your Med herbs where this mound of crushed stones is?'He points to the pile of Nat's questionably procured leftover York paving stone.

'I hear chequerboard herb gardens are all the rage at the moment.' I escort Bernie to the other end of Lottie. 'We could design one to look like a chess set with paving slabs as the "white" squares, and squares filled with herbs as the "black" squares.'

'I've never played chess,' says Nat. 'I'm more into Snakes - or rather earthworms - and ladders!'

'Oh, no, Deborah,' Bernie shakes his sweaty head which is glistening with sunlight. 'Paving should always be kept to a minimum. We have to think of maximum yield and preserving life underground.'

'According to the Great Tit,' says Nat, 'you can grow some herbs from seeds, whilst others are best bought as young plants. Herbs once established will spread faster than poor little Sammi's nits.'

'Talking of cleanliness,' I block the image of Sammi and his nits, from my mind, 'wouldn't it be heaven to soak in a bath filled with home-grown lavender and chamomile?'

'Bet I can find us an old bath to actually grow 'em in Deb.'
'You could make lavender bags,' Bernie suggests.

'I hear they're a great natural moth repellent,' I add, 'those moths just love my cashmere.'
'Funny that, I don't have moth problems,' Nat shrugs her shoulders and heads off into the polytunnel to transfer the cabbage seeds we planted last month into larger pots. Miraculously, they have sprouted little shoots.

'How about planting salad herbs beside the area where we are going to build your cob oven,' Bernie grins. 'Fill it with rocket, chives, parsley, and nasturtiums. Chives. beautiful purple flowers also attract bees.'

#NTS: Nasturtiums. Aren't they a flower?

Bees, I shudder. I'm still smarting thirty years later after a school-girl sting I received on my derriere.

Bernie continues, 'I'm sure you know that bees pollinate over seventy percent of our vital flowering/fruit crops in the UK. That's equivalent to one in three of the mouthfuls of food we eat. But did you know that within the last couple of years, there has been a drastic decline in the bee population? We don't know why - possibly agricultural, chemical or loss of habitat factors. What we do know is that any future reductions will have a significant impact on food security. The BBA are running a Beekeeping course this Spring which Toby and I are planning to attend. Perhaps you'd like to join us?'

'I'd love to come, Bernie,' I link his arm. 'After all, we must all do our bit to help endangered species.'

'Oh, bee-have Deb!' Nat laughs. 'Get it? bee spelt with an extra 'E'! Now what else shall we grow next to the barbie?'

'Tarragon,' I beam. 'Beloved of French chefs. I just love a rich béarnaise sauce.

'I heard that tarragon was once used to treat snake bites,' says Pete, walking up to us. 'Might come in useful here.'

'How about growing fresh mint?' I walk over the area designated for our Pimms patch. 'Couldn't you fancy a delicious cool drink? Terrible how hot it is for the time of year.' I smile at Bernie and await his lecture on climate change.

'Well my fave herb is basil,' Nat chirps in. 'We'll grow it in our deep-crust pizza bed.'

'Did you know that basil protects against evil and is sacred to Krishna? Every Hindu is buried with a basil leaf,' Bernie smiles as he lifts a brochure out of his hessian rucksack, 'Talking of which, I've got great news. I've got a new job.'

'Good for you mate,' says Pete. 'I'll get the beers in.'

Bernie explains. 'I'm starting at Green Endings Funerals. Their coffins are reusable.'

'Talking of getting back to your roots,' Nat looks at me. Both of us try not to burst out laughing. 'How about growing horseradish? It's the root that's used for …'

'With Green Endings coffins, it's only the inner lining which is used in cremation,' Bernie flicks through the brochure with Pete, 'the outer is made from bio-degradable card, or bamboo …'

'Hail fellow allotmenteers,' Ben-G joins the cortege. 'I read in my man Dougie's book that we can plant outside now, so I bought these as my contribution,' he hands us a packet of seeds.

'Ben-G, that is so kind of you,' I hug him. Never has a packet of artichoke seeds been more welcome.

Jerusalem artichokes: Once established are impossible to get rid of. Are perennial. Much like Bernie's coffins. Next year in …

'Whilst Jerusalems are not the prettiest, they are rugged, weatherproof, and not fussy about soil. They'll be ready in May,' Nat looks at the picture on the packet. 'They look a bit like your knobbly knees, Deb. Ever thought of getting those varicose veins done?'

'What's the difference between Jerusalem and globe artichokes?' asks Pete.

'You can't plant globe's artichokes until April,' continues Bernie. 'Would you like to look at my new brochure?'
'I want to grow Globe artichokes named after Shakespeare's theatre,' adds Ben-G.

'But then artichoke can cause excessive flatulence in some people,' Nat turns round and pats my tummy. 'Prone to it are you, Deb?'

LITTLE GREEN BOOK

Sowing from seed: Tarragon 'Artemisia dracunculus' in pots next month in the green room. Will plant out in final position in garden when seedlings are 4" high in late April.

We also plan to pot chamomile and parsley seeds at the same time. Nat says she is going to collect old tea pots and sow chamomile seeds directly in them. Chin chin.

Basil is a late starter. Can't be sown in pots in the green room until April and transplanted outside late May. Nasturtiums have edible flowers. They look beautiful in salads or added to crustless sarnies with mozzarella, toms, olive oil and balsamic ...

Growing from small plants
Thyme after thyme. Lemon thyme, sage, lavender, chives, mint. All going to be planted outside in April/May.

Four seasons in one day. Does not refer to the weather, but to the Jerusalem artichoke tubers we planted in on quarter of our pizza crust bed. They can grow up to 2 metres high. Have just seen a wonderful recipe for slicing Jerusalem shavings and adding to a stir fry ...

BBA. British Beekeepers association. Fifteen thousand members in UK. Now, seemingly, plus one, according to email just received from best friend Bernie.

Chapter 17
World cabbage day

It's world cabbage day. Enough said.

MARCH
beware the ides of...

Chapter 18
Transition date

Toby has invited me on a Transition town date. Transition Towns are an international movement of communities coming together to reimagine and rebuild our world.

'So how did you get on with your garden purchases?' he asks, as we walk into Willesden Town Hall. 'Did you buy a decent pair of secateurs?'

#NTS: Sequators. Why is he asking me about some kind of noun? Not the opening topic I had imagined on our date.

We join the crowd who are sitting on chairs laid out in a large circle. The chatter hushes as a bespectacled man sits down in the centre. He takes out a sandwich from a plastic carrier bag and removes the plastic packaging with its Tesco label.

'Global oil production has begun its inevitable decline,' the speaker lifts the sandwich.

#NTS: Snack-time? Couldn't he have had breakfast before he left home? Am feeling a little peckish after long bus journey here.
I rifle around in my bag for my beef and horseradish sandwich.

'Do you know the carbon footprint of this sandwich?' the speaker asks as he separates the mangy sandwich layers. 'This ham is from intensively reared pigs - and we all know how energy heavy livestock farming is.' He lifts up a droopy lettuce leaf. 'This salad has been pumped full of pesticides. The bread is made from white flour ground in factories and the plastic packaging from oil.'

I firmly shove my sandwich back into bottom of bag.

He continues, 'As fossil fuel production goes into decline, we need to find ways of living without cheap oil. The resurgence of community is going to play a key part in this. Energy descent is ultimately about energy ascent - the energising of communities. From oil dependency to local resilience.'

'Hear, hear,' shout out several members of the crowd.

'Our work should be preparing communities for transition - hence the name Transition Town. Together, we will rebuild local agriculture and food production.'

#NTS: Growing your own. Isn't that what I'm already doing?

'We must scale up on renewables,' he raises his voice, 'create localised energy micro grids …'

#NTS: Have turned my washing machine to thirty degrees. Perhaps my central heating doesn't have to be on all day.

'We need innovative new building materials made from the low tech recycling of plastics, paper and glass.' Speaker lifts large clump of clay. 'We must rediscover local building materials like this clay.'

I resist the temptation to shout out how my best friend Bernie is building us a cob oven.

'We must all encourage the local gift and sharing economy ...'

#NTS: Nat and the local gift economy. Seems like Nat's been getting lots of seeds, etc., for free. Wonder what she/we have been giving in return?

'We've launched our own local currency,' someone shouts out. 'Seventy percent of all shops and businesses are now accepting it. Our money now helps the community it serves.'

#NTS: Local currency. Not sure what Stu and banker chums would have to say about it. Best not tell him.

'In terms of fashion ...'

My ears prick up at the speaker's mention of *my* area.

'... Over seven billion items of clothing end up in our bins each year.' The speaker shakes his head. 'Our throwaway culture has left landfills bulging at the seams. Fashion waste decomposes in landfills producing methane - a gas twenty times more toxic than CO2. Did you know that cotton growing accounts for eleven per cent of the world's pesticide use?'

#NTS: Cotton - pesticides - eleven per cent! Even with my poor grasp of maths, this figure does sound incredibly high.

The speaker stands up. 'So let's reuse all our fabrics and grow materials out of low energy fibres like hemp which has served mankind for thousands of years. Hemp is fast growing. It's gentle on the land and requires no chemicals.'

'Did you see Hen's cape?' Toby whispers in my ear. I certainly did, I think, recalling Hen's crumpled cape after disappearing with Toby round the back of the polytunnel the other week.

'Hen made it from a recycled curtain,' says Toby.

A curtain? I can't believe Nat was right.

'Did Hen tell you about the poor injured frog we found round the back of the polytunnel that day?' Toby asks. 'We had to use her cape as a blanket. The good news is we put the frog back in your wildlife tank.'

I feel a big (recycled) smile appear on my face, on the basis that I'm kinda soo on message with all this

Transition Town local stuff. And that Toby is not shagging Hen.

The speaker stands up. 'Let's all stand up and shout out, "I'm not afraid of a world of less stuff."'

'I'm not afraid of a world of less stuff,' everyone shouts out.

#NTS: I'm not afraid of a world without stuff. Apart from shoes, face cream, several flights each year … the list goes on.

Oh God, what about the new company car Stu is pondering over? I can learn to ride a bike, can't I?
I close my eyes, imagine myself at an AA meeting of the future. Hi, I'm Deborah. I'm addicted to fossil fuels.

'This is not a lecture about how dreadful the future could be, but an invitation to join the hundreds of communities around the world who are taking steps towards making an abundant future.' The speaker sits back down.

'Where do I sign up?' I jump up.

'You have already, Deborah, by your actions,' Toby smiles at me, links my arm, and leads me to the lunch table where a lady dressed in a hemp apron hands us a delicious bowl of spinach soup.

'Are you enjoying the nettle soup.' A rather dour looking man dressed in a horrid brown suit joins us. 'Hi, I'm Hilary.'

#NTS: Poor bloke with a name like that. Must have been bullied rotten at school.

'What's your interest here?' he asks.

'I'm Deborah, I'm a fashion designer. I've got a ...'

'Deborah is going to be designing a range of zero-energy clothes.' Toby comes up to us. 'Hello Hilary, good to see you. How's it going with DEFRA and the shadow cabinet?'

'Are you designing a range of zero-energy furniture?' I ask him. 'I just love those cute little wooden, FSC approved, cabinets that ...'

'I think the afternoon session is about to commence.' Toby yanks my arm. 'Shall we sit back down? Good to see you.' He shakes Hilary's hand, and whisks me away.

'The rise of carbon dioxide concentrations has led to a dangerous global temperature rise above pre-industrial levels,' the speaker continues with his lecture on global climate destabilisation.
I pull my sleeve down to hide the tan I acquired the other day whilst basking in sun.

'Yet, glacial retreat in the Himalayas, heavy monsoons in India, droughts in Australia - disasters we have recently witnessed, will seem like a stroll in the park if we break the one degrees barrier. This will see Mount Kilimanjaro completely bereft of ice, an almost complete collapse of the Great Barrier Reef, and islands submerged by rising sea levels.' The speaker presses a button and several slides appear on a big screen containing apocalyptic images. 'A two percent increase would bring dreadful heat waves and increased drought. Three percent threshold would bring about the complete collapse of the Amazon ecosystem and the threat of conflict over water supplies around the world.'

I place my hand across my mouth and gasp, uncertain whether I'm upset more about the conversation topic, or the stress of trying to digest nettle soup without letting out a loud belch.

'Anyway ...' The speaker ends by showing a slide of a child clasping a handful of freshly dug potatoes. 'With his vision for a New Sustainable Food Policy will you please welcome onto the stage this afternoon's esteemed speaker, the Right Honourable Hilary Benn, Shadow Secretary of State for the Environment.'

LITTLE GREEN BOOK

Non secateurs: Two sentences that don't merge into one concept: I am an urban, sophisticated woman of the world. I don't know who Hilary Benn is.

9 pm. Drinking large g&t to repress feelings of hideous embarrassment. How am I ever going to face Toby again?

10 pm. Have drunk two more.

11 pm. Stu just arrived home from work. Couldn't believe I chatted with famous politician Hilary Benn today. Says he's a hero. Son of Toby Benn … or is it Ben Toby? Have just googled. It's Tony Benn …

Cultivation*: 'I am not afraid of a world without stuff.' My new personal mantra. I close my Conde Nast Traveller magazine, take in a deep breath and chant: 'I am not afraid of a world without stuff. I am not afraid of a world without stuff*

Chapter 19
Feeling Chit?

I am. Not only with worry how I'm ever going to face Toby again, but because Nat just told me that, far from a date, Toby invited her yesterday as well.

Chitting potatoes. Refers to the process of letting seed spuds sprout half-inch shoots indoors, before planting outside. Seed potatoes are specially developed for planting.

'According to the Great Tit, we're late chitting these.' Nat places several seed potatoes on her orange kitchen window ledge. There's a plaque next to it: 'Grow your own dope. Plant a man!' She races on, 'We should've started these late Jan.'

'Apparently there are over five hundred different varieties of potatoes,' I read out from 'The Untold History of the Potato,' a book laying on Nat's table. 'Potatoes can be grown three times a year. Earlies, planted outside in April to be ready in June. Second earlies, planted late April, ready July. Main crop potatoes planted in May for a September-Dec harvest.'

'We'll have rosemary roasted Xmas spuds!' Nat cheers. 'And creamy dauphinoise,' I add.

'Talking about chips and old blocks, my Pete loves wedgies,' Nat lifts several cartons of eggs out of a LIDL shopping bag.

'In my day, spuds were planted on March 17th - St Paddy's Day,' Dora walks in holding poor little Sammi's hand. 'Did you know that potato blight, the most serious potato disease, was responsible for the Irish famine of 1800's?'

'How old were you then Dora?' Poor little Sammi grabs an egg out of a carton and proceeds to play catch with it.

'How do you like your eggs, Deb?' asks Nat, adding half a dozen eggs into the frying pan. 'I'm easy! Get me some brown sauce outa the cupboard.'

She explains how we're going use empty egg cartons as tomato seed trays, adding how when the seedlings are big enough, we'll plant them out in the garden, egg box and all. Their closed lids act as built-in propagators.

Tomatoes. Arrived from South America into Europe in the 4th Century. Were originally regarded as dangerous member of the deadly nightshade family.

'Did you know that the first tomatoes to arrive in Italy were called pomi d'oro - yellow apples.' I, well versed in Italian culture, tell Nat and Dora how I worked in Milan for three years as a fashion designer for Bottega Veneta.

'Think I've tried their tomato sauce. It's well tasty!' Nat fills an egg carton with compost and adds two tomato seeds to each compartment.

#NTS: My illustrious fashion career. I sigh. Twenty years designing for the biggest fashion brands only to be made redundant last year. No future job in sight …

'Talking of history,' asks Nat, 'did you know that until the 1880's toms were classified as a fruit in order to avoid paying tax! Bet your Stuart knows some good tax scams.'

'Stu is no more a tax specialist than Bottega Veneta is a tomato sauce.' I pause, unsure how to describe what Stu's job actually is.

'If you were a tomato Dora, bet you'd be an heirloom!' Nat laughs. 'I'd be a hot tomato, my Pete's the beefsteak, and Poor little Sammi's a cherry,' she smiles as she watches Sammi tip a whole packet of tomato seeds into one section of the egg carton.

'I guess I'm a plum.'

'No Deb, you're totally sun-dried!' Nat points to my arm. 'Only joking, but is that fake tan?'

'No, it's from other weekend.' I look down at my tanned arms and décolletage carefully on display through my white linen shirt.

'Anyway, "omelot" smarter than I look,' laughs Nat, lifting the frying pan off the stove, and placing three eggs on a. hands it to Sammi.

I watch this rather heavy child scoff down his eggs, only to immediately discharge a less than free range fart. Sunny side up. Which is more than can be said for the weather. We look out of the window as, unbelievably, it starts to snow.

Deciding to leave the egg cartons filled with tomato seeds on the window ledge, we quickly devour the eggs which, according to Nat, were as poached as my mood this morning. We put on our coats, and dash outside.

'Beware the ides of March.' Ben G, stands in Lottie, his arms outstretched to catch falling snowflakes.

'OMG – little garlic shoots have appeared and the snow is covering them.' I rush over to our bed shaped like a light bulb.

'That's called the cotyledon,' explains Nat. 'It's the first leaf to appear after a seed has germinated. Can you believe that very question was on "Who Wants to be a Millionaire," the other night 'Stupid woman got the answer wrong and lost sixteen grand.'

'It's like a white doily out here,' Dora smiles as she picks up a handful of snow and throws it at poor little Sammi.

Sammi throws a snowball back, narrowly missing Dora who ducks down. It hits me squarely in the face. I lift up a ball of snow, hurl it at Nat, and finding myself overcome by fit of giggles, and rush to take cover in the green room.

Around me, tiny cauliflower and cabbage shoots have popped up (I believe the word is germinated) in the trays. They look so fragile. Ephemerally beautiful. So full of hope. I outstretch a finger to gently touch them. My cold breath fogs up the plastic cocoon now draped in soft white snow. It's as if I am viewing the world through a layer of fine voile. Outside, there's raucous laughter as Pete joins in with the fun. A swish of a snowball lands on the green room roof. The silence of our winter garden further disturbed by a distant beat of salsa.

I hopelessly root around in my jacket pocket to find that my mobile, with its salsa ringing tone, has fallen out. It now lays buried, sprouting missed calls and taking root somewhere in the snow.

LITTLE GREEN BOOK

Spud-u-like! - our potato planting calendar

First early: Plant outside April. Harvest Jun
Variety*: Accent.*
Chit Feb/March
Good for boiling
Need 10 weeks in ground.
Second early: Plant outside late April. Harvest July
Variety: Lady Christ
Good for new potatoes
Need 13 weeks in ground.
Main crop: Plant outside late May Harvest Sept/Dec
Variety: King Eddy's
Good for roasting
Need 15 weeks in ground
Depleted crop:
Variety: Couch potato
Good for nothing.

The ten missed calls prior to finding my phone turned out to be from Lee, an arborist. He'd arrived along with a ton of free eucalyptus and willow wood chipping for our paths. We transported twenty wheelbarrows of Lee's load through our winter wonderland. My nose glowing redder than the robin who accompanied us on the wheelbarrow.

7 pm. Collapsed on sofa. As Stu is away yet again, perfect son, James, cooked us gourmet dinner of baked beans on toast!

Chapter 20
Seedy Sunday

A Seedy Sunday is not an all-day-lie-in with one's husbondage or lover, but an event which brings together growers to exchange and talk seeds.

I have bribed James with two extra hours of computer time tonight, to escort me to the Seedy Sunday in Stoke Newington today, and a bonus hour if he pretends to be interested.

Having driven (and hidden car round corner) we enter the hall expecting it to be empty. Surely no-one comes out on a frosty Sunday morning like this. The hall is packed. Tables filled with seeds and small plants, chock-a-block with people milling around chatting, swigging hot cider. The hum of animated chatter is accompanied by a backbeat of, err … heavy metal music.

'Do you know I daydream about seed catalogues,' Delia tells Dougie as I approach them.

'At the NSALG we always order ours on Boxing Day,' Dougie downs the contents of his glass.

'I always do it on Thanksgiving,' adds a lady with a broad American accent.

'Bet you do!' Says a gorgeous young man wearing a Che Guevara T-shirt. He rifles his muscled arm, with a tattoo of a tree running up the length of it, through his long jet-black hair.

'Actually, I've already got my Thomson and Morgan catalogue,' I join the spirit of bonhomie.

'Oh no Deborah, one should only buy from The Real Seed Company, Garden Organic, or smaller Independent seed companies.' Delia nods to the American lady, who looks horrified.

'Or just nick 'em,' winks the young man who introduces himself to me as Che, a guerrilla gardener from Hackney.

'Have you yet joined the Heritage Seed Library, Deborah?' asks Dougie.

'Hey Mum, come and look at this,' James takes my hand and drags me away from my impending catalogue of disaster. 'There's a veg seed over here called Lazy Housewife!'

The Heritage seed library. Not so much a catalogue, as a club. Literally. James leads me to the Heritage stall. It's being run by several guys and girls who look like they've been up clubbing all night. They're bopping away to loud rock music which is belting out. Must say, I rather like the psychedelic T-shirts they are wearing with its logo: 'I dig my heritage. Gardening is so the new rock n roll.'

'Heritage seeds refer to cultivars no longer grown commercially in modern large-scale agriculture, as they are not on the official EU Agricultural list,' says a girl wearing an ivy crown and red Doc Martin boots. 'Many heritage veg just don't conform to the requirements of industrial-scale agriculture,' she sighs.

'Many are de-selected because of their lack of commercial productivity, or ability to withstand mechanical picking,' a chap holding a bunch of daffs shows me a packet of Uncle Fred's pea seeds.

'Or are too delicate or perishable to survive cross-country shipping,' a skinhead raises his dark shades. 'But mainly, they are too variable in shape or size.'

I push my agriculturally-listed, perfect, Marks and Spencer apple firmly back into my designer bag.

'But most cynically of all, it costs thousands of pounds to get onto the official agricultural register,' Red DM girl shakes her head sending her ivy crown flying. 'It's an amount too prohibitive for many heritage varieties.'

'It's just another capitalist conspiracy' they cry in unison. 'Heirloom Gardening is a reaction against this trend.'

'Did you know that fifty years ago, farmers saved their own seeds rather than buying more each year,' Delia walks up to us.
'For subsistence farmers in developing countries, it is still crucial,' Che joins the group.

'Seeds were handed down from one generation to the next like family heirlooms - hence the name heirloom veg.' adds Dougie - monarch of his glen.

Rewind fifty years. Darling here's the jewels, but more importantly, the peas …

'As plant weeding techniques became more sophisticated and pest control developed, this led to large investment into seed companies and the dominance of multinational seed companies and their F1 hybrids.'
#NTS: F1 what?

'Garden organic is a charity which grows Heritage or Heirloom seeds. They're called first generations as they were passed down through generations of farmers. Second generation hybrids, the antithesis of these, are those which have been genetically engineered by the multinational seed companies mixing two different varieties,' explains the red DM girl.

'As F1 hybrids are the result of a cross between breeding and often sterile. No good for seed saving. They fast contaminate global seed supply which threatens the purity of seeds.'

'So it's getting pretty seedy out there!' I regret my poor joke even before it leaves my lips.
'I'm afraid the loss of genetic seed biodiversity facing us today may lead to catastrophe far beyond our imagining,' Delia wipes a tear.

'The Irish potato famine in 1840s was proof of how dangerous it is to be too dependent upon a few species of plants,' Dougie looks at me gravely.

I shake my head in agreement.

Che continues,'at the Heritage Seed club we are looking for seed guardians. Why not give a gift of an adopted veg from our heritage seed library?'

He hands me a packet of peas called 'Gravedigger.' Bernie would surely love them.

'Hey Mum, why don't we adopt this Crapaudine beetroot?' laughs James. 'It says here it was used by the Romans over 1,000 years ago.'

'I do like a veg with history,' reflects Delia.

I rather like the look of this red-tipped lettuce, Merveille de Quatre Saisons. I lift a packet. 'It reminds me of the wonderful meal I had last month at ...'

'Would you like to make a contribution for them?' Che winks at me.

'What Che is trying to say,' Delia explains, 'is that in the 1970's the EU passed a law making it illegal to sell vegetable cultivars not on the official national list of any EU country. One cannot buy Heirloom seeds - but one can make a *contribution* for them.'

'Whilst it's illegal to sell seeds, mum, it's not, to sell the envelope containing them!' James (Basildon) Bond adds his comment in the dark, as suddenly the lights go out in the room.

I imagine lots of shifty envelopes being secretly exchanged, hushed whispers, codeword: Grandma Ethel's asparagus. Early blood turnips. Password: Dr Hinkelhatz hot pepper …

There's a pat on my shoulder. I jump and turn round as the lights go back on. In front of me, Dougie is squeezing Delia's bottom.

'Hey Mum, check this one out,' James comes running up to me, 'it's called Squashed Stu, I've offered to become a seed guardian of it for Dad …'

LITTLE GREEN BOOK

Sowing the seeds -
Heritage Seed Library: On James' insistence, we spent twenty-five pounds to join the club, but will have to pay nothing for the seeds. For our 'contribution' we get to choose six packets of heritage seed varieties every year, and get access to its huge network of seed swappers.

F1: is not the Monte Carlo Grand Prix which Stu has been lounging around all day watching, but nasty hybrids.

Must convince Nat we should only buy seeds pollinated by natural means, wind, insects, birds.

Chapter 21
Gutted

I'm not. But our peas are. If you have wet soil or a problem with mice (aargghh!), it is advised to sow seeds in a length of plastic guttering. I just hope that the water leaking out from Mr Parkeeper's roof has nothing to do with the plastic piping Nat 'acquired' last night. We are going to sow our peas into it today.

With the snow and subsequent frost now as thawed as our planting schedule, we have lots of catching up to do. Toby has therefore called in the troops: The Hampstead Scouts.

'There's a beautiful smell in your garden,' a broad-shouldered, oh-so-long-legged scout called Nick tells me, as he leans his taut body (aren't those brown shorts a little too small?) over our broad bean bed. He starts to build a bamboo cage to support our growing crop. 'It must be that eucalyptus mulch on your paths,' he smiles as he places a bamboo stake every foot along the outside of the bed, and another behind every tiny broad bean shoot which have appeared. Running a length of green garden wire around and in between the stakes, he finishes the cage, stands up and skips off to join his other five scout buddies.

#NTS: Mrs Robinson. Here's to you … Can't believe I'm really gawping at a teenager.

'Dyb dyb dyb. Fancy a bit of pole dancing then?' sings Nat, skipping up to me. 'They need lots of support.'

Don't we all, I fan away my middle age flush with a packet of Musselburgh leek seeds.

'Talking of support,' Nat whispers in my ear, 'I opened a letter addressed to that opera singer at Flat 18 by mistake.'

'I didn't know an opera singer lives there. Stu loves …'

'Anyway, guess what? She's claiming child tax credit and hasn't got any kids!' Nat hands me a packet of seeds. 'Whilst we're on the subject of money, I bought us these Moneymaker aubergine seeds which we can sow now. Hope they're a great cash crop!' She roars with laughter.

I follow Nat into the green room. We get to work sowing aubergine and carrot seeds into little pots filled with compost, and place them on a table.

'Apparently, these Healthmaster carrot seeds contain three times more beta-carotene than other varieties,' I read out the info on seed packet.

'Better than what?' Nat laughs. 'Talking of health, I think we should grow smoothies.'

Smoothies indeed. I watch Toby enter Lottie walking alongside a no-nonsense-looking man dressed in perfectly-pressed green shirt and shorts.

'Hi dee hi, Tob,' Nat sticks various fingers up to him in an attempt to offer some sort of Scout's greeting.

'Roger Lyntton. Scout leader.' The man briskly shakes my hand. 'We scouts don't just wear green but think green. Here today to earn the first part of our smallholding badge.' He lifts a whistle out of his pocket and gives it a shrill blow.

The scouts line up to salute Roger. They start digging our chippie, peas and cabbages bed, whilst we prepare the ground for parsnips and leeks.

Parsnips. A slow-growing crop. Stays in the ground for nine months. Parsnips thrive on frost as it turns starch into sugar. We have purchased a brand called Avon resister, as it is resistant to canker.

'You can tell a plant has canker by its brown scabby skin,' Roger informs Nat, as they dig away and sow four seeds at six-inch intervals.

'Bit like my sister-in-law after she came back from Tenerife last week,' says Nat singing that scout classic: 'Ging gang gooly ...'

'I can't wait to make you some of my cream of parsnip soup served with homemade partridge sausage rolls,' I smile at Toby.

'Bet you'd prefer a bowl of my cock-a-leekie any day, wouldn't you Tob?' Nat offers.

'Do you know that leeks - which won't be ready until November, stay in the ground as long as parsnips,' adds Toby, in the soup, (but ever the politician).

'Talking of taking a leek, could I use your loo?' Boy (if you can call him that) scout Nick, comes up to me. I lead him indoors.

'You haven't got a ciggie?' he asks, winking at me. 'I'm dying for a quick puff.'

'Sorry, I don't smoke. Brownies honour,' I giggle as I cross my fingers behind my back. I pinch myself to stop all temptation of retrieving a ciggie from my secret stash hidden from Stu, and share one with him.

#NTS: Here's to you Mrs Robin ...

Smoking the pipe of peas. *Peas* sown outside at this time of year are at the mercy of rodents in search of an easy meal. I rejoin Toby and Nat in the green room, where they have started to sow Meteor, an early variety, into the length of plastic piping.

'The great thing about sowing your seeds into this,' Toby strokes the pipe, 'is that once the peas have germinated and the chance of frost has passed next month, you can transfer the pipe directly into the ground. Your tender shoots will not be disturbed.' He places his hand on my shoulder.

'Oh, tender is the night,' I feel my face blush a deeper shade of purple than the beetroot we turn our attention to.

Beetroot. Not the stuff sold in jars and packed with chemicals and colours. Real beet is full of antioxidants and is great for the immune system.

'I like to slowly bake them like potatoes, rip off their tops, and serve dripping with garlic and sour cream,' Toby slides his hand down my arm. 'Or grate them rough and raw, gently sprinkle all over with golden ...'

'Burpees Golden.' Nat relegates beetroot back to the pickle jar as she lifts a packet of seeds. Toby removes his hand from my arm to take them.

'I bought these Burpees beets to plant late Spring,' Nat tears open another packet. 'The one we're sowing is called Bolt-hardy, an early variety.'

A while later our sowing is interrupted by Mr Parkeeper, who storms into the green room. 'That's my new length of feckin' guttering pipe,' he shouts as he lifts the pipe and empties out all of our carefully sowed peas and compost onto the ground. 'I've got a feckin' leak. I've had to call the plumbers in. Cost me eighty feckin quid.'

'Look Mr Parker, I'm sure there's a logical explanation to all this,' Toby looks enquiringly at me. I look enquiringly at a packet of rocket seeds.

'And as to you, you politico dipshite, I'll have you in the press as an accessory.'

The gutter press, that is. I keep my less-than-conciliatory pun to myself.

'Everything all right in here?' The green room door opens. Roger Lyntton and scouts squeeze into the already packed space.

'Your all gonna feckin' pay for this,' yells Mr Parkeeper.

'I already have arsehole,' Nat yells back, 'and don't swear in front of children.'

Boy scout Nick winks at me.

'What I'm trying to tell you is that I've got the receipt for it here, so just pipe down,' Nat fishes out a B&Q receipt from her jacket pocket.

We all lean over to look at the details on the receipt which, unbelievably, does seem to indicate the recent purchase of a length of plastic piping.

'So lettuce all be friends!' Nat slices open a packet of 'salad bowl' seeds and leads the scouts out to plant our first lettuce seeds of the season. I remain behind to place the compost and fallen peas seeds back into the pipe.

I reflect upon how Nat had just managed to earn her own proficiency badge - getting herself out of a knot

LITTLE GREEN BOOK

Keeping doubts at bay

10 pm: Laying in the bath, as much shattered from long day in garden as row have just had with Stu. He can't understand why I am getting so involved with this 'silly eco food-growing thing'. Thinks our weekly Ocado food delivery is adequate. No doubt he also thinks I should be a) sipping tea on day out with nice ladies at RHS Wisley, whilst dreaming of a herbaceous border, as opposed to sharing tepid tea with Nat fantasising about Toby (and boy scouts) after - b) having nails manicured in Primrose Hill. That would be a vast improvement on their current caked mud colour, which he hinted I should polish for dinner with his banking colleagues tomorrow night.

I submerge my body, proud dirty hands et al, into the bubbles and pick up one of the bay leaves I had scattered in the bath. Funnily enough, before today, I had never even noticed that there was a bay tree in my garden ...

Accurate record of what was sown today. Scouts honour:

Sowed in the Green room:
Carrots: Healthmaster. Plant outside April
Aubergine: Moneymaker
Tarragon: Artemisia Dracunculus
Peas: Meteor (in pipe) Transfer pipe outside April
Sowed outside:
Parsnips: Avon Resister.
Beetroot: Burpees Golden.
Leeks: Musselburgh
Lettuce: 'Salad bowl.'

Good housekeeping:
When we transplant the carrots outside, we'll place them next to the leeks as part of our good bedfellows, companion planting plan. Aha, it's all starting to make sense!

Not so good housekeeping. Budget breakdown*:*
Spend to-date bought forward	*£500*
Cost of mines a shish purchases	*£ 40*
Herbs, potatoes and artichokes	*£ 40*
Heritage seed Library	*£ 25*
Total spend to date	*£605*

Excludes cost for pipe of peas. Asked Nat for receipt that she showed to Mr Parkeeper today. Strangely, she was reluctant to give it to me. She finally admitted that she found it on the floor at B&Q.

More like taking the peas.

Chapter 22
Astronomical gardening

Does not refer to spiralling Lottie costs, but the practice of timing gardening and cultivation activities to coincide with phases of the moon. Lunar gardening - which Nat now calls 'loony' gardening.

We have a new member of our gardening fraternity: Gaia —earth goddess. She recently moved into No.7, a lucky number in numerology, or so she tells us. Her name is really Gale Fisher (Nat's sister who works at the council has seen her rent book).

Gaia has just finished lecturing us for two hours on bio or in our case not-so-bio-dynamic gardening, a system developed by Rudolph Steiner.

'We must treat this garden tool like a magic wand,' Gaia lifts a fork and strokes it.

'Well I call a spade a spade,' Nat shoves her spade back in the mud. Her sense of humour is waning like the root veg Gaia has suggested we plant during next week's waning moon.

'Since prehistoric times man has gardened by the phases of the moon with all its inhalations and exhalations,' Gaia takes in a deep breath as she weeds our leafy veg bed. 'Moon gardeners co-ordinate their activities according to the moon's path, drawing sap up into the sky when it is ascending, and down to earth on its descent,' she smiles up at the sky.

'My Pete loves mooning, don't ya babe!' Nat shoves her bum out at Pete, who joins us.

'How actually does it work?' I ask as Gaia raises her Aztec poncho up over her mop of frizzy plum hair to reveal a long crushed velvet dress. It's a deeper shade of amber than the mug of mugwort tea she sips.

'The Moon affects plant growth through its pull on water,' she lifts a sheet of card out of her hessian bag. It contains a lunar calendar. She points out several facts. 'Each moon phase lasts for six to eight days. At the time of the new moon, when gravity is strong, its pull on moisture causes seeds to swell and burst. It is therefore a good time for planting crops that produce seeds on the outside - broccoli, strawberries. Whereas plants that produce yield above ground should be planted during waxing moon. In its second phase, increased moonlight creates optimum conditions for leaf growth, tomatoes, bean, peas ...'

'Talking of beans, Deb, have you seen our beans and pea shoots which are popping up?' Nat grabs my hand and drags me to the green room.

'At the time of the full moon, energy is focused towards root growth,' Gaia calls out as she follows us. She sticks on a metal pole. 'We must not plant anything during the days of new or full moon.'

'What do you call a clock on the moon?' asks Nat, who like me, is clearly in desperate need of a change of subject. 'A lunar-tic!'

'To sum up,' Gaia raises her voice above our raucous laughter, 'when the moon moves into a different sign it becomes barren or more fertile.'

'I always read my horoscopes in Hello magazine every week,' nods Nat. 'What star sign are you?'

'I'm Virgo. Barren and moist,' Gaia smiles.

'Are you barren as well, Deb?' Nat giggles.

'Actually, I'm a Gemini,' I reply.

'I'm Leo,' Nat adds, 'we're gonna have a wicked party out here in August.'

'You know that tonight is a very special night. It is the eve of the Vernal equinox,' says Gaia, looking up at the sky, which has turned a foreboding shade of grey. 'Why don't we all join hands and say a prayer ...'

'I've gotta go,' Nat announces and dashes off, leaving me alone with Gaia and the egg she lifts out of her bag.

'Happy Eostre,' Gaia hands me the egg.

'Thanks, but I'm just about to cook dinner.' I refrain from adding how actually Easter was not till next month. It's official. Gaia is even battier than the sleeves on her dress.

I thank her for a stellar afternoon, jump on my broomstick and fly back indoors.

WHAT & WHERE IT'S AT ...

1. *Onions and garlic: Growing!*
2. *Pimms patch*
3. *Nettle beer: No comment*
4. *Pizza patch: Jerusalem artichokes in one quarter.*
5. *Jack n his beanstalk: Aquadulce Claudia beans growing*
6. *Courgettes: Can't find where we dug trench!*
8. *Chitted spuds to be placed in tyres next month*
9. *Fruit bushes*
10. *Apple and pear trees*
11. *Bath time.*
12. *Gro-bags*
13. *Oil cans*
14. *Lettuce be friends: Seeds sown.*
15. *Beeten up: Bolthardy beetroot seeds sown*
16. *Parsnips: Avon Resister seeds sown.*
17. *Leeks: Musselburgh seeds sown*
18. *Loony gardening: Gaia's dynamic bed. She's going to design in yin-yang shape. According to Teutonic mythology, Eostre was the goddess of upspringing light. Suspected Gaia's hue of hennaed hair - last seen in the 1970s, had German roots.*

Seeds sown in green room...
19. *Organic tomatoes in egg cartons*
20. *Meteor peas in pipe*
21. *Armado caulie*
22. *Savoy Siberia cabbage*
23. *Healthmaster carrots.*
24 *Moneymaker aubergine*

SPRING

APRIL

Storm in a B-Cup

Chapter 23
Brassicas. Mine's an A cup

Are not some form of Vivienne Westwood lingerie but fast-maturing crops of the cabbage family.

We are planting spinach and summer cabbages 'under the cloche.' It's not a term, according to Nat, which refers to Pete after his late return home from the pub, but a plastic cover we are placing over our plants, to keep them warm.

Talking about heat, Dora has bought out an old net curtain to cover the ground and warm up the soil. I wonder why there's a bra attached to it?

'What size is your cup then girls?' Toby laughs as he watches Nat untangle said grey bra and hold it up for all to see.

'Talking of cup sizes, isn't that T-shirt a little too tight for you, Deb?' Nat turns round to face me.

#NTS My cup does indeed runneth over.

I look down at my purple "I dig my heritage" T-shirt carefully on display over my shapely Myla bra. 'As you probably know Toby,' I flutter my eyelashes, 'this T-shirt is from the Heritage Seed Library.'

'Talking of heritage,' says Dora as she takes the bra from Nat, 'we can fill this with manure and dangle it above a bucket of water for a few weeks to make manure tea. In the Summer we can support growing pumpkins in them -'

'A support bra,' Nat bursts out laughing.

'It also works with stockings,' Toby winks at me, 'I love a pair of seamed fishnet stockings. Hen wears them -'

Holey hosiery! So Toby has also noticed. Hen's penchant for wearing fishnets.

Dora continues. 'In my day we used to say that if you can sit in soil comfortably with a bare bum then it's warm enough to sow outside.' She lowers her body onto the ground.

'Be careful love, you know you're prone to haemorrhoids,' advises Nat.

'Even though it's, er, technically Spring, it's still a little chilly and I don't think the final risk of frost has yet passed,' Toby helps lift Dora up before she puts her words to the test.
'Anyway Tob,' says Nat, 'have you heard about our new volunteer? Her name's Gaia, or dire gaia – DG, as I'm gonna call her.'

Nat's use of the abbreviation 'DG', not to be confused with leading fashion house - Dolce and Gabbana - who I worked with for many years.

'Sadly she won't be helping out for a few days as it's the new moon.' Nat looks at the lunar calendar Gaia has now super-glued to the green room door!'

Talking about small moons, *Brussels* are miniature cabbages. Ugh! We've all heard the term, a dog is not just for Xmas, well now it appears the same applies for Brussels.

Sprouts are the latest health-eating sensation due to their cancer-busting mustard oils which give them their characteristic bitter flavour.

'The Brussels we are planting today are called Sanda. They're from the Real Seed Company,' I hand the packet to Nat.

'It says here they have nice round tight balls,' she reads, 'personally, I like a nice tight …'

Cabbages fall into three categories. Summer hearting varieties which should be sown in April for a September crop. Winter hearting/Savoys, sown May for a December crop, and Spring cabbages, sown July for an April crop.

'Oh well,' Nat laughs as we walk into the green room to view the Savoy cabbage seeds we sowed in January – completely the wrong time of year. Miraculously, several seem to have germinated and formed two-inch shoots.

Nat flips open our Great Tit bible and reads out loud. 'Now that there are two sets of leaves on them, we should 'harden' them off. That means placing them outside for a few hours each day to avoid shocking them with a sudden change in temperature. We will then transplant them into the brassiere bed. 'Talking of harden offs ...' Nat grins and looks down at Toby's crotch.

'Hard what?' Hen comes bounding into the garden. 'Sorry I'm late, what have I missed?' Hen asks as she takes off her coat to reveal elegant long black stockinged legs shooting out from little tweed shorts.

Fishnets. Damn - I didn't say it out loud did I? 'Er ... we've just sown brassicas, and are about to plant Cavolo Nero in the polytunnel.'

'Yum, I love kale,' Hen licks her lips.

'It's fabulous in an Italian dish called Robillata,' I look at Toby, who is busy staring at Hen's legs. 'When I was a fashion designer in Milan we used to ...'

'Do be careful not to get clubroot. It's the biggest problem you'll have with brassicas,' interjects Hen, preventing me from sharing my fashion credentials.

'Shall we go see the nettles growing around our onions, Hen?' I reply. 'And do be careful not to get your legs stung.'

Talking of Icebergs. *Lettuces.* There are four different types. Romaine, Crisphead, Butterhead, and loose leaf.

'Did you know that a shop-bought bag of mixed lettuce is washed in twenty times more chlorine than a swimming pool?' Toby explains as we walk over to our lettuce be friends, bed. 'It's one of the most chlorinated products out there.'

'I see you are sowing cut-and-come-again loose leaf lettuce,' Hen smiles at Toby, 'it always works for me.'

I bet it does. I keep the thought to myself.

'Cut and come again is the quickest way to grow salads,' Toby quickly adds. 'They should be sowed in rows and their leaves cut when five to eight centimetres high, leaving the plant in the ground to re-grow for successive cuts.'

'According to the Great Tit, we should sow lettuce seeds every two weeks to ensure a constant supply.' Nat opens a packet of seeds. 'I'm looking forward to sowing little gem lettuce seeds next month for my little gem, poor little Sammi.'

I add, 'And I plan to sow the Marvel of four season seeds I procured from the Heritage seed library, followed by Amorina,'– a Lolla Rossa. It has an intense rosette of deep Bordeaux red leaves.'

'If you were a salad dressing, which would you all be?' Nat interrupts my attempts to impress Toby with my ode to lettuce, 'I'd be marie rose coz I love all things pink!' She chuckles.

'Toby would be caesar,' Hen laughs.

'Dora would be blue cheese as she's often got an odd smell! Only joking,' Nat chuckles. 'I'd be a classic Italian made with the finest virgin olive oil.'

'Funny, I always find it too acidic,' Hen shrugs her shoulders. She continues, 'I think a homegrown salad needs no dressing at all. It's perfect undressed.' She slides her hand down the seam of her stockings to smooth them out. 'Talking of perfection, have you seen the beautiful little pink blossom buds which have appeared on the plum tree?'

Damn Hen and her perfect little pink buds.

'Talking of undressing,' Nat adds her own observation, 'did you know that the Egyptians thought lettuce was an aphrodisiac ...?'

LITTLE GREEN BOOK

What we planted outside today ... bit of a cupful

'Picasso' spinach: Harvest May onwards
'Sanda brussels: Harvest Oct onwards
'Amorina' lolla rossa lettuce: Pick in 8-10 weeks
'Marvel of 4 seasons loose leaf lettuce: Pick in 10 weeks
'Salad bowl' lettuce: Pick in 6-8 weeks

WHAT WE PLANTED IN THE GREEN ROOM:
 'Red drumhead' cabbage: Harvest Aug
Cavolo nero - black kale: Harvest September onwards

... it's sleaves even more ruffled than I am

Chapter 24
Four seasons in one day

'If you were a pizza topping, which would you be?'

Psychologist Nat asks a week later as we dig over our quarto stagione pizza patch to remove the thick crust of weeds which have encased it.

'Pete's a sloppy Guiseppe, poor little Sammy's full of capers, and Bernie, you'd be the spinach one that gives a donation to charity,' she laughs. 'Deb, I bet you'd say Toby's the hot chilli!'

Talking of hot, Toby will not be around for two weeks. He's whisked Grace off to the South of France.

'How lovely to jet off to the Côte D'Azur for Easter,' I change the subject as a gust of un-balmy wind sends my beret flying.

'Jet – Deborah, hardly,' says Bernie, snarling at me in a less than charitable way. 'They've taken the train to Avignon and will cycle to the coast from there.'

'Bicyclette, bien sur,' I add not wanting to distract him from the fantastique job he is doing preparing the building materials for our cob oven. I close my eyes, imagine Toby in tight spandex shorts and maillot jaune whizzing along on his chopper.

'So what are we going to plant in here?' Nat studies our pizza base. It's so far topping-less, save for the artichokes growing encouragingly in one quarter.

'A lot of *peppers*.' I look at the pile of free Daily Mail seeds packets which Nat seems to have ordered on behalf of every home in the street. 'They're absolutely delicious when layered over the freshest mozzarella di buffalo from ...'

'Watford. We must support our local food producers, Deborah,' Bernie looks up as it starts to rain cats and ... er ... wood pigeons.

I yell as a large bird deposits a slimy white excretion over my new jacket. I quickly try and wipe it off.

'Is that a Canada goose jacket, Deborah?' Bernie glares at the label. 'A product of cruelty.'

'Time to plant these peppers under cover,' Nat comes to my rescue leaving me no time to remark how I'd bought it in a charity shop. She grabs my arm and we dash into the green room.

#NTS: Canada Goose. Cruelty?

Chilli strength varies considerably between varieties. Nat has decided to grow Thai Dragon. It's the hottest.

'Deb, why don't you place these seeds which I've scattered between two damp kitchen towels in your airing cupboard? It'll help speed up germination process,' Nat explains as she shoves two soggy towels in my Canada goose jacket pocket. She pats me reassuringly on the shoulder and links my arm.

Armed with a tray of burgeoning little tomato shoots to transplant into a quarter of our pizza patch - even though it's still early in the season, we head back to Bernie.

'Happy Easter to you all for next weekend,' Pete comes into Lottie holding a tray of hot cross buns, 'I never know if it's meant to be happy or not.'

'That Robert Powell Jesus movie makes me sob every year.' Nat stuffs a bun in Bernie's mouth as his hands are covered in clay.

'Talking of Easter and eggs,' Bernie attempts to speak whilst chewing, 'broken egg shells are the best organic solution to stop pests from destroying your crop.' He scoops a handful of broken egg shells from his pocket and scatters them over our leek and parsnip plants. 'Make sure from now on you save your eggs. You do use good ones don't you?'

'All my eggs are good,' Nat winks at Pete. 'They're farm fresh! Talking of eggs Deb, I've had several of mine frozen?'

'Farm fresh eggs are the worst, most cruel, produced by caged hens who live short wretched lives, living on wire mesh floors in racks with space less than a sheet of A4 paper ...'

'She means they're fresh from the local Farmers Market,' I add, unsure whether to be more upset by Bernie's words, or the unpleasant dribble of butter coagulating on his chin.

'Whilst on the subject of eggs,' Bernie glares at Nat, 'I hope you're regularly cleaning the egg larvae forming on the rim of your wormery?'

'Did you know that the cross on a hot cross bun symbolises the solar wheel in Pagan cosmology,' DG - Dire Gaia, walks up to us and swipes the last bun off Pete's tray.

'In Latin, Pagan means one who lives in the country. Life and death are not seen as personal ego-based conditions as feared in Judeo-Christianity.'

'What religion are you then Gire?' asks Nat.

'A pantheist?'

'Would that be a pink pantheist?'

'Bernie - have you er ... met Gaia?' I introduce them as Nat and Pete burst out laughing.

Leaving them to get acquainted beside DG's loony bed which she has designed in shape of yin-yang symbol, Nat and I turn our attention to planting our Accent, first early potatoes.

'Chips. Big, fat and greasy, that's how I love them,' I nod in agreement with Nat as we place a line of tyres along one strip of Pete's chippie bed. We fill them with compost and plant five well-chitted tubers into each tyre.
Nat explains, 'when the leaves pop up above the compost, we earth em up by placing another tyre filled with compost on top. We keep doing this until we have a tower of tyres filled with lotsa lovely spuds.'

'It says here that coriander is two herbs in one,' I read out from the Great Tit as we sow coriander seeds. 'Their leaves can be used for chopping and sprinkling. But it's also a spice. If we leave the foliage at the end of the season, the plant will produce hard round buff peppercorn-sized seeds which form the spice garam masala, used in Indian cookery.'

'Talking of korma,' replies Nat, 'I popped round to the recycling centre and saw some chairs going free that would look great in your garden.' She races on before I can rather meanly add how I doubt we have the same taste in furniture.
'I'm starved. I know your Stu is away working agaaaain, and James is on a sleepover.' She links my arm. 'Fancy popping to the chippie with me? They do a great chips in curry sauce?'

LITTLE GREEN BOOK

Green room:
Pepper, 'carnival mix.' Basil 'organic sweet Genovese.'
Courgettes –

Most stylish room:
Popped along to the recycling centre Nat mentioned and
O.M.G - found to-die-for chairs. Someone had thrown out
four Phillipe Starke 'Louis ghost' chairs, now on display in
my garden.

Cultivation:
Don't think I'll be sampling chips in curry sauce again any
time soon!

Uncultivated:
Canada goose. Fur trim made from wild coyotes

Chapter 25
Potluck

Florence. Vivarosa. Mara de Bois. Not the names of my fashionista friends, but types of strawberries.

We are growing strawberries in terracotta pots as it stops the slugs from nibbling them. Today, we are going to plant, 'Elvira,' an early fruiting variety.

Talking of fashionista friends, I've invited the girls around for a tea party today in Lottie. I survey the tea table: crustless cucumber sarnies, Laduree macaroons, a vintage teapot, cups, and saucers all laid out on a white linen tablecloth with matching napkins. The Phillipe Starke chairs surround it.

'So girls, what do you think of my little eco-garden?' I proudly ask an hour later as the girls stroll in, sharing air kisses and protestations for having gone A.W.O.L (absent without lunch) for too long.

'Oh no, Deborah, everyone calls it an allotment these days,' says Fliff, donning her boxing (Orla Kiely, yellow-flowered potting) gloves. She strokes Percy her poodle, who is dressed in matching dog coat.

'Yes, darling, allotments are the new buzzword.' Phoebe wipes the mud off her red Marc Jacobs high-heeled wellies. They are sooo in. 'What a fashionista you are.'

She pats me on the shoulder. 'It's so unlike you to be ahead of the pack ...'
The wolf one. I keep my thought to myself.

'By the way, how's Stuart,' she continues, 'I thought I saw him at the Connaught bar last week. You weren't with him. Must have been another work do ...?'

'So what do you think of our bespoke cob oven?' I quickly change the subject away from Stu and lead them over to the cob oven. 'We roasted fab veg in it last night.'

My little lie is somewhat more caramelised than the veg.

'Oh, I was wondering what that odd little structure was.' Fliff looks dismissively at the oven with its wonky dome perched on mismatched bricks.

'Did you know that gardening is the new pilates,' Phoebe strokes her tresses of glossy blonde hair and straightens out her Pucci scarf. She shoves an Elvira plant in a pot, mixes in some compost, and sits back down exhausted from her exercise.

'I must say Deborah you are looking a little more trim. I was a little concerned about the amount of weight you have been putting on ...'

'Talking about a good feed,' I insert a much-needed segue, 'when the strawberry flowers it will need to be fed every ten days with a tomato feed.'

I turn around as there's a loud barking. Tikka and Marsala come charging into Lottie. They sniff out Percy, who has found his own good feed and has his nose dipped into our wildlife tank.

'Ahoy matey, come and see what I've found!' shouts Nat, as she and Dora follow tout-suite (more-like bath suite). They stagger in, lugging some kind of … er … bath on a pallet with wheels.

'That fancy store in Primrose Hill was throwing this out,' says Nat.

I rush over to take the weight from Dora who is gasping for breath. 'But this is a brand new cast iron bath,' I stare at the bath with its gleaming gilt taps. 'It would retail for over a thousand pounds. Why would they be throwing it out?' I reduce my question to a whisper.

'Dunno! Probably damaged.' says Nat shaking her head. 'Pete said it had been left out on the kerb.'

'Er, girls … meet Natalie and Dora, my colleagues in Lottie … our eco-garden.'

Fliff and Phoebe walk up to inspect the bath.

'Charmed,' Fliff dons her gloved hand to Nat who grabs it and gives it a good shake.

'Where did you say you got this bath from? asks Phoebe.

'We're going to grow lemon thyme and lavender in it,' Nat races on. 'Make it a sensory soak.'

'And I've bought over this teapot from the church to sow chamomile and parsley seeds into it.' Dora lifts a teapot out of a bag.

The term 'any more tea vicar,' is seemingly now relegated to the church canon.

'Talking about tea ladies, I think it's about that time.' I scuttle off into my kitchen.

'Heel dog, heel,' I hiss as I return with a tray of tea, passing Percy, who is trying to hump Tikka behind the green room.

'Talking about heels, I'm buying some fab new ochre Jimmy Choos,' Fliff continues, clearly oblivious to what her beloved pet is getting up to behind her.

'Yes, we were thinking of getting Chinese tonight,' Nat who has inveigled herself into my tea party, scoffs down … three (doesn't she know they're Laduree) pastel-shaded macaroons.

'Anyhow, Deborah,' Fliff lifts a macaroon off the plate, 'we were wondering what had been keeping you sooo busy. Everyone in the industry knows you're 'in-between,' jobs. Thought you might have a secret lover stashed behind your suedes!'

'Well, Deb does fancy Toby like mad,' Nat gulps down her cup of tea.

'Toby?' Phoebe's tone does little to hide the fact that she finds it unbelievable that I might be able to secure a new job or a lover. And not necessarily in that order. 'Who's Toby?' she asks.

'So tell me, ladies, have you seen Christopher Kane's latest collection?' I, future Lady Chatterley, change the subject.

'Yes, we must build our cane collection around our Jack n beanstalks bed. It's getting wild over there,' says Nat.

'OMG,' Fliff slides her hand along the Ghost chair she is sitting on, 'I love these, are they from Heals?'

'Talking of heels,' I once again change the subject, 'have you seen the new range of hunter wellies?'

'And talking of hunting, Deborah, how is the job search going? It's been quite a while now. You poor thing, you must be feeling desperate.' Phoebe asks in a voice more sickly sweet than the morsel of macaroon she deigns to place to her lips.

Nat replies. 'Didn't Deb tell you about the meeting she had last week, talking to Hilary Benn – the government's DEFRA Minister, about designing a range of hemp clothes? I'm sure you all know that hemp is an eco-fabric, unlike the cotton top you're wearing,' Nat pauses to point at Phoebe's paisley Prada blouse, 'it doesn't need tons of water and herbicides to grow.'

Joy upon joy – I look at their flabbergasted faces. I feel like hugging Nat, but instead, I pop a whole macaroon into her mouth.

'You know hemp is made from yon cannabis plant,' Ben-G walks out carrying a joint. He inhales a large puff. #NTS: Hemp - marijuana. What's the link? I rack my eco-brain to no avail.

'Talking about pot,' I change the subject. 'We went to Arthur Pott Dawson's restaurant last night. Stu thought it was fabulous.'

'Well met ladies. I'm Ben-G. You're gonna love this one,' he lifts up a packet of seeds and waves it in front of Fliff, who is desperately trying to fan away his smoke. 'I bought us this Stonehead cabbage.'

He winks at Phoebe. 'Any of you fair maidens wanna come plant it with me?'

His words are drowned out by the roar of a loud drill. We turn round to see Nat, sporting snowman earmuffs, has started to drill. She points in the direction of the bath. 'Gotta drill holes for aeration.' She grins, and drills away.

'Fancy a Pimms?' I shout out to Fliff as Phoebe, unbelievably, takes up Ben-G's offer, and follows him into the green room.

Fliff follows me to our Pimms patch. She stands around watching as I plant the Elvira strawbs and mint plants in two sections of the bed. Pete has brilliantly bordered it to look like the shape of a bottle. Salut.

'Aagggh! There's a frog leg hanging out of Percy's mouth,' yells Fliff in a piercing scream that's even louder than Nat's drilling.

It's not however as loud as Phoebe's howls of laughter coming from the green room. Tikka's howls of something I daren't even think about. And a loud snoring. Dora has fallen asleep on the bird table.

'Oh God, no! I think Percy's just about to throw up,' Fliff bursts into tears as Percy charges up to us and discharges his dejeuner all over my strawberry pots. 'Percy Throwup,' Dora sits up, 'I used to have a thing about him.'

'I think you mean Thrower, Dora,' I look at my pot with its wilting strawbs.

The pandemonium continues as Nat turns her attention to getting holey (drilling) the vicar's teapot, a giggling Phoebe and Ben-G stagger out of the green room, clearly stoned. Fliff stares at Percy's stained coat and starts to screech in a witch-like warble certain to send all the remaining frogs, eye of newt, toe of frog, leaping back into the wildlife tank for cover. Wish I could join them.

Potluck. Am not sure would be the phrase I would use to sum up today!

LITTLE GREEN - THE COLOURS - *ARE-REALLY-COMING-AT-ME* - BOOK

Harvest: 2 hours later. Stonehead cabbage: Medium-sized, firm, short-cored, round-head reefers which means there is very little time lets get wasted when preparing for cooking. Holds for a long time without spliffing. Each well-flavoured head rolls up and blows back in at about 4lb on average. Plant with good grass in Pimms patch with Elvira strawberry plugs flavour enhanced by Percy's offering. In herb bed smoking sage, moon juice, and oregano with Ben-g who is to marry Joanna.

Chapter 26
Wiggly woo

The myth of Percy and the frog is nothing, however, compared to the myth of Persephone and the worms. Only in this story, Gaia, the witch, is real ...

One beautiful Spring day as Persephone, daughter of Demeter, the Greek Goddess of the Harvest, saw the most enchanting flower: A narcissus. As she reached down to pick it, her feet began to tremble. The earth was split in two. From a crack in the ground, a giant arm reached up to grab her. It was Hades, God of the Underworld. He dragged her off below to Hell.

Demeter searched for Persephone. She was so upset that she stopped performing her worldly duties. All plants on Earth stopped growing. There were no more harvests. When all the children around the world starved, Persephone's father, Zeus, wielded his thunderbolt. Terrible storms flooded the Earth.

Finally, Hades relented and agreed to return Persephone. As she was leaving, he offered her an apple to eat. Persephone, who had refused all food, was so hungry, that although she knew that those who ate anything in the underworld were never allowed to return to earth, she thought it would be fine if she only ate the pips. But this put a curse on her. Ever after, she was forced to return to the underworld for four months each year. Whilst Demeter was overjoyed to have her daughter back, and restored life to Earth, ever since that time, she withdraws it for four months each year. This is the period we know as Winter.

'Any questions children?' asks Gaia through her black-painted lips as she finishes her story. She throws out the arms of her long black hooded cape and snarls as she hands round apple slices to the quivering children.

'When you said we were going on a trip to a nursery, I thought it would be Petersham garden nursery, not poor little Sammi's nursery!' I whisper to Nat.

My head is banging as much from my 'trip' with Ben-G to the green room last night after the girls left, as having to listen to DG's terrifying story. She has stunned a group of trembling children into silence.

'And why on earth did you invite her?' I hiss.

Nat shrugs her shoulders. 'I thought it would help poor little Sammi get into the big school here if we offered a free fairytale and gardening session.'

'I need to go …' a pretty little three-year-old girl with golden plaits bursts into tears.

'I'll … er, just help her pop to the loo, if you wouldn't mind holding the fort,' the teacher looks down at the embarrassed-looking girl's pink skirt. It's now turned a shade more magenta as a result of a wet patch. She quickly whisks the girl out of the room.

'I want my mummy,' another little girl starts to scream as DG forces an apple slice into her mouth.

'Wanna go home,' another girl sobs into my ears and jumps on my lap.

I wanna go home too, girlfriend, I feel like sobbing back.

'How about a joke children,' Nat jumps up. 'What do you call it when worms take over the world?' She lifts up a large Lidl carrier bag and takes our wormery out of it. 'Global worming!'

'Are you a witch too?' My fear of the suitability of Nat's choice of classroom props or jokes remains unvoiced as a little boy spits an apple seed out of his mouth onto my jacket.

Burberry bile! Don't kids recognise a designer Burberry jacket when they see one? I swapped it yesterday for Canada goose jacket in a St Johns Wood charity shop.

Cue the start of an apple pip pitting contest as several other boys join in the fun. They spit away, adding their own imprint to my now-stained jacket.

'There's a worm at the bottom of the garden …' I sing, trying to distract them.

But to no avail. Poor little Sammi (oh, for Hades to grab him) grabs the wormery out of Nat's hands and drops it on the floor. The lid falls off and the worms seize their chance to escape their underworld.

The classroom door bursts open. In walks a man, his eyes burning with more fury than Zeus. He lifts his trident (actually, it's chalk) and looks at the hysterical girls, which include Gaia, who has now jumped upon the desks to escape the worms that are wriggling all over the floor. Some of the boys are still mid apple spitting contest, whilst others brandish knives, which poor little Sammi has procured, and are trying to chop the worms in half.

Zeus, it transpired was actually Mr. Streetar, school head teacher. The man accompanying him, an inspector from OFSTED.

And no, his name was not ... as poor little Sammi saw fit to ask ... Wiggly Woo.

LITTLE GREEN BOOK

Talking of monsters ...

The honey monsters: I'm laying in bed plastered with oat/ honey face scrub in prep for big bee-keeping date with Toby tomorrow. Haven't seen him since his return from hols.
I take in a deep breath before chanting the LithuanianGoddess of the Bees' positive mantra, which

DG told me to repeat one hundred times tonight: 'I am not afraid of bees … I'm not afraid …'

'After all they're just mortal bee…ings,' I chuckle at Nat's final words before she set off for her two-week family camping trip to Devon. I'm actually going to miss her.

I look out of the window into the darkness, and shiver as the indecisive Spring weather finally makes up its mind whether to rain or smile and starts to bucket it down. The only buckets and spades I fear Nat will be needing will be those to collect leaky rain and dig their tent out of soggy sand. But knowing glass half full Nat as I now do, I'm sure she'll still have a great time.

Chapter 27
The bees knees

'Bees have six legs, a three-part body and a hard exoskeleton,' Sidney, a dapper elderly gentleman sporting a green stripy blazer and pressed handkerchief in his breast pocket, presses a button on his slide projector. A graphic picture of a bee's anatomy flashes on the screen behind him. 'Beekeeping brings together people interested in the countryside, agriculture, food, science and ...'

What about people interested in having a day out with Toby?

I keep my mis-beehaved thought to myself and look around the community hall in Mill Hill East where Sydney's lecture: 'An introduction to bee-keeping,' is entering its second hour.

Sid explains, 'beekeeping, or apiculture, from Latin apis - bee, is the maintenance of honey bee colonies in hives. A beekeeper or apiarist keeps bees in order to pollinate crops and collect honey. It's one of the most ancient human skills ...'

Ancient skills. I study Sid's bushy but perfectly trimmed white Edwardian moustache. Why does no one have moustaches these days? Maybe I should start campaign: #NoMowMoustacheMay

'Bees are kept in an apiary, and live in large colonies.' continues Sid. 'The Queen Bee is the only breeding female in the colony ...'

I look around at the men who sit raptly listening to his every word. Why am I the only woman here? My queen bee eyes settle on Toby, who is sitting next to me. He smiles at me, his tanned hand squeezes my pasty hand reassuringly.

'The queen is the only sexually mature female in the hive. She's capable of laying half a million eggs or more in her lifetime.' Sid tweaks his moustache as he flips onto a rather explicit slide of a male and queen bee ... er... mating. 'At the peak of the breeding season in early Summer, a queen may be capable of laying three thousand eggs in one day. Her mating fight is otherwise known as a nuptial fight ...'

'I like a good old-fashioned nuptial fight don't you, Deborah?' Toby winks at me.

' ... A male drone will mount the queen bee and insert his endophallus into her. Male honey bees are able to mate seven to ten times during a mating flight ...'

'Only ten!' Toby's soft lips brush against my cheek as he whispers the secrets of his boudoir into my ear.

'... After ejaculation, it is ripped from his body ...'

I lower my gaze, my cheeks as much burning from Toby's touch, as from trying to process how what had started as a thoroughly boring lecture had turned from bee porn ... into schlock horror.

Sid races on. 'The emasculated drone then dies quickly ...'

'Not quite *le petit mort* then!' I listen to everyone burst out laughing, as I realise with alarm that whilst pondering how I wish I'd had my ears de-waxed so I could hear Toby's secrets, I'd voiced my rather inappropriate joke out loud. All male eyes are now upon me.
'Very funny, young lady!' Sid points at me. 'After a short break and final lecture, it will be time to meet the bees. It's sure to be today's *climax*.' I'm sure I hear him place emphasis on his final word. 'In the meantime, please enjoy our snacks and don't forget to buy this month's copy of 'Bee Craft.'

I quickly dash out of the room, leaving Toby and the rest of the ogling drones to turn their attention away from me and swarm the plates of honey sandwiches.

'Colony Collapse Disorder (CCD) is a frighteningly new phenomenon in which honey bee colonies are drastically disappearing,' Sid continues his lecture half an hour later.

He shakes his head despairingly. 'In 2015, forty per cent of all bee colonies in the USA disappeared. Colony losses have a significant impact on food production. One in three mouthfuls of the food we eat is bee-pollinated. That's why we need bee *lovers*, people like you!' He points at me.

'What's the reason behind this CCD?' asks a gentleman in the front row.

'Some scientists suggest it is down to radiation from mobile phones which interfere with the bees' navigation systems,' answers Sid.

Toby leans against me. 'Did you know, Deborah, Indian studies show that men who heavily use their mobile phones have reduced sperm counts?'

My hips start to throb. Damm. It's my mobile phone which I placed on silence. It's now madly vibrating in my jeans pocket.

'Anyhow, fellow apiarists, now's the moment you've all been waiting for. It's time to meet the bees.' Sid lifts up a large white trilby hat, pops it on his head, and pulls down a long white veil over it. Philip Treacy watch out!

'There's no point getting a bee in your bonnet!' a man in the back row calls out.

'Novice beekeepers usually also wear gloves and a hooded suit.' A wisp of Sid's moustache gets entangled in his veil as he tries to speak through it. 'If you wear a ring, it's worth removing it when handling bees.'

My two-carat diamond ring. I don't think so. I shove my hand firmly into my jeans pocket.

'So if you would like to get changed into these suits.' Sid hands around several white astronaut suits. 'Make sure your trousers are tucked into your socks to prevent bees from entering.'

Toby hands me a suit. 'And don't worry honey, I won't look!'

#NTS Pants. Am wearing old graying, M&S knickers. Oh God no.

Did Toby really just call me honey?
'Honey, get it,' Toby laughs as he lifts up a jar of honey.

'Defensive bees are attracted to the breath,' says an enthusiastic man already changed into his space suit. (Buzzy B. Aldrin) walks up to us. 'But then there's nothing like a sting or two to focus the mind!'

Talking about focusing the mind, I focus mine on praying. Please God, Lithuanian Bee Goddess, don't make me have to go and meet the bees. I promise to do two extra hours weeding tomorrow. I'll even collect and distribute the worm tea. Just give me a sign.

'Yes a sting on the face can lead to more pain and swelling than a sting elsewhere,' Buzzy B smiles.

My hand (avec ring) wedged into my jeans pocket next to my mobile starts to tremble. And talking of stings. There is a sting to this tale.

The call I answered was from Stu. He's on his way home from work with an unbearable rash all over his neck and was furious.

I excuse myself, husbondage emergency et al.

I rush home, beset by a horrible thought. Just what did happen to Nat's chilli seeds I put in the airing cupboard the other week? They didn't get wedged in-between Stu's shirts, did they?

Chapter 28
Sister act

'In 1838 when the Cherokee People were driven out of their homeland by the US government, their treacherous march became known as the Trail of Tears.

'One evening, around the campfire, the Elders called upon Nunne'hi - immortal being of the skyworld, and told him of their people's suffering and tears. He told him of their fears that the sisters of the tribe would not survive the journey. The next morning as the women awoke, they found their trail ahead strewn with growing plants. Like the plants, their strength began to grow. They found the courage and determination to continue their journey and rebuild the Cherokee nation ...'

Hen pauses from her storytelling, and lifts up a packet of French bean seeds. 'These beans are one of the heirlooms they managed to keep with them. They've been passed on from generation to generation ever since.'

'That's a beautiful story.' St Grace wipes a tear from her eye.

Hen braids her hair into a long plait, to complete her Minnehaha Cherokee look. Pocahontas Grace picks up a fallen (wood pigeon) feather and places it in her hair. This leaves me wrapped in a pashmina, to shield off the drizzly weather, looking more like rattling blanket woman.

'We are going to sow these beans today in line with the three sisters' Native American planting method, growing sweet corn, beans, and squash in a single bed.' Minehaha Hen hugs Pocahontas Grace. 'According to an Iroquois legend, corn, beans, and squash are three inseparable sisters who thrive together.'

'Corn provides a natural pole for bean vines to climb up,' Haha Hen slides her arm around Poca St Grace's waist.

'And the nitrogen of beans add fertility to the soil,' Poca St Grace smiles back.

'Whilst the large pumpkin leaves provide shade for the beans and corn.' They draw me into their sisterly group hug.

#NTS Pumpkin pooper! If St Grace, the fertile soil, Hen, the long-legged bean, that leaves me as the fat pumpkin leaf.

'All three have so much in common,' declares Poca Grace as she watches me trying to cover my tummy rolls with my pashmina.

Actually, the only thing I think we have in common is that we all fancy Toby like mad. I keep my un-sisterly thought to myself.

Talking of sisters doing it for themselves, group pow-wow-hug over, they both jump up and dash out into

Lottie, leaving me to sow all the 'Squashed
Stu,' 'Cinderella pumpkin,' and 'Sweet nugget sweetcorn
seeds.'

'Spring you have soggy legs and a muddy petticoat ...'

I rejoin the sisters a while later, to find HaHa Hen dancing
and reciting poetry whilst scattering a line of 'Trail of
tears' French bean seeds into our broad bean bed.

'Very ... er poetic, did you make that up?' I ask.
'Good gracious, no, it's Spring Onmipotent Goddess by
E. E. Cummings,' she chastises.

'Drowsy is your hair, your eyes are sticky with dream ...'
Poca St Grace continues waxing lyrical. 'Are you not a
poetry lover, Deborah?' she tuts.

Our shared moment of sisterly love clearly over.
She continues, 'By the way, where's the bean compost
trench my Toby built? I thought we could use it as the
base to make a teepee for that charming little lad,
Sammi.'

'I'm afraid Sammi charmingly played pick up sticks, and
picked up all the labels so we don't know where anything
is in Lottie.' I reply with a sweet smile.

'Talking of Toby, he told me about your day out with him. I
hear you're not exactly a bee lover either.' Poca St
Grace's smile is sickly sweet. But I'm not fooled.

'Talking of days out, I went foraging on the heath yesterday to find chervil for my homemade pesto.' HaHa Hen closes her eyes. 'The trees were so laden with clusters of pink and chartreuse blossom drooping at the tips.'

'Yes, Toby and I had a wonderful day laying in the park under blossom trees. I never realised how tickly those petals could be.' Poca St Grace giggles as she sows a line of shade-loving Webb's lettuces in-between beans.

'Talking of blossom, or rather in our case a lack of it,' I change the subject. 'Our pear tree leaves have red rust spots on them.'

'Pear leaf blister mite.' Poca St Grace drops the packet of seeds causing them to sprinkle everywhere. She rushes over to the trees. 'Poor darlings must have had their feelings hurt during the planting ceremony.'

'Have your trees got these feckin red spots on them too?' We are joined by a real-life shady character.

'Oh, hello there Mr. Parkeeper,' I say.

'It's Parker. Are yous taking the piss?'

'Sorry, I did mean, Mr. Parker,' I stutter 'You remember St … I mean … Grace. She's a pomologist. I'm sure she can help.'

'Too late I've burnt the feckin tree.'

'You've done what?' St Grace's eyes well up.

Mr Parkeeper lifts up a saw he is carrying and strides towards our pear tree. 'I'm not having any of your hippy diseases affect my roses.'

Poca St Grace bursts into tears.

'Let our trail of tears water the seeds of future growth,' recites HaHa Hen.

'Er, so sorry, I've got to go. I'm late for a lecture on er… pruning,' I add as I dash out of Lottie with one thought in my mind: Nat, please come home!

Sister Act. Indeed.

LITTLE CHARTREUSE BOOK

Cultivation - Pot laureate:

'Weeds are flowers too once you get to know them.'
Zen

6 pm. In Lottie, poetry book clutched in one hand, spade in t'other. Bent over pear tree Mr Parkeeper had started to dig up, and tree-loving Sisters HaHa and Poca hadn't bothered to re-plant.

6:10 pm. Have just put on reading glasses. On closer inspection of son's old book of children's first verse, have discovered that quote is not a Zen koan, but from Winnie the poo:

'Don't underestimate the value of Doing Nothing, of just going along, listening to all the things you can't hear -'
Winnie

6:15 pm. Starting on long list of 'to do' jobs, super glued by Nat onto DG's loony calendar. Miss her chirpy chatter.

8:15 pm – Strike last comment. Sooo don't miss her at all. I stretch my stiff back after two hours of work.

-Have transplanted carrots outside and dug little chive plants around their perimeter.
-Dug nasturtium seeds around edge of brassiere bed in line with good bedfellows plan.

-Transplanted toms into slice of pizza, and placed marigold seeds around edge of crust.
-Tarragon transplanted next to coriander in herb bed.
-Transferred 'Armado' caulies and 'Savoy Siberia' cabbage outside into brassiere bed. Several of them drooping in the pots. Think the term is called pot bound.
-Sowed some more courgette seeds (two per three inch pot) our first batch have not germinated.
-Given sweetcorn, pumpkin, and squash seeds in the green room a good watering.

8:10 pm. I down tools. Might just try a sip of mead I bought to share with Nat on her return tomorrow. I sit down on wooden beam bench. Feels strange to be in Lottie on my own. Can't believe it's already six months since we started all this ...

I take in a deep breath. It's as if I can smell the vivid tartness of ripe apples; leaves fresh sappy and sharp. Wonder if pear blossom smells differently to apple blossom? Guess I'll have to wait to next year to find out. I imagine a utopic world where streets are lined with apple and pear. New friends chatting as they pick fruit ... A drizzle more mead which is rather nice ... A drizzle more rain. Also nice. Smell of earthy sappy moss, garlic, water weeds springing out of wildlife tank, gurgle of frog spawn ...

MAY

Best in shoe...

Chapter 29
All is wellie

It's Sunday morn. I'm woken by an insistent knocking on my front door. I open it to find that my missing new wellie… now planted with mint … has turned up. Along with Nat.

'Yoo hoo, Deb.' She pulls me into a bear hug and hands me large glass of Pimms. 'I know how you posh girls like your cocktails,' she laughs. She bends down to pick a mint leaf out from my wellie and pops it in the glass. 'It's Pimms o clock! Did you miss me?'

Unsure whether to bemoan that my new designer wellies cost me a fortune, or that it is 8 am, I take a sip of the Pimms (it *has* got mint in it … it's almost mint tea) and follow Nat round to Lottie.

Overnight, an eight-foot carved wooden pole covered with strips of ribbon appeared.

Dire Gire - DG, is beside it, bending over a wooden (salad bowl). 'It's said that maidens who bathe their faces in early morn Beltane dew, will radiate beauty all year round.' She explains, as splashes her face with water from the bowl.

'What the bloody hell is this?' yells Nat, as we gaze at the large pole dug into the ground between our chippie bed

'It's our Maypole. It's May 1st. Happy Beltane, girls.' DG throws out her arms.

'Belt what?' asks Nat, as a length of ribbon uncurls in the un-May-like breeze, and whips across her face.

DG continues, 'Beltane, May 1st is a celebration of fertility. It's the union between the May king and queen. The entwining of ribbons during the maypole dance is a symbol of their sexual union. Jarvis, my new boyfriend, carved this for us out of a hawthorn trunk.' She sighs with contentment. 'We've been up all night a-maying - making love in the woods. Beltane is the time of fecundity …'

The thought of DG and this Jarvis at it is not an image I would've chosen to dwell upon at this time in the morning. I swig back my drink.

'Well, we're not having any fuck-unditys of any kind going on in here,' adds Nat. 'You'll put the frogs off.'

I look over at Nat through my rose (more-like Pimms tinted) glass, and we burst out laughing.

'Anyway, what are you girls doing up so early?' asks DG. 'You need to save your energy for our pole dancing later.' 'Shame I'll miss it. We're going to Oxford for lunch.' I smile.
'And we got back from Gloucestershire late last night,' says Nat. 'Pete had a narrow escape at a stilton cheese rolling championship when a man came hurtling down a hill with a seven-pounder narrowly missing him. He's

been up all night with a terrible migraine. Gotta play Nurse Natchet all day! He's well cheesed off!'

'Poor Pete,' I reply, trying to stop myself from chuckling. Nat winks at me conspiratorially.

'You should give Peter a tincture of willow bark. I'll make you one,' DG offers. 'Plus garlic to help with blood pressure, sage for his breathing. I must dash.' She jumps up, 'I've had raspberry leaves boiling for over two hours to help with my pmt.'

I look over at our raspberry bushes, unsure whether to be more disturbed by the lack of leaves on them, or the surplus of personal information inflicted on us by DG.

'Anyway Deb,' Nat turns round to check she's gone. She lifts a rubber glove, poor little Sammi's sand bucket, and a giant empty ice cream tub out of a carrier bag. 'We're gonna plant salad, strawbs, leafy herbs, edible flowers, and mint, in all sorts of containers and shoes. Bet you'd love that, High-Heeled gardener that you are! You just have to add drainage holes in the bottom.'

As Nat hands me a bag of compost, I turn my attention to the purchase of a wardrobe padlock.

She races on. 'Thought we'd have a competition to see who can grow plants in the most unusual container. We'll call it 'going potty!' The kids will love it. This will be a great pole to display them on.' She slides her hand down DG's maypole.

Lifting up a box of nails, she starts to hammer one into DG's maypole. We try and suppress a fit of giggles, as we get to work.

I fill the ice cream tub with compost, whilst Nat sifts it into the rubber glove. She opens a packet of rocket seeds.

'Let's have a rocket race,' she suggests. 'I'll grow mine in this old football.' She lifts up a plastic football that has been sawn in half. It's even more deflated than DG will be when she sees what we've done to her pole.

A while later, with the products of our container competition hanging like emblems of victory … scalps on our totem pole, we turn our attention to transplanting aubergine plants from the green room into gro-bags.

'Next month we can plant cucumbers in these old cooking oil tins.' Nat places little pepper plants into the cans which we've filled with compost.

'Wow, look at our 'Lolla Rossa' and 'Marvel of Four Seasons,' lettuces,' I call out. 'We only planted them six weeks ago and they're already four inches tall.'

'And the garlic's almost ready to eat,' Nat calls back.

I walk over and we look at the garlic with its six-inch shoots. 'The Great Tit says when the leaves crinkle and turn brown they're ready to eat. I reckon it's a couple of weeks away.'

The sun comes out as we continue to sow 'Romaine' and more 'Salad bowl' seeds in our Lettuce-be-friends bed. Nat chats away about her holiday and bursts out laughing as I tell her all about my bee-keeping escapade, and HaHa Hen and Poca St Grace's sister act.

I take a bite out of the gooey brie baguette which Nat shares with me and realise that we've become really good friends.

I look over at *my* hanging mint wellie, the sawn football, and bulging compost-filled rubber glove - it's finger almost pointing conspiratorially at us. I chuckle at the sight of DG's wooden bowl (might actually have a go at splashing in it later when Natalie is not around.) I smile, beset by a feeling of contentment.

All is well(ie) in the world.

LITTLE GREEN BOOK

Getting mashed: *Today we also transplanted our pipe of peas in chippie bed. We 'earthed up' the potatoes as the plants are poking their little green heads above the soil. First crop of creamy mash surely only a month away.*

I'm sitting in bed adding up how much of our grant we have left. Last count £600 spent. Wonder what that strange loud drilling noise is outside?

Chapter 30
Cyclanthera explodens – Exploding cucumber

The loud noise that started late last night turned out to be Nat, who was drilling holes in our oil cans and other 'going potty' containers to allow for drainage.

What's not as certain is why she had chosen to do so at midnight.

Talking about sending sparks flying, James gave me a May Day pressie this morning … a packet of exploding cucumber seeds. According to the information on the packet: 'When mature, they burst open at the slightest touch, flinging their seeds out across the garden. The fruit can be used in salads or cooked. No need to deseed them first as they do this for you at the slightest provocation!'

Whilst generally I'm not one for regifting, I thought I might pass them onto Mr Parkeeper who might like to have go …

HEALTH WARNING. DANGER OF EYE INJURY!
HARD SEED IS EJECTED AT GREAT SPEED.
DO NOT HOLD RIPE FRUIT NEAR FACE.
DO NOT ALLOW CHILDREN TO PLAY WITH FRUIT.
WEAR EYE PROTECTION WHILE HARVESTING

Chapter 31
Raised bed. But is it a four-poster?

It's a beautiful early Summer's day. The blue sky is beset with puffy little Constable clouds. The beds are filled with variegated hues of green which seem to imperceptibly grow and change on an hourly basis. The seeds are swelling in the sunlight, which is warm upon my face.

'If you raise the soil, you speed up the life process of ...' My attention is reluctantly drawn back to Bernie, who continues to drawl on about the merits of raised beds. The only one of current interest to me is a sun bed with comfy cushions, recliner button, and a drinks holder enclosing a chilled white wine spritzer.

'With a rectangular bed, you can also plant crops closer together,' winks Toby, sidling up to me. 'Their roots can grow deeper instead of spreading out sideways.'

#NTS: A bit of internal springing with Toby. If only... I smile at the thought.

'Asparagus is an example of a crop that benefits from growing in a raised bed. They're in season now,' Bernie digs away at one of the last bare patches of ground in Lottie.

'I read in your Country Life magazine, Deb, that nuns who feared that the *shape* of asparagus would excite young ladies, banned it from their schools in the 19th century!' Nat pokes me in the ribs. 'Bet you've had a go?'

'I certainly have not …'

'Anyway,' Bernie sighs impatiently, 'whilst it's a perennial which can last for many years, you can't pick asparagus for the first two years.'

'I'm all for a bit of *delayed* gratification,' says Toby, placing an emphasis on the word delayed. He smiles at me and continues to thin out the leek seeds.

'Did you know that all crops benefit from the presence of radish seeds,' shares Dora, as she walks up to us.

I close my eyes to shut out the image of Dora and radish seeds and concentrate on my daydream: Toby and I are in a (raised) four-poster bed draped in a mosquito net, a canopy of vines, giant strawberries, and asparagus crowns climbing around us. The stars are twinkling overhead …

I open my eyes as Toby walks up to Hen, who has just arrived. He puts his arm around her. The mosquito net of my imagining is now no more than a fruit cage. The stars, mere fruit flies buzzing irritatingly around me. The climbing fruit turned perennial bindweed.

'A lazy bed is one which is bounded by boards and soil piled up in the middle to create a ridge upon which veg is grown.' Bernie slides his hand over his bald head. It's now turned a rather unpleasant shade of strawberry in the midday sun.

'We're gonna grow herbs … sage, thyme, and basil in this bed boarded by railway sleepers.' Nat draws our attention to several long planks of wood which have appeared and are now piled up by our wildlife area.

The 10:45 from Euston is now delayed because of … I keep my derailed train announcement thought to myself.

'Where ever did you get them from?' asks Hen.

'Talking of beds, what type of bed does everyone kip in?' asks Nat, changing the subject. 'Pete and me have got a fairytale cast iron Bedknobs and Broomsticks bed. I bet you sleep on a roll-up futon Bernie!'

'I like to sleep at the top of a bunk bed,' Dora shovels two sage and thyme plants in a wobbly line next to our basil plants.

'I like to sleep surrounded by natural wood, don't I, Tob?' Hen smiles at Toby. 'Wood so lovely dark and deep its promises to keep …'

'Bet that means you're always pining for it!' chuckles Nat. 'Get it … pine … as in the wood!'

I sigh with relief as everyone (except Hen) bursts out laughing, drawing attention away from Toby and me having to share the secrets of our boudoir. a) I don't wish to hear about his and Grace's *lit d'amour,* b) couldn't possibly admit to having a bed with a TV that pops up at the end, and c) How does Toby know about Hen's bed? What was that someone once said about making your own bed and …

'Anyhow, time to move onto the strawbs.' announces Bernie.

We follow him to the Pimms patch.

'We need to place some hay under these Elvira strawberry plants,' he says lifting a bundle of straw from his backpack. 'The reason for laying straw under them is that as the fruit develops, their weight will cause them to droop on the ground and rot.' He places a wedge of hay under the plants.

'Look at the darling runner this has sent out,' Hen lifts up a strawberry plant and traces her navy blue painted nails along its trailing stem. 'When the joyous fruit swells, we should protect them with netting.'

'I'll ask Dora if she needs that net curtain hanging up in her front room?' suggests Nat.

I avert my gaze from Hen's navy blue polish as Toby lifts several plants out of a box.

'These 'Mara de Bois' are a perpetual which will fruit all through the summer.'

'Oh how joyous and redolent with the fragrance of the wild woods ...'

'We've got curds,' Hen's latest poetic moment is interrupted by Dora's squeal of delight coming from the brassiere bed.

We all rush over to look at the little pale green cauliflower florets. They're bathed in sunlight, shaded by large white outer leaves bent over them for protection.

'Aren't they beautiful,' Nat declares.

'They certainly are,' I reply.

'Gosh is that the time?' Hen looks at her watch, 'I must dash. Got a big audition. If any of you are going to Chelsea next week, I'll see you there.'

'Think you'll find they're playing away next week. Big match against the Reds,' replies Nat.

'Er, perfect,' Hen frowns, clearly confused by Nat's response to what was meant to be a poke at the fact that she had tickets to next week's Chelsea flower show and assumed we didn't. When in actuality ... courtesy of Delia, Nat and I, floral dresses et al, will also be treading its lofty aisles.

'Talking of perfection,' Toby tears the tip off a long garlic leaf and pops it in my mouth, 'bet you've never tasted anything like this before.'

My protestations about the edibility of garlic leaves are immediately put on hold as my throat is filled with a strong pungent aroma, a sweet oakiness, tingling, zesty …

'Repeat after me Deborah,' Toby munches on his bit of leaf, 'I've never tasted garlic bursting with so much flavour before.'

Repeat it, I did. As unfortunately so did the garlic on me. All night.

LITTLE GREEN BOOK

Today's bed-hopping:

Toby into Hen's wooden bed…

Brassiere bed:
Chocka full of different sized & shaped crops.
-We removed the cloches from the 'Romanesco' caulies and 'Savoy Siberia' cabbages, now that the 'fear of frost' has passed.
-Transferred red cabbage 'Drumhead,' outside ready for August harvest.
-Transferred 'Cavolo nero,' plants outside.
-Sowed 'Belot' Winter caulie and 'January King' Winter Cabbage, ready for an end-of-year harvest.

Chippie:

-Planted 'second earlies,' 'Lady Christ' potatoes – should have gone in late April. Whoops.
-Little white and yellow flowers have appeared on our 'Accent' first earlies – must be a sign that they are almost ready for harvest.

Four seasons Pizza:
-Transplanted remainder of peppers from green room into one quarter of the pizza-shaped bed, and basil into the last available quarter.

Cor: Our last sowings of courgettes have grown into plants with big fat leaves. Transplanted them out into bed next to peas.

Bath time:
-Planted 2 lemon thyme and lavender plants.

Pimms O'Clock:
-Placed 'Mara de Bois' strawberry plants in tyres filled with compost, a bin liner, and supported by hay.

On track:
-In Nat's railway sleeper bed we planted sage and thyme plants next to basil seeds.

Off track:
Note writing suspended for the night due to need for second dose of Rennies-garlic-leaf-indigestion-abating tablets.

Chapter 32
Wild at heart

'Burpees …! These golden beetroots are not a new trendy cultivar but made their debut in 1828. And look at these candy-striped beets?' A man wearing an artist's smock & beret slices a beetroot in half to reveal a pink and white candy-striped interior.

Nat and I stand gawping beside a stall shaped like an artist's palette. It's filled with a display of strangely coloured, psychedelic plants. We are making our way down Main Avenue at the Chelsea Flower show. I smile with delight as Chelsea is proving to be not just a gardening show but pure theatre.

'Or how about these Cosse Violette purple French beans, which turn green when cooked?' A lady dressed in a long paint-splattered dress picks a purple bean out of the palette-shaped bed. 'At Technicolour Seeds, it's all about the colour …'

Beret man continues, 'These Tozers turn golden-yellow.'

'There's no need for that kind of language,' Nat nudges me. 'I thought this was meant to be a posh event.'

He hands us a packet of 'Tozer' Brussel sprout seeds. 'Madam might also be interested in this Red lettuce dazzle orange sunset cauliflower, or how about these purple carrots' deep purple seeds?'

'This reminds me of the time Pete and I dropped aci …'

Thanking beret man for the information, I drag Nat away by the hem of her surprisingly ladylike floral skirt. I'm determined to enjoy an afternoon of hemlines…not hemlock.

We continue to stroll down Main Avenue.

'Hi there sexy, it's Deborah isn't it?' asks a rock-god sporting black shades and long Jesus hair as he walks up to us. 'We met at the Stokie seed exchange. I'm one of Southwark's guerrilla gardeners.'

'Oh yes, nice to see you again, er …'

'Che.' He takes off his T-shirt sporting a 'resistance is fertile' logo, to reveal a sweaty torso that's lean, tanned and oh so muscular. 'It's a hot one today, isn't it?'

#NTS Hot? Most certainly.

I keep my middle-aged flush to myself.

'Allotment art needs to be utilitarian,' a girl hands me a leaflet made out of an old piece of cardboard. 'Wanna come see our zone?'

Nat and I follow Che and the guerrilla girl to their stand. In front of us, a bath which has been sawn in two and plumped up with cushions has been turned into a sofa. The old bath taps are now a drinks dispenser. Words which describe the merits of watering plants with 'grey bath water' have been graffitied onto a shower curtain, and a hose has been attached to the bath's plug hole.

'With guerrilla gardeners, it's all about the artistic use of found and reused materials,' says topless Che, as he douses himself with the contents of a metal watering can.

'Yes, just look over here,' Guerrilla girl forces my attention away from Che to stare at a bunch of strawberries growing out of a bidet. 'Yes, a bidet!' she adds, 'it's about applying thrift and restraint.'

With slightly less thrift or restraint, I excuse myself on the basis of needing a cool drink. I open my site map to track down the nearest champagne bar and pause by a lush wall covered with greenery.

'In vertical gardens, plants are rooted in fibrous material anchored to a wall … Oh hello Deborah …'

I turn round to see St Grace dressed in a white lace dress. She pauses from talking to the group surrounding her. 'I didn't know you were coming to Chelsea.'

You and Hen, both. I refrain from adding.

'Lovely to see you too.' I reply. 'I hear green roofs are the new big thing,'

'Yes, Daddy has one on the roof of his hotel,' she smiles. 'They're marvellous for thermal insulation and carbon sequestration.'

#NTS: Daddy's hotel? Sequest what?

St Grace continues. 'Daddy's living wall is irrigated by an automated drip system fed from rainwater collected from the rooftop. It was inspired by Patrick Blanc's vertical garden at the Musée du Quai, Paris.' She takes a long swig from her flute of champagne. 'Tobs and I are going there next weekend.'

'Talking of Toby, er ... are you not here with him?' I manage to mumble. Did I really hear St Grace share that her papa has a hotel in Paris?

'He's over there busy with some kind of TV interview,' she flutters her eyelashes. 'You know how it is.'

Actually, no I don't. I want to reply but am prevented from doing so by a man in a green tux.

'There's a marvellous green roof at the Laurent Perrier Show Garden,' Green tux man extols. 'The rhythms and spacing of its plants are so bucolic ...'

'Poor sick plants.' butts in Nat, as she walks up to us.

Tux man continues. 'I adore the Daily Telegraph show garden with its uneven paths and forbidden fruits ...'

Nat links my arm and drags me away.

In the distance, we spot forbidden fruit - Toby. He's flanked by a crowd of ladies. He looks so handsome in his beige linen suit, crumpled in all the right places. His tanned face is glowing in the sun. His blue eyes beam into a TV camera.

He turns round, waves at me and gestures for me to join him. I hear the pounding of my heart … and …

'Tally ho girls …' It's RHS Delia. 'Do come and have tea in our Wisley show garden.' She whizzes up to us. 'I won't take no for an answer.'

Reluctantly I watch all prospects of Toby and I … future celebrity interviewing, TV chat show hosts fade into the flowery distance.

'Be there in a jiffy!' I turn round to hear a lady standing beside me, call back to Toby. He's clearly waving at her, and her matching peach satin hat and shoes. Not me. I duck down wishing that the bejewelled ground would swallow me up.

'Deb, why's your face gone a brighter shade of red than this raspberry?' asks Nat, as she picks a raspberry out from her glass of champers and pops it in my mouth.

We follow Delia into the Wisley show garden. We walk along a path of sweet-scented wood chip, surrounded by long grass dotted with yellow and pink wildflowers.

A long table covered in white linen and rose petals is nestled in the centre of the garden. The sun shines down on bone china plates, tea cups and saucers, and dainty silver cake forks. An assortment of crustless sandwiches and dainty cakes are piled high on tiered cake stands. An assortment of crusty ladies dressed in floral tea dresses is seated on gilt chairs around the table. They carry dainty handbags and wide-brimmed straw hats.

'Our Wisley wildlife meadow is designed to provide a home for butterflies, bees and all forms of wildlife.' Delia stands up as a bee buzzes around her. She swats it dead with her serviette.

'Do try the wild fruit jam sandwiches,' a lady we are introduced to as Lady Rosie Huntington Brown, hands us a plate of sandwiches.

'Charmed.' Nat holds out her hand

'Wisley, the flagship garden of the RHS, is undoubtedly one of the great gardens of the world.' Delia gestures for a black-tied waiter to pour us a glass of champagne. He hands us a raffia basket of scones. She continues, 'The rosemary in these scones is of course grown at Wisley.'

I lift up the Wisley brochure in front of me and study the grand house surrounded by formal gardens which according to the blurb, was gifted to the Society in 1903.

'This carnation petal cake is absolutely wonderful.' A lady stands up revealing several layers of her chiffon dress which have unfortunately been tucked into her lilac rather large knickers.

'Ladies,' Delia calls us to attention. 'Did you know that in recent years over ninety-five per cent of the UK's wildflower meadows have disappeared? Just look at the beauty of this Tufted vetch and Nipplewort,' she points to several purple and yellow flowers.

'Flowers called tufted vetch and nipplewort! Bit rude, eh, Deb?' giggles Nat as she digs me in the ribs. She downs her glass of champers.

'I always say there's nothing like the scent of this Myrrhis odorata … Sweet Cicely. How do you do.' Another lady turns to face Nat.

'How do you do too? Can you pass me a tart please, Cicely?'

Nat shakes her gloved hand, mistaking the plant, that the woman lifts up, with her name.

'Why garden with native wildflowers?' Delia asks. 'Native plants are adapted to our climate and soil conditions. They provide nectar, pollen, and seeds. Food for our native wildlife. Unlike natives, common horticultural plants often require fertilisers and pesticides to survive.'

'Natives also require less water due to their deep root systems which increase the soil's capacity to store water,'

Lady Rosie adds. 'And of course, wildflower germination can be improved by scarification.'

'Sweet Jesus, I think I'm going to faint …' All eyes turn to Nat who has suddenly gone rather pale.

'What is it, my dear?' Delia asks with concern and starts to fan her with a Wisley brochure.

Nat replies, 'It's the great Tit …!'

'No dear, the ornithology garden is at the other end …'

'Fuck me, he's coming towards us. Bollocks, where's my shittin lipstick,' shrieks Nat.

I look up to see Alan Titmarsh … the Great Tit …TV garden celebrity extraordinaire walking towards us.

Nat jumps up with such force that bangs against the leg of the tea table. It buckles and collapses. The carnation petal cake goes flying to the ground. Plates of sandwiches, meringues, strawberry tartlets, and scones minus their rosemary, hurtle down over chiffon and crepe de chine. Around me, the ladies shriek. Pandemonium breaks out in the Wisley show garden.

Now … in more ways than one, truly wild.

LITTLE GREEN DIARY OF AN ENGLISH COUNTRY LADY

Chelsea buns: *Unfortunately the Great Tit didn't don us with his presence. Possibly something to do with Nat and the upturned tea table and the havoc she caused.*

I don't think our pumpkin will turn into a carriage and we will be invited to the Chelsea ball next year.

After beating a hasty retreat, we came home to work on our very own show garden ... and what a show Lottie had put on. In the space of a day there had been so much growth and change.

Three sisters: *Talking of Cinderella and balls, our first job of the evening was to transplant our Cinderella pumpkins, Squashed Stu & Sweet nugget sweet corn little plants into our Three sisters' bed. Owing to the amount of space the pumpkins are going to need, we appropriated Dora and poor little Sammi's wartime bunker ... as yet unexcavated. We also sowed more French bean seeds due to the non-appearance of the first 'sisterly' batch that Minnehaha Hen sowed last month.*

Mine's a pint: *Pete joined us. Having regaled us for the tenth time with Nat's Great Tit story ... now more embellished than DG's maypole, he started to dig a nettle beer can-and shaped bed. Is now the time to go tee-total?*

Blank canvas: *Pea-casso. Going to design a bed with multi-coloured peas, beans edged with ornate frames. Jack 'n the beanstalk: Our 'Aqueduct' broad beans, plump and drooping (like Pete after an hour of diggin!) are almost ready to harvest. Their blue-grey foliage and clusters of creamy pinky flowers interspersed with snow white pea, and scarlet runner bean flowers look beautiful.*

Four seasons pizza: *Transferred green room tomatoes from 3" pots into 10" pots. Will soon transplant outside. Talking of Four Seasons ... most important job of all. Find out where St Grace's papa's hotel is, and what it's called.*

My salad days (nights)
9 pm. We downed tools and dispatched a grumpy James (come out to ask where his dinner was) to procure a bottle of chilled Chablis. Nat walked around picking Lolla rosa and Salad bowl lettuce leaves. Snipping the frilly leaves, carrot tops and greeny-purple beetroot leaves, she mixed them all together in an empty terracotta pot. She sloshed them with water and lo and behold ... our first salad was ready to eat.

I looked down at the pot, overwhelmed by a feeling of pride. Until this moment, I never really believed that we'd be able to eat anything that we'd grown.

Returning with the wine, James ordered a load of pizzas and sat down to join us. We started munching on the raw leaves, happy and cosy in our own garden. As Nat said, Lottie was the best show garden of all.

Summer
June
Game set and mulch

Chapter 33
Pest control

'There's many a blackfly twixt bean flower and beanfeast,' shares Ben-G, as we stand around on a cloudy first day of June listening to Bernie's lecture on pest control.

'Slugs eat twice their own body weight every day, and turn lettuce and brassica leaves into lace.' Bernie strokes a giant broad bean leaf which is now covered with lattice-like holes.

'Talking of lace, did you see that dress Grace was wearing at Chelsea?' I whisper to Nat.

'Yeah, bit virginal, wasn't it?' she replies.

Whilst on a sartorial subject, I look over to DG's maypole. A peach silk hat, planted with parsley, has been added to the motley collection of planting containers. It's a hat I'm certain I saw filled with large bouffant hair at Chelsea last week. A hat worn by the woman Toby was calling to join him for the TV filming … I grimace at Nat. She winks back at me.

'Another organic method of slug control is to plant a yoghurt carton filled with beer. Slugs are attracted by the smell of the beer, and drown.' Bernie grins as he lifts an empty (Tesco – aha!!) yoghurt carton out of his rucksack.

'Pissed as a newt,' Pete chuckles. 'Bit like our wonky maypole.' He points to the maypole which is now tilting due to the weight of odd containers … and one naughtily procured hat, on it.

'It's now more like our leaning tower of pisser!' Nat roars with laughter.

'Talking of drinks, anyone fancy a cuppa?' asks Bernie …

'I'd love one,' I reply, only to watch Bernie pick up a watering can which is reeking of decaying nettles imbued in a rank brown water.

'This is nettle tea.' He places the odorous can under my nose. 'It makes a rich plant feed. Helps deter pests and prevent fungal disease. Plants need nitrogen for leafy growth, phosphorous for healthy roots, and potassium to stimulate fruit and flowering. The best all-rounder is my homemade nettle tea.'

'I will go root away the noisome weeds, which without profit suck the soil's fertility from wholesome flowers.' Ben-G takes the can from Bernie and splashes it over the bed of winter cabbages we've just planted.

'Time to blitz these bind weeds sneaking up everywhere,' says Bernie, as he digs out a weed that is wrapped round one of our beans. 'They'll strangle our plants. It's where the phrase getting into a bind comes from. If you leave them laying around, they'll spring back to life.'

'Return of the plant snatchers, a blockbuster movie coming to a garden near you …!' announces Nat, as she turns her trowel into a microphone.

She tosses a clump of bindweed over the fence into Mr. Parkeeper's garden, just as he walks out into it.

Mr. Parkeeper is carrying an evil-looking plastic bottle of Weedol fertiliser. He takes off the lid and starts to liberally spray his crops with it.

'Plants are like kids.' Bernie shakes his head at the sight of his actions.' They need the right encouragement and a weekly feed to grow up strong and healthy.

'Bit like my poor little Sammi,' agrees Nat.

'They do not need spraying with weedkiller,' says Bernie.

'Perhaps only occasionally …' Nat's chuckle turns to yells of abuse, as Mr. Parkeeper, chucks the empty bottle of Weedol over the fence into Lottie.

He turns round to snarl at us, the sunlight gleaming on his dentures.

'If you were a movie baddie who would you be?' asks Nat as she watches him disappear indoors. 'My Pete would be the Joker. Dire Gire looks like that Cruella de Vil. Bern, you'd be Darth Vader, as you're always wearing a Star Wars T-shirt. Deb, you'd be …'

'Can we get on with making the nettle tea,' snaps Bernie. His impatient tone suggests he considers Nat is now the main garden pest. He continues, 'All you have to do is fill an old pair of tights, or something, with nettles, sink it into a water butt, and …'

Interrupting Bernie to tell him that she had to pop out to fetch something, Nat dashes off.

'Look at our teapot,' says Dora, walking up to us with the vicar's teapot. It's now brimming with green leaves. 'Doesn't this chamomile smell delicious? It will make a nice strong brew?'

'This is parsley.' Bernie plucks off one of the leaves and chucks it to the ground.

'Look what I've got, everyone!' cries out Nat as she rushes back into Lottie. She's carrying a couple of pillowcases. 'I thought we could brew our nettle tea in these.'

Nat hands me one of the pillowcases. It's a freshly laundered, Egyptian cotton, double-ply pillowcase as embroidered as Nat's forthcoming story of its provenance.

#NTS Tea leaves. Rhyming slang.

'You did say you wanted to keep the garden organic, Deb,' she smiles at me.

'Anyway, any signs of other pests bothering you?' Bernie stuffs the other pillowcase with nettles, ties a knot at its end, and drops it into our water butt.

'Me, no,' I reply, failing to add how I couldn't, of course, speak for any of our neighbours and their empty washing lines.

LITTLE GREEN BOOK

DG's loony bed: Still barren. Not because of any lunar activity, just plain fury over her maypole. We sowed 'Christmas Drumhead' cabbage seeds into it. They'll be ready for Christmas dins. Plus 'Sunset' caulies to add a burst of sunshine orange onto Spring dinner plates.

Chippie: Planted 'King eddy' main crop spuds in tyres and placed on chippie bed The giant green leaves growing out of our first early 'Accent' tato-tyres are a sign that the potatoes are ready to harvest.

Pimms patch: Sowed seeds of NON-exploding cucumber variety into pots in the green room. When 6-8 cm tall in a few weeks, will transfer outside into gro-bags in Pimms patch.

-Hurrah! Strawberries are coming into flower. Fed potash to fruit bushes.

Chapter 34
Freegan hell

Dire Gire's new lover Jarvis has come round to help out in the garden. He is a freegan.

'We freegans are not just dumpster divers who forage for food in dustbins,' he explains as he takes off his Ray-Bans, 'but are making an ethical stand against supermarket globalisation. It's our way of eradicating the environmental impact of the food we eat and stores benefit from having less waste to dispose of.'

I stuff my Gingsters pork pie wrapper into the pocket of my linen shorts and carry on with my second hour of weeding.

'Making use of discarded meat also brings purpose to the needless slaughter of animals.' He lifts several sweaty chicken drumsticks out of his pocket and offers one to me. I politely decline.

'And of course, the environment benefits from having less waste rotting in landfills and the emission of harmful gasses in the atmosphere,' DG takes a giant bite out of one.

'The long-term goal of freeganism is the complete restoration of society without the need for a monetary system.'

DG looks up lovingly into Jarvis's blue eyes as she listens to his every word. His every public school, *plummy* word.

'You'll have to excuse me, I am a little fatigued today,' he lays down on the chair DG fetches for him. 'I've just returned from filming a Channel 4 TV programme called, "Dumped." I had to live on a rubbish dump with seven people for three weeks, surviving on food that had been thrown away. All of us living together in cramped conditions amongst tons of rubbish.' He wipes his hand through his blonde hair. 'As you can imagine, it's taken its toll on me.'

'My poor darling.' DG snaps off a broad bean leaf and fans him with it.

Jarvis continues, 'Although it has given me an idea to start a social enterprise offering motivational courses for corporate companies on dumps. I'd charge several hundred pounds per participant. I would, of course, run free taster sessions for friends,' he smiles.

#NTS Free tasters. Every pun intended.

'I hear you're in the fashion industry, Deborah?' He smiles at me. 'Perhaps your colleagues might benefit from ...'

I imagine my fashionista friends: Phoebe cloaked in a fetching bin liner and matching hessian sack. Fliff in her glad rags.

'Talking of fashion,' DG continues, 'just look at Jarvis's fantastic flippys. Their soles are made from recycled car tyres …'

#NTS: Jimmy Choos now consigned to the pit stop.

'Leather and man-made materials make Jarvis and me sad.' DG takes off his flippys and starts to massage his foot.

'I'd rather not wear any clothes at all,' sighs Jarvis.

'What about you, Deborah?' asks a sexy voice. It's one I haven't heard since Chelsea.

I turn around to watch Toby saunter into Lottie. He blows me a kiss. I look down, my face blushing more brightly than the dandelion I pick.

'Watteau. You're that local eco chappie.' Jarvis uncurls from his lounger and outstretches his arm to shake Toby's hand. 'Jolly good show. I might be able to offer you some advice. I'm a freegan. Just been on this TV programme called …'

'Did you know that there are a number of folklore beliefs related to dandelions?' Toby walks up to me, completely ignoring Jarvis. 'Blowing their fluffy seed head away in one go means that you have a passionate lover. If any of it remains, your lover has reservations.'

He loves me, he loves me not. I lift the dandelion to my quivering lips …

'Hello, young lovers.' Dora comes out into Lottie carrying a wobbly tray stacked with a teapot, cups, and a packet of jam tarts.

'I've made us a cuppa with the chamomile flowers I've grown.'

'Er … let me help you,' I drop the dandelion and rush to help Dora as the tray tilts perilously in my direction.

'Did you know the sap of a dandelion stem makes invisible ink?' says DG, pouring the tea. 'You can write your lover a secret message with it.'

'I'll write you one then, shall I?' Toby winks at me.

NTS# Dandelion dreams. Toby? Secret? Message? Where is that bloody dandelion I dropped?

'Here's mud in your eye.' Jarvis lifts the cup that DG hands him and drinks down what is in fact … parsley tea.

#NTS: Mud in eye. There's no mud on any part of Jarvis's body, due to his complete lack of effort in the garden today.

Jarvis laughs as he scoops the last of Dora's rich tea biscuits off the tray. 'I'll take these home for my dinner.

One can only dream of a fillet mignon in the Waitrose bins tonight!'

Before Toby and I can mutter, 'little gem,' he jumps up and pulls out several of the lettuces that have grown in the strangest places due to a shocked St Grace dropping seeds mid-apple-tree-gate with Mr. Parkeeper last month. Putting his arm around DG, they head off.

Toby whispers into my ear. 'Give me your hand, Deborah.'

Would happily do so, but sadly it's taken. I keep the thought to myself.

'Close your eyes,' he demands, 'and follow me.'

I link Toby's arm and let him lead me down the garden path (probably in more ways than one)

We pause. Toby dips my hand into something soft, cold, and crumbly … Agggh … It's mud.

He's dipped our hands into a tyre of potatoes. He clasps my hand tightly and we dig deeper into the tyre. Together we explore its viscous folds. Our arms caressed by the silken … what now feels like … oh so sexy, soil. My heart starts pounding as we slowly root around. We feel something hard and round.

We lift it out to see a beautiful potato covered in mud. It's our first harvested potato. A perfect nugget. A jewel. Toby cups it in my palm and covers his palm with it.

'Well done, you.' He turns round and kisses me on the cheek.

'Now don't you go making any fancy-pants dishes with these spuds. Just boil them and serve them with some freshly picked chives tossed in butter. I will think of you tonight eating them.' He bends down, picks a clump of chives topped with little purple flowers. They're more perfect than the most perfect bunch of red roses. He hands them to me.

Locating the fallen dandelion, he lifts it off the ground, blows it and …

LITTLE GREEN BOOK

Talking of fancy recipes, jewels, and dandelions, saw a fab dish on Masterchef tonight:

Jewel risotto
Wash 150g of dandelion flower heads in cold water Cut off the ends, peel back the green sepals, freeing the petals.

Saute onion in olive oil with two cloves of garlic.

Add 300g of arborio rice. Stir into the onions and then pour in 125ml of dry white wine.

Once absorbed, gradually add a ladleful of stock at a time, allowing the rice to soak up the liquid before adding more.

Cook for at least 30 minutes. Add 125g of fromage frais or yoghurt - plus 100g of grated parmesan and the dandelion petals.

Serve immediately, drizzled with olive oil.

But talking of a recipe for disaster:

Cheesed off cauliflower
Agggghhh. Our cauliflowers have been destroyed. There are scores of little yellow round eggs on the underside of their leaves ...

Chapter 35
Chicken nuggets

Talking further on the subject of jewels, recipes, and lovers, when it comes down to it, it's only the real ones that count.

It's my birthday today, happy b'day to me. For I'm a jolly good …

So where did my real-life lover, Stu … (yes, I know it's been a while) take me to dinner tonight? I'll tell you where … to the most fab, gastronomic restaurant of them all … Chez Lottie.

I still can't stop laughing about it, but as part of my birthday pressie, Nat arranged for Stu and me to have a romantic dinner in the garden. A meal prepared by a chef whom Nat booked, and instructed to use as many ingredients as possible from Lottie.

It all started at eight, when hand in hand, Stu led me out into the garden for a supposed quick glass of champers. In front of me, a table had been laid with white linen. Tea lights sparkled as warmly as the lovely June evening. A bunch of yellow roses (not I hope from Mr. Parkeepers garden) were perched in a vase in the centre interspersed with sprigs of rosemary.

Stu sat me down, placed a napkin on my lap, and handed me the menu:

Deborah – The High Heeled Gardener

Birthday menu

Berry bubbly

*

Mixed lettuce, beetroot leaves, and pea
shoots served with local goats cheese in a
chive dressing topped with chive flowers

*

Chilled vichyssoise of broad beans

*

Grilled garlic chicken stuffed with sage,
sauteed with spring onions and boiled
potatoes served with rocket and nasturtium
flower salad ...

We ate the most delicious dinner ever, accompanied by copious amounts of champagne. I couldn't stop giggling as I plundered Lottie for as many squishy-looking berries as I could find.

I opened my pressies to receive an M&S cashmere jumper from my mother: an annual subscription to something called Farmville from James:; a friendship band from DG and a packet of football cards from poor little Sammi. The grand finale was a peach night dress from Nat. The same one she'd seen me spying her wearing. What a hoot! Just don't mention the word flannel nightie in front of my other fashionista friends!

I popped a lone rocket leaf into my mouth and smiled as I looked around Lottie. For in many ways, my best pressie of all had been my newfound respect, a reverence, for where our food comes from.

In many ways, that is, but not all … It was desert time.

Stu bent down and lifted a box of crispy crème donuts which he handed to me. I opened it to discover a little Tiffany's package nestling within the sweet peaks and doughy domes. The icing on my cake. I opened the box to find a beautiful bracelet of white gold.

Stu tenderly lifted my hand, wrapped the bracelet around it, and told me how proud he was of my little garden hobby, and how surprisingly delicious the produce was. He understood how tough it must be on me watching James … now a teenager, become less dependent upon me … how much he knew I was secretly hurting about not being able to get a job, and watching the fashion industry … now the domain of next season's designers, slip from my grasp. He held my hand and told me how I had changed, but looked more beautiful the older I got.

I won't ruin the memory of the evening by dwelling on his mention of the job interview he told me he'd been invited to attend next week in Dallas, USA. He was absolutely certain it wouldn't amount to anything.

#NTS: Debbie, certainly does (not do) Dallas!

Stu wrapped his arm around me as we listened to the birds nesting down for the night. I swear I even heard a croakin' at my feet. We watched a butterfly flutter past (aggh … hope it's not one of those white ones hell-bent on desecrating more of my produce). We sat in silence watching the tea lights flickering in the sultry breeze and the sky turn as black as our … (when was the last time I filled it?) compost bin.

Chapter 36
A right bunch

'Darling Debo, it's been too long!' declares Phoebe.

I place my phone on speaker mode and continue to listen to Phoebe's news, as I dig up bundles of garlic.

'I'm calling to wish you birthday felicitations,' she continues, 'but also in my professional capacity as fashion editor of Flair Magazine. I've got exciting news for you, darling. I want to send a team down to your little allotment thingy, to do a photo shoot. The concept is to link veg growing with fashion ...'

A fashion shoot for Flair Mag? My heart starts to pound. I imagine Nat dressed as a giant butternut squash. Dire Gire sporting a Carmen-Miranda-veg-head-dress. Hen, with her stringy green bean legs.

'Yes, I was only talking to Lilly Cole last week about her veggie ventures. Everyone's at it.' Phoebe lowers her voice. 'I thought as you were *still* out of work, you poor sad darling, you could style the shoot for me ... consider it my birthday gift to you. By the way, where did Stuart take you for dins last night?'

'The garden,' I smile as I look over at an empty champagne bottle laying in-between the strawberry and mint plants.

'*Where?*' The tone of disdain in Phoebe's voice is as dry as the soil in our brassiere bed.

'Nat … er … Stu booked a chef who cooked an amazing dinner using ingredients from the allotment.'

'I'm sure it was fab … and I guess, with no job, you must be watching the pennies,' Phoebe sighs. 'But listen, darling, about this shoot. I don't mean to rush you, but I do need ideas asap?'

I look across at the table. It's empty after last night's *priceless* dinner, except for the vase of roses mixed with rosemary and a wisp of a chive stem with its purple flower laying elegantly across it.

'How about models munching edible bouquets,' I blurt out.

'Edible what?'

'Bouquets filled with rainbow chard, rosemary, dried chillies, carrot tops, even purple beet leaves, marigolds, pea sprouts, borage … anything and everything I can grow that's colourful and edible and …'

'What a simply divine idea, Debo, darling. There I was, thinking your heels had lost their wedge!' Phoebe titters.

'How's July 12th for you? Pop the date in your diary. I always said what a great team we are, always coming up with the best ideas. Now I must dash, darling. I'm going to lunch with Naomi … By the way, Fliff and I have your birthday pressie. It's a voucher for a Jo Malone anti-ageing facial …'

" Pom-Pom Chive Shoes "

LITTLE GREEN BOOK

Garlic: *can be stored for several months. When the garlic foliage starts to turn yellow and crinkle … something Phoebe and Fliff clearly think my skin has done … it's time to dig it up. Garlic is good for warding off evil spirits. Must munch some next time I meet Phoebe!*

Flowering onions: *Have just spent an allium-inating three hours on the internet researching edible flowers for my SHOOT! Who knew there are over four hundred species of edible alliums (leeks, chives, garlic etc.) Their flowers have the strongest flavour. Other edible flowers include: lavender, squash blossom, basil, thyme after thyme. Chrysanthemums have a tangy, slightly bitter taste ranging from a faint peppery to mild cauliflower flavour. Marigolds are great in salads as they have a citrus flavour*

Chapter 37
Longest day of year

'Looks like your crops have gone leggy.' Hen snips off several of the little yellow flowers which have appeared atop our rocket.

'Like you in your cropped little shorts.' I keep my jealous thought to myself and smile at Toby who carries on watering the chippie bed.

'Cutting off the flowerhead helps plants concentrate on their growth.' Hen points her secateurs perilously towards the pretty purple chive flowers.

Aaggh! I watch the edible bouquet I'm nurturing for my big shoot … far from going to pot, disappear *from* the pot.

As she and Toby walk over to the carrot bed, out of the corner of my eye I spot Toby cup one cheek of her derriere. It's as perfectly formed as the cabbages I start to water.

'Gosh, it's a sweltering one today,' she calls out as she dips her hand into Toby's can of water and slowly showers it all over her body.

'It certainly is clammy.' I take off my shirt, leaving my new (push-up) halter neck top on display. 'I think there's going to be a storm.'

'Every cloud engenders not a storm,' quotes Ben-G walking up to us. He looks up into the sultry early evening sky.

'Oh dear, Deborah, you've got a gardener's sun tan!' Hen points to the T-shirt lines on my body. They're as white as the broad bean flowers she continues to snip. Unfortunately, my halter neck top has only served to reveal the unsightly white patches.

'You should garden naked like I do when I'm home.' She lifts up a tray of courgettes.

'Yes, your buds are perfect.' Toby takes the tray from her.

'Feeding plants will also help delay premature bolting.' Hen looks coyly at Toby.

'My Pete never has that problem.' Nat strolls out into Lottie holding a (much-needed) bottle of Pimms.

#NTS: Veg growing is soo the new sex.

'We need to transplant these courgettes as the pollinating insects will not be able to reach their flowers in the polytunnel,' says Hen, walking over to the empty space next to the pea bed. She starts to dig a courgette trench

'Insect pollination may be poor this year and we will have to help plants "set" fruit by hand'

'You mean give 'em a hand job,' chuckles Nat.

'The first thing to do is check whether the courgette flowers are male or female,' Hen sighs, clearly un-amused by Nat's comment.

I try and stop myself from giggling as Hen lifts the courgette plant which Toby hands her. She starts to stroke it.

'Let my words, like my veg, be tender,' she waxes lyrical. 'Next season, we should look out for a pathenocarpic variety.'

'Pathe what?' Nat frowns. 'You need a blinking GSCE in Greek to understand all of this.'

'Pathenocarpic varieties are those which will set seed without being pollinated,' explains Toby as he plants the courgettes.

#NTS: Bonking zucchinis. This conversation was going a little far for me. I dash off to get a bottle of lemonade.

'Merrily met this litha ...'

I return to find Jarvis and DG standing arms stretched, wearing hooded long white robes and wildflower crowns.

'So good of you to come to our Sonnenwende Summer solstice party.' DG hands round glasses full of a strange-looking brown potion with bits floating in it. 'Tonight is Midsummer's Eve, the night of magical happenings. The night when the veil between the fairie world and mortal world is at its thinnest.'

'A night where anything can happen,' chants Jarvis.

'I'm well up for that.' Pete looks at Ben-G, who nods in agreement.

'So let's start by sharing a cup of marigold, thyme and hollyhock tea. It's a gateway to the fairie world.' DG hands round the awful-looking liquid.

'I don't need tea to see any flippin' fairies,' laughs Nat. 'A nice magic mushroom will do!'

'I'm more of a Pimms girl myself, anyone care to join?' I look inquiringly over to Hen and Toby who are now at the other end of the garden. Hen is perched atop his strong shoulders, her long legs dangling like the small white flowers they are picking from a tree.

'Swift as a shadow, short as any dream; brief as the lightning in the collied night,' says Ben-G, knocking the brew that Jarvis hands him.

'Make my Pimms a strong one,' adds Nat, as DG and Jarvis drape a garland of daisies around the maypole, which has become their outdoor altar. They sit cross-legged around it, raise their hoods, and start to pray.

'We celebrate the Mid-of-Summer, held in honor of the Blazing Sun God. All of Nature vibrates with the fertileness of the Goddess …'

Emptying out poor little Sammi's mini watering can, Nat pours half the bottle of Pimms into it. She adds a smattering of lemonade, some freshly picked mint and borage flowers, then stirs it in with a bamboo cane. Having toasted all the blazin' gods, she takes a large swig from the can.

There's distant giggling from the other end of the garden. Toby and Hen are hidden behind green room.

'On Midsummers Eve, freshly picked herbs and flowers are considered to be exceptionally potent.' DG finishes her prayers and lifts several green twigs out from a bin liner. 'We're going to weave willow garlands of St Johns Wort, burdock and thorn to hang on all of the neighbourhood doors and windows for protection. Here's a piece of willow for you, Deborah. Place it over your left arm then slot it between the fourth finger of your right hand and …'

I grab the Pimms watering can from Nat, and take a big swig.

'I know a bank where the wild thyme blows, where ox slips and nodding violet grows,' Ben-G starts to rap.

'I'm a professional tabla drummer,' adds Jarvis. 'Do you play an instrument, Deborah?'

'Rimming the glass when she's had a few!' chuckles Nat.

Jarvis continues, 'Let's all sit down and form a fairy ring. Faeries love music. Wood from the elder tree lends itself to making whistles, as their branches contain a soft pithy core.'

Ben-G turns an empty terracotta plant pot upside down, lifts a trowel and starts to drum on it. 'Quite over-canopied with luscious woodbine,' he raps, 'sweet musk roses and eglantine ...'

'Ssshh! I can hear something,' DG interrupts. 'It might be the fairies. I have psychic hearing abilities. I'm clairaudiant ...'

'Clair who?' Nat whispers in my ear. 'That's not what it says in her rent book.'

'Look what we've got,' says Hen. She and Toby come bounding up to us.

'This is for elderflower champagne.' Hen hands me a cluster of little white flowers.

'How delicious,' I reply. Eager to demonstrate my edible flower appreciation skills, I pop a flower into my mouth.

'No, Deborah, stop!' shouts Toby. 'You can't eat the raw flowers. They're poisonous. Spit it out.'

He whacks me on the back with such force that the flower projectiles out of my mouth and lands on his pale blue linen shirt. I feel myself blush a shade more crimson than the rose which Hen hands me.

'If you're interested in sampling edible flowers, try this,' she tuts. 'Its flavour is reminiscent of strawberries and green apples, sweet with subtle undertones ranging from mint to spice ...'

'Debs is gonna be using edible flowers to style a high-profile magazine fashion shoot,' says Nat, jumping to my rescue.

I look apologetically at Toby, who is still trying to wipe soggy elderflowers off his shirt.

'Tobs, we've got to dash to the sustainability meet?' interjects Hen.

The only shoot she's interested in is 'shooting off' with Toby. She links his arm, and like two threads in an inedible daisy chain, they walk off.

'Open yourself up to the spirit of the garden.' DG drops to her knees and looks up to the golden sun which is now reaching its zenith. 'Learn from Saturn and maintain your borders ...'

'Think we'll maintain ours,' Nat and Pete take off their wildflower crowns and march back indoors.

Longest day of the year. I munch on my rose petal. It certainly was starting to feel like one.

NOT SO LITTLE GREEN GROWING LIST.

Have tried to write a list of everything growing in the garden. Holy hollyhocks … can't believe it but we have over fifty edible fruit and veg. With £65 added to budget for Seafeed, potash and basil making new total £745, we now have around £250 left.

Fruit bushes:
Lots of bonny-looking leaves but v. little fruit.

Fruit trees:
Nasty orange patches on pear leaves. Am having to madly snip off.

Brassiere bed:
Armado Caulie: Picked first caulie I can't believe it. Feels like such an achievement.

Red cabbage: Have disappeared.

Savoy Siberia/ January king: Large grey-green leaves curling in to form tight little balls. Beautiful.

Cavolo nero: Lovely silver-grey leaves growing.
Picasso spinach: Eating leaf by leaf.

Sanda brussels: Growing on long stems, look like little Xmas baubles. Will be ready Oct.

Loony bed:
'Christmas Drumhead' cabbage seeds and 'Sunset' caulies. Both vanished into the less than (bio) dynamic sunset.

Lettuce b friends:
Salad bowl. Eating lots of it.

Rocket. Lives up to its name and runs to seed v. quickly. Will have to plant some more.

Nasturtium. Cropping up all over the place.

Beeten to a … Enjoying eating beet leaves (and showing off the fact)

On track:
Lemon Thyme, Sage, Chives, Tarragon. Am picking and cooking with most nights. Basil and coriander plants have vanished.

Spud-u-like:
Second earlies. Growing nicely.

Chippie:
Accent first earlies. Mashing-boiling-sautéing. Smashing! Tomatoes. Bonny 9" plants with lush green leaves.

Peas. Sweetest peas ever. Poor little Sammi thinks they're candy.

Light bulbs:
Garlic. Nat placing on a nightly basis outside DG's flat.
Onions. Weeping and eating.

Two and a half seasons:

Pepper. Have placed grow bags in one quarter.
Tomatoes. Lovely yellow flowers growing on them. Fruit soon to follow.
Artichoke. Have been choked.
Marigold. Our pizza crust is stuffed with beautiful orange flowers.

Sisters most certainly doing it for themselves:

French beans. Nearly one-foot tall, wrapping themselves around bamboo poles.
Sweetcorn - have 3" leaves.
Squashed Stu - have 2" leaves.

Dora and poor little Sammi's war bunker:
Putting hay beneath swelling pumpkins and squash.

Bathtime:
Lemon thyme. Beautiful and plentiful.

Lavender. Love rubbing leaves across the palm of my hand.

Jack n pea n courgette and beanstalk.

Broad beans. Branches are covered in nasty-looking black things but have still managed to pick loadsa beans. Great served raw with chunks of parma ham!

Courgettes. 3" leaves.

Pimms patch:
Mint & Strawberries. Growing rampantly.
Cucumber. Transferred out into Pimms patch.
Wild borage. Am sooo never going to eat wildflowers again

Leeks. Have long pencil-thick stalks. Will be ready Oct

Carrots. Lovely frilly 6" leaves

Chives. Plentiful with beautiful purple pom pom flowers

High Tea. Jarvis still enjoying Dora's parsley tea!

Rosemary. Our little bush is still there and thriving.

Nettle beer. Nettles are everywhere but in Pete's beer bed!

Parsnips. Long green wispy leaves growing. Plan to dig up in Oct.

Radishes. How many more radishes do I have to eat?

Green room:

Looking like a mini Kew Gardens hothouse with a mix of various cabbages and leaves. Poor little Sammi has once again removed labels.

Next month we will plan what to sow to extend our season and for … (must remember to use this word next time I see Toby) 'overwintering.'

Potluck maypole:

Moving swiftly on … as is the angle of the pole towards the ground.

Edible flowers:

Despite Hen's best efforts, Lottie still abounds with a glorious canvas of colourful, edible flowers, including a few roses sticking through (more like pulled through by Nat) from Mr Parkeeper's garden next door.

Cub 'ism:'

Whilst on the subject of roses and art read a fab idea in Vogue mag. Place rose petals (non-Weedol treated) in an ice cube tray. Fill with water. Freeze … and lo and behold … rose petal cubes to float in one's cocktail.

JULY

Top of the crops …

Chapter 38
Who dares not grasp the thorn should never crave the rose

Talking of roses, Mr Parkeeper is escorting a group of la-di-da Hampstead ladies on an art tour of his garden.

He's dressed in a well-ironed brown suit. Terracotta stripes run along the length of it like the crevices in our parched earth. He sighs as he looks up into the leaden sky. He's followed into his garden by several septuagenarian ladies who carry heavy sketch pads and watercolour sets.

His warning for us to stay out of Lottie during his tour has fallen not only on deaf—but ear-muffed ears. Pete continues to drill stakes in the ground. He's rigging up a giant screen for us to watch the Wimbledon final this afternoon. Nat, who is helping Ben-G with his drama homework shrieks, 'Go, bind thou up yon dangling apricocks ...'

Talking of homework and dangling apricocks, Ben-G is mortified. As part of his school project on Shakespeare's use of garden imagery, he has been given the role of Queen Isabel in his school's non-binary production of Richard II. As Nat rather, unfortunately, expressed, 'Romeo and Julian surely a panto away!' I remind him that in Shakespeare's time, all boys played girls' roles.

Politely declining Nat's invitation to play the role of the old gardener, I carry on weeding … and earwigging

'These "Freckle Face" miniature roses are an unusual spotted white and pink blend bloom,' says Mr Parkeeper, wiping the sweat off his forehead as the sky turns a shade more charcoal than the pencils which the ladies start to sketch with. He continues, 'They have a moderate fragrance with twenty to forty petals. He points to another rose. 'These Brass bands fully petalled rose changes from orange yellow buds into a virtual fruit salad of …'

'Oy, what sport shall we devise here in this garden to drive away the heavy thought of care?'

All eyes turn to face Nat, who in full thespian mode, stands aloft in yon Lottie belting out her first line.

'Man, that's my line,' Ben-G, aka Queen Isabel, enters stage left. He's wrapped in a long crimson velvet curtain and carries a copy of the play in one hand and a roll-up in t'other.

'But stay, here come the gardeners, let's step into the shadow of these trees.' Ben-G takes a bow as he looks across the wire fence to his unwitting audience.

Mr Parkeeper raises his voice to draw the attention of the startled ladies back to his lecture. 'These Hot Chocolate floribunda roses have exquisite warm chocolate orange blooms carried in clusters on a bushy …'

'These noisome weeds, which without profit suck the soil's fertility from wholesome flowers.' Ben-G gathers his billowing skirt and crouches down behind the broad beans.

'Did you know there is a language of roses,' asks a lady with an interesting shade of blue hair. 'Floriography was a Victorian means of communication by which flowers were used to send coded messages to express feelings which otherwise could not be spoken. Whilst an open red rose meant I'm full of desire for you, a yellow one symbolised friendship, more than passion.'

#NTS Yellow roses. Like the bunch that Stu gave me for my birthday …

'Why is that black-skinned fellow hiding behind that bush wearing a dress?' asks another lady in a quivering voice.

Mr Parkeeper is undeterred. He continues, 'These Golden shower yellow roses turn to cream then …' He pauses to look up to the heavens which threaten a torrential downpour more than golden shower.

'Gardener, for telling me these news of woe, pray God the plants thou graft'st may never grow.' Ben-G rips several roses from the bush poking through from Mr Parkeeper's fence. He stands up and throws the petals up into the rain. It starts to pelt down.

'What the feck are you doing to my roses?' Mr Parkeeper yells. 'How feckin' dare yous.' Opening up his secateurs he charges towards the fence separating him and Ben-G.

#NTS: Good fences make good neighbours. What do crossed ones suggest?

'Mr Parker, may we please take shelter in your house?' asks the blue-haired lady, whilst the rest of them rush around trying to gather their possessions getting absolutely soaked by the downpour.

'Bollix to the lot of yous.' Mr Parkeeper turns back round, bolts into his house and slams the door shut with a thud louder than the clap of thunder.

'So musical a discord, such sweet thunder,' laments Ben-G, as I quickly call out to the ladies to follow me into the green room.

Some thirty minutes later, the rain is still lashing down upon a sea of rose petals, swamping strawberries and pounding on our crops. Invertebrates are dashing for cover, frogs gurgle in freshly filled pools, ladybirds take shelter under the straw, whilst aphids are swept down broad bean leaf waterslides.

The la-di-da ladies and I are huddled together in the green room watching Ben-G and Nat's performance. Some might claim it's more wooden than the makeshift chair tree stumps the ladies perch on, but we are enjoying every minute.

'When I have pluck'd thy rose, I cannot give it vital growth again. Its needs must wither …' proclaims Desdemona Nat, laying on the floor shrouded in Dora's old net curtain. Othello Ben-G leans over her, his sopping curtain cloak dripping all over her.

'I'll smell thee on the tree.' He snogs his dying Desdemona.

'Yuck, get off me you perv …!' Nat pushes him away.

Talking of smells, the lovely aroma of honeyed rain percolating through the green room is suddenly replaced by a rather nasty whiff. The pillowcase that one of the ladies is sitting upon, bursts open to release a less-than-salubrious smell. It's our nettle fertiliser.

'I kiss'd thee ere, I kill'd thee, no way but this to die upon a kiss.' Othello slumps down on top of Nat.

'Oh bravo, bravo,' a roar of applause breaks out around the green room. 'That was simply marvellous.'

'We should toast your great performance,' suggests the lady with hair now a shade more lavender than our plants.

'Coming right up ma'am.' Ben-G jumps up and fetches several bottles of Hen's elderflower champagne which have lain fermenting in the corner.

'I always said the optimist sees the rose bush, not the thorns.' Nat offers a swig of wisdom along with the surprisingly delicious bottles of premier cru(de) which she hands around the room.

Swigging it back, I look out through the filtered light of the misted green room to see Lottie has been transformed into a technicolour world of rich greens, luscious reds, purples and invigorated yellows, which the paintbrush of rain has all mixed together.

'Shame the rain's gonna stop play at Wimbledon isn't it, Deb?' Nat calls out to me as she and Ben-G assume a 'still life mid-tomato pose.' They continue to be sketched by the ladies.

'Not that you're too worried about the weather as you are bugging off to France tomorrow. How long are you going for again?'

'Two glorious weeks.' I smile at the thought of the two lovely, lazy weeks lying ahead of me where the only digging I'll be doing is into a large plate of fruit de mer.

'And don't worry,' Nat continues, 'I'll text you *every day* to update you on what's going on in Lottie. By the way … in case you're worried … I put your passport back in your bag. Must say I didn't realise you were quite that old.'

LITTLE GREEN BOOK

Talking about good vintages -
Hen's bubbly (at least Toby thinks so) elderflower
champagne recipe.

Ingredients: Makes about 6 litres
4 litres hot water
700g sugar
Juice and zest of four lemons
2 tablespoons white wine vinegar
About 15 elderflower heads in full bloom

1. Place hot water and sugar in a large container, stir until
the sugar dissolves, top up with cold water to make 6
litres of liquid in total.
2. Add the lemon juice and zest, vinegar, flower heads
and stir gently.
3. Cover with clean muslin and leave to ferment in a cool,
airy place for a couple of days. Take a look at the brew,
and if it's not becoming a little foamy and obviously
beginning to ferment, add a pinch of yeast.
4. Leave the mixture to ferment, again covered with
muslin, for a further four days. Strain the liquid through a
sieve lined with muslin and decant into sterilised strong
glass bottles with champagne stoppers or sterilised
screw-top plastic bottles
5. Seal and leave to ferment in bottles for at least a week
before serving as chilled as I intend to be … en
vacances, over the next couple of weeks.

Au revoir!

Chapter 39
Farmville

Not to be confused with Frejus, our gorgeous holiday destination en France, but an app where folk farm their land, grow veg and share tips on organic fertiliser. Virtually.

So strong is the current worldwide appetite for food growing and nature, that Farmville now has millions of members who log on to tend their crops. Millions plus ... two. James and I have been lounging around the pool on his phone, now into our third hour of Farmville tilling: Our exhausting endeavours rewarded by Stu's supply of chilled glasses of lemonade and vino rose.

Talking of tasty bouquets ... of the flower variety, the only blight on my perfect horizon is when I turn on my phone to check my texts. I can't believe it. Phoebe has cancelled my edible bouquet shoot. She claims the space is needed for an article on anaerobic digesters. And talking of blight, according to Nat's text, our peas have it.

I turn off my phone and place all thoughts of decimated petit pois, swelling plums, pollinated cucumbers and bolting flowers to one side. It's time to get back to the hard work of making sure that all traces of my alleged gardener's tan have been replaced by an all-round tan, one that's as lustrous and golden as the calamari the waiter places down in front of me. Albeit not quite so crinkled and deep fried.

LARGE GREEN ... MORE SOFT PORN THAN SOFT BACK ... HOLIDAY BOOK ...

'Oh no you mustn't,' moaned Deborah as Toby's hands slid down towards her ...'

Chapter 40
Big butt. No sweat.

'St Swithin was an Anglo Saxon Bishop who requested on his deathbed in 970BC to be buried in a churchyard where the rain would fall on him. When monks removed his remains to a shrine in Winchester Cathedral, there was the mother of all storms. It rained for the next forty days. Since that time, legend states that if it the sun shines on St Swith's day, it'll be a boiling hot Summer ...'

'Is it St Swithins Day today?' I ask Nat, as I follow her bleary eyes, around Lottie. It's seven the morning after my late-night return from France. We are inspecting the crop damage caused by the heatwave gripping England in its clammy paws.

'No idea.' Nat shrugs her shoulders. 'Jesus, is it hot or am I just having another flush?' She wipes her brow which looks as shrivelled as the beetroot she picks.

'Bleedin' menopause. Not mulch fun! Anyway, good hols, was it?'

'Talking of mulch,' Bernie skips into the garden and welcomes me back with a big wet bear bug, 'you really should spread a layer of bark chip over the soil to help keep the moisture in.'

'You should also chew on this comfrey leaf to help with your menopausal symptoms,' says DG, handing me a dagger-shaped green leaf.

I hand it to Nat and wipe away Bernie's sweat which is now glazing my new white strapless top.

'Water loss is a very serious issue now.' Bernie removes his black string t-shirt to reveal a torso that is paler than our unwatered courgette leaves. 'You need to buy a big water butt.'

'Talking of butts,' Nat calls out to me as I go to fetch the hose, 'put on a bit of weight in La France, did you, Deb?'

'STOP Deborah, you can't use that,' Bernie shouts at me.

'Haven't you heard about the hosepipe ban?' DG screeches.

'Er … no,' I sheepishly reply.

'I've always claimed that hosepipes are the enemy of the organic gardener,' Bernie adds his sprinkling of wisdom 'but now with the hosepipe ban, people are having to find ways round watering. Mulching, which slows down evaporation of water from the soil, is one.'

'Well you know what I always say,' Nat winks at me, 'water your kids. Mulch your spouse, and fertilise your neighbours!'

'I'll show you a self-watering trick using an empty plastic water bottle.' Bernie lifts a blue towel printed with a Hitchhikers Guide to the Galaxy logo out of his bag.

'Talking of watering your kids, I've found a great way around the hosepipe ban,' Nat whispers in my ear. 'I don't water the plants, just poor little Sammi! As it's too hot to give him a shower indoors, I've had to hose him down at least twenty times this week outside in the garden!'

'That Mr Parkeeper does it in the middle of the night' Pete joins us. 'He thinks no one is looking.'

#NTS: Hosepipes at dawn. I chuckle at the thought.

'Did you know a fifty by twenty food garden uses two thousand litres of water a day?' Bernie swabs the beads of sweat on his forehead. They're glistening more brightly than the sun on the Cote D'Azur.

Bernie continues, 'Watering plants every day will damage them, as the roots will go to where the water is. As a light watering never sinks much below the first few inches of topsoil, this is where the strongest root formation will be. One should always direct water at roots and prioritise.'

#NTS Priorities. Where's tan-viewing Toby?

'According to Steiner, shallow-rooted plants need lots of water or they turn tough and woody.' DG lifts up a bottle of Badoit and douches it over her body. 'Lettuces are particularly touchy about getting enough water. Carrots rebel if they get too much, whilst strawberries sulk by producing small crops of hard fruit.'

'What about moody melons?' Nat nudges Pete. They roar with laughter.

'Did you know that soft fruit bushes can be watered with recycled water,' says Bernie. 'You should use grey water by rigging a hose to your bath …'

#NTS Grey what? All images of the sparkling blue sea vanish down the plughole.

Bernie races on. 'Grey water includes water from laundry, dishwashers, baths, and showers. But not from the toilet. That's called black water. It's best not to use kitchen sink waste water as this contains traces of grease. This water can be put to use for toilet flushing and …'

'So what do these yellow leaves on our tomato plants indicate?' I swiftly change the subject.

'Split toms occur as a result of stresses to the skin. This is caused by plants being alternately wet and dry at the roots. God, it's boiling.' Bernie looks up into the glaring sun. 'Climate change is a frightening thing.'
'I've just googled the temperature and it's due to reach thirty-two degrees today.' DG shakes her head.

We all nod in agreement. Talk about frightening things, and skin stresses, I look down at my peeling legs. 'Anyway, good to see you all.' I turn round to walk indoors. Time to apply that moisturiser

'Surely you're not going anywhere, Deborah?' Bernie sighs. 'It's time for our winter planting meeting. Didn't you get the texts I sent you on holiday?'

LITTLE GREEN BOOK

Bernie's self-watering plastic bottle trick. Abra(cap)dabra:

-Remove the cap from a large plastic water bottle. Cut a small hole in it and replace the cap.

-Cut off the bottom of the water bottle. Recycle the cut end.

-Turn the plastic water bottle upside down. Bury the capped end in the soil as close as possible to the base of the plant that you wish to water.

-Fill the plastic bottle with water. The water will slowly drip into the soil through the hole in the plastic bottle's cap.

Chapter 41
Cultivated relationships

'The aim of pruning is to remove unproductive wood and encourage new growth,' says Dougie as we huddle around an apple tree, listening to his lecture on fruit tree health.

'Yes, we must cultivate trees like we do our relationships,' enthuses St Grace. She takes off her Orla Kiely gardening glove and smiles at what looks like a ring gleaming on the fourth finger on her left hand.

'Holy mother, this aubergine looks like Pete's face after our row last night,' Nat calls out from the gro-bag she's leaning over.

'It's swelling and turning purple.'

#NTS Holy nuptials. Talking about relationships ... was that an engagement ring I just saw flashing on St G's finger?

'I hope Peter's okay?' St G puts her arm around Nat.

'I'm only joshing with you,' chuckles Nat. 'He's only got a small black eye!'

I try and steal a quick look at St Grace's fourth finger, but it's now concealed by a cluster of apple tree leaves which she curls her hand around.

'I always see pruning as a form of living sculpture,' St G continues. 'Personally, I'm a fan of Verrier candelabras.'

And I'm a fan of leaving this morning to curl up its un-pruned branches and consign all thoughts of rings to those on the bark of a tree, I sulkily think. I want to slink back indoors to catch up on the final episode of *Married at First Sight Australia*.

'By the way, how's Toby? We haven't seen him for yonks,' Nat asks St G.

'Do you two have any *news* to share?' I hesitantly ask.

'Well, yes we do …' Grace quickly whips her hand back into the glove. 'Have you heard about poor Tob's arm? He slipped on a packet of humus crisps outside the library and dislocated his shoulder.'

'He should contact Claims Direct,' says Nat 'The lady at no.15 got three grand for …'
'Oh no, poor Toby …' I cry out.

'Back to pruning,' Dougie sighs, the note of impatience in his voice dryer than the apple tree branch he starts to snip. 'Prune, you must. I've just had the most dreadful exeeeeeeexperience with apple sooty blotch. The first thing you do is nip the top off the tree to encourage side shoots …'

'I'm gonna practice on poor little Sammi's hair.' Nat slaps me on the shoulder.

'Anyway,' Dougie sums up, 'I heartily recommend you buy 'Pruning Made Easy. Published in 1977, it is the only pruning manual you'll ever need.'

'I'll put it on your Xmas list, will I Deb?' Nat roars with laughter.

LITTLE GREEN BOOK OF CULTIVATED RELATIONSHIPS

Who needs a sunny day when you have blazing bright yellow courgette flowers?

After Bernie and St G finally finished their running lecture, which was as dull and grey as the sky, Nat and I went a-a-harvesting. We picked several courgettes and lots of oh-so-sweet peas. We plundered the prickly gooseberry plants bursting with enticing green purplish berries.

Bean there! We composted our withered broad bean plants. We admired the pretty red beans on the French bean plants. Beans surely a few weeks away.

Our pumpkin leaves seem to be growing by the minute. They're now as big as my hand!

Talking of hands and other cultivated relationships, there's no news on the RING. Nat claimed she didn't spot anything, it was just sunlight gleaming on St G's finger.

Chapter 42
Happy Christmas

'Happy Christmas, Deborah.' Toby leans over and pecks me on the cheek.

'Thanks, er … you too, Toby, but aren't your kind wishes a little early?

#NTS: Mistletoe. Just where is it when you need it. Wonder if wild rosemary would do?

'How's your arm?' I ask, my eyes scanning down his tanned, muscular, un-bandaged arm. Little golden hairs are bristling upon it like our baby pumpkins emerging from golden flowers.

'Oh, it's fine. Just a false alarm.' He sidles his un-dislocated, potentially-betrothed shoulder up to mine. 'But in terms of Christmas planting, I'm afraid we should have met up and got started weeks ago.'

Couldn't agree more. I refrain from voicing my comment which is as sour as the lone blackcurrant he pops into my mouth. Not that I've seriously counted the four-and-a-half-weeks—sixteen tan-diminishing days, that I haven't seen him for.

'But there are still some Christmas crops we can sow.' He smiles and lifts his finger to slowly wipe away the blackcurrant residue coating my lips. He pops said finger into his mouth and licks it. 'And there is an empty bed here.'

#NTS: Empty bed. Ooh yes Toby, let's climb in it.

'I've got a pressie for you,' he leans over and slides something out from a large envelope.

My heart starts to race.

'Carrots,' he winks at me. 'These "Giant Reds" are very vigorous.'

Talk about dangling a …

'Every Xmas I gorge myself on these served with roasted parsnips oozing with caramelised honey.' He hands me the packet of seeds, his hand lingering on mine. 'Don't you just find swede, oh so sexy, especially when mashed and whipped with …'

'Any other glad tidings to impart?' I ask, firmly fixing the image of a boiled turnip in my mind. I'm unprepared to indulge in any more veg fantasising until I know the truth about him and St Grace. And their nuptials.

'Oh, I'm just very busy with starting to plan next year's local council elections.' He slices opens the carrot packet. 'Hope I can count on your vote?'

'On the first day of Xmas my true love gave to me …' My political cross-questioning is interrupted by Nat, who skips up to us.

'I've got a great idea.' She looks down at DG's loony bed. 'Let's grow the twelve crops of Xmas in here. This round bed looks like a Xmas bauble! Our new bauble bed!'

#NTS: Political ponderings. Whilst I hold deep political beliefs, I can't seem to remember which party Toby is a member of!

'I don't understand why the "Christmas Drumhead" cabbage seeds you sowed last month didn't grow?' Bernie strolls up to us. 'Although their name is misleading, they should have been ready for harvest by September. I've just popped round to donate a packet of Swede seeds. They are excellent in Welsh cawls.'

'Late night cawls,' Nat yawns. 'That was me last night with the girls!'

'Turnips.' Bernie licks his lips. 'They're also lovely in Winter stews. My mum cooks 'em every night. The brands I recommend include "Manchester Market" and "Snowball."'

'Er Deb, you might want to take a look in this.' Nat hands me Bernie's new gleaming trowel to show me my reflection in it.

I lift it up to see a set of lips an unfortunate shade of smeared blackcurrant stare back at me.

'But the most important crop we must of course plant for Christmas are new potatoes.' Toby winks at me. 'We plant 'em without chitting in large pots so that they can be moved under cover in Autumn.'

'And what about winter radishes, Deborah?' Bernie turns round to face me. 'They grow a dark shade of red. Just like the colour your cheeks have turned.'

LITTLE GREEN BOOK

On the twelfth day of Xmas
Toby gave to me,
Eleven peas-a-piping,
Ten sexy suedes a leaping,
Nine giant red carrots dangling,
Eight maids Tobe-a-milking,
Seven frogs a-swimming,
Six time-a-nite Tobe-a-laying,
A golden ... is it or is it not ... engagement ring?
Four calling birds,
Three blushing radishes,
Two turnip doves,

And a ...

The twelve homegrown crops of Xmas dinner.

1. *Cabbages:* Growing well. Will pick/freeze in Autumn
2. *Leeks:* As above
3. *Parsnips:* As above
4. *'Sanda' Brussels:* Looking good. Ready in Oct. Will pick 'n freeze. May grow till Xmas
5. *Cavolo Nero:* Lovely long silver grey leaves growing. May also grow till Xmas depending upon frost.
6. *'Carlingford' new pots:* Gonna order
7. *'Giant Red' carrots:* Sowed Toby's sexy seeds in bauble bed.
8. *'St Joan' swede:* As above
9. *Turnip:* Am behaving like one. **Ridiculous** crush on Toby must stop right here.
10. *Sage n other herbs:* Will pick as available
11. *Lettuce/garnish:* Will sow in green room in Sept for smoked salmon blinis
12. *Blackberries:* Will freeze in Autumn 'n dribble over ...

Actually all this talk of the twelve crops of Xmas
has got me in the mood for a little festive cheer.
Pour myself a nice large Pimms ...
'Once in royal Toby's city ...

Is he engaged, or not?

Chapter 43
Feeing comfrey

'Then I'll begin …'

It's a perfect, languid Summer's eve. Am reclining on new (FSC-approved) wooden deckchair, glass of Pinot Grigio in one hand, hoe in t'other. I'm dozing off listening to DG drone on about the healing properties of wild herbs.

'For thousands of years, herbs have been used in complementary medicine for their spiritual properties.' She plucks a yellow flowers from a raspberry bush. 'Many herbs grow wild, like Agrimony. It's a remedy for people who keep their troubles hidden under a mask of pleasure and happiness.'

'Agrimony, I have enough of that in my life!' says Nat as she tries to untangle the net around our fruit bushes.

DG sighs, 'the sad clown masking his inner hurt by being the life and soul of the party is an Agrimony archetype. She hands me the flower. 'In Chaucer's time, Agrimony was mixed with Mugwort and vinegar to cure a bad back. It was even recommended to be taken with pounded frogs and human blood.'

'I've heard that cabbage vinegar is a great hangover cure.' Nat grabs my wine glass and takes a generous swig. 'It also relieves constipation. The painter who lives at no.17 suffers from ...'

'Vegetables and herbs also have vulnerary uses.' DG smirks at me, correctly guessing it's a word beyond my comprehension. 'They can be turned into beauty products and ...'

#NTS: Skin Creams. My ears prick up at the mention of two words I surely can understand. My two-hundred-pound jar of Le Prairie soon to be replaced by a free jar of Le (wild) Meadow.

DG lifts a plastic container and removes its lid. 'This cucumber compress contains homegrown cucumbers and onions which I've grated and chilled, then mixed with yoghurt. It makes a refreshing summer toner.' She steeps several cotton wool pads into the mixture.

I glance down at the gloopy-looking concoction. It brings a whole new meaning to the term knowing your onions.

'We could make nettle hair conditioner.' Nat casts down her net and jumps up. 'I could approach Lidl to sell it for us. What about sage bubble bath & rosemary nit shampoo? We could go into production. Save you lookin' for a job, Deb!'

'I'm a *resting* fashion designer, thank you, Natalie,' I snap.

'Did you know that a tincture of holly is used for treating symptoms of anger, Deborah?' DG pats me on the shoulder. 'Gosh, you are a little tense aren't you? But back to nettles, they really are an underrated plant. The small stinging hairs on their leaves can be neutralised by drying or cooking. Their young shoots have been used for hundreds of years to treat painful muscles and joints.'

'Bloody hell, this is lovage?' exclaims Nat, picking a cluster of the celery-like leaves growing in between our fruit bushes.

'Yes, they were once revered as an aphrodisiac in Medieval Europe.' DG leans over and sniffs the leaves.

'I've heard they're a great remedy for smelly feet!' Nat picks several leaves and sinks them into a bucket of water. She hands me a bamboo cane to stir the concoction. 'Here's one for our production line, Deb.'

'Nat, you and I are most certainly not going to start any kind of eco-business …'

'My nan used to make a wicked lovage cordial.' A tear wells up in Nat's eyes. 'She used to mix crushed lovage seeds with four ounces of sugar and a pint of brandy.'

With that much brandy, no wonder it's called a cordial. I keep the thought to myself and stir Nat's potion de pieds.

'And, of course, you girls surely recognise those comfrey leaves,' says DG, picking a pink bell-shaped flower.

'I read in one of poor little Sammi's picture books that in olden days scattered comfrey leaves were a remedy for a girl ruing the loss of her virginity.' Nat pokes her hand into our tyre of second early potatoes. It's brimming with bonny green leaves and little white flowers. 'I think these are ready to harvest now.'

'Did you know that before paints and chemical dyes existed people made dyes from natural plants, animals and minerals?' says Dora, scurrying up to us carrying a plate of olives. 'Hello, land girls!' She lays down on the chair next to me.

'In Roman times, it took thousands of snails to produce a small amount of the colour purple, which, by the way, was Queen Cleopatra … my alter-ego's favourite colour,' adds DG. 'Have I ever told you about the regression therapy I had in which I was taken back to the time of …'

'People also used the dead dried bodies of cochineal insects to make a red dye.' Dora scrapes a ladybird onto her finger and places it atop an olive. 'Maybe poor little Sammi and I could experiment with making dyes. There's a whole world of unseen insects below our very feet

Anyway, anyone for an olive?' Dora hands me the plate. I pass the plate and all its contents straight onto Nat.

'From this garden, we can make a yellow dye from onion skins, brown from comfrey, red from dandelion roots … Oh, these are delicious.' DG scoops up a handful of olives. 'What are they stuffed with?'

Nat interjects, 'I read in Grazia Mag that a good way to darken greying hair is to comb it through with an infusion of sage. Anyhow, it's time to start planning my birthday party for next week. I've invited everyone. It's gonna be our big summer barbie bash, isn't it, Deb?'

I lay back on my chair, close my eyes. I try to forget Nat's use of the word *'our'* bash and reassure myself that her reference to greying hair was aimed at DG … not me. I concentrate on feeling the long shadow of evening wrap its warmth around the garden emitting a buttery sweetness into the still air. I imagine the unseen insects of Dora's edict scampering around making their dins.

Talking of Dora, who has dozed off, her loud snores would surely frighten away even the most stalwart of spiders. And talking of dins, I look at my watch, horrified to see it's almost 8 pm. A starved James would be back from rugger practice soon, eager for his (homemade, sort of) chicken and sweetcorn pie.

I stretch out and start to sit up, but feel my efforts hampered as DG places two sodden cotton wool pads over my eyes.

'Cor, that's bliss,' says Nat, who's clearly been offered the same treatment.

My eyes tingle with a lovely zingy freshness as DG lifts my flip-flop-less feet and places them in a bucket filled with a warm concoction.

Leaving all thoughts of corns … both the sweetened and pedicure varieties to one side, I let out a deep sigh of contentment and concentrate on enjoying my beauty therapy. Feeling comfey, actually, I most certainly am.

'You know what Gire, you're actually all right,' Nat adds.

'Now girls, just lay down and relax,' DG whispers. 'You're both going to enjoy the fascinating story I'm going to read about the hundred different varieties of comfrey that Lawrence D Hills discovered in 1954. He listed all their uses, of which particular interest is the "Bocking 14" cultivar of Russian Comfrey and it's …'

LITTLE GREEN BOOK

To make herb/wildflower ointment:

Heat 60g of selected herb in 500g petroleum jelly over boiling water for two hours. Strain in jar. Leave to cool.

We will dye for you:
Steep herbs in a bowl of boiling water for 8 hours before simmering for 2 hours. Cool solution. Add garments. Simmer in a commercial mordant solution to fix colour.

Wonder what my new little white midriff would look like dyed purple? Perhaps I'll dig up some beets later, and James and I can embark upon a science project.

Just had an email from Toby asking me ... ol' blackcurrant lips ... to go 'swan upping' with him the week after next. Cool cochineals!

What actually is swan upping?

Schwarzwurz:
The best recipe with comfrey leaves is a Teutonic fritter. YOU vill need:
Comfrey leaves, as required. 1 egg. 2oz plain flour. Half a pint of milk. Half teaspoon salt. Oil for frying
Leave the stalks on the comfrey leaves and dip into thin batter made from egg, flour, milk and salt. Fry the battered leaf in oil for two mins

Guten appétit

August

Shear magic …

Chapter 44
Getting caned

Despite dreadful weather warnings, the night of Nat's party is a gorgeous one.

Having been banned from Lottie all day in order for Nat and Pete to 'set dress' the garden, I walk out fashionably late (five outfit changes later) to find Lottie transformed into a magical oasis. Every fence, twig, and plant has been festooned in fairy lights. Their luminosity is only surpassed by the glow of the gold sequins on Nat's dress. Guests are lounging around on bales of hay, their pungent farm fresh aroma mixing with a delicious woody smell coming from the cob oven. I must admit it all makes for a rather lovely setting. Maybe the evening won't be as painful as I'd imagined.

'Yoohoo, Deb, try one of these' says Nat, rushing up to me.

'I can't believe your Stu's in New York again and gonna miss this brill party. It's far more glam here, don't you agree!' She hands me a Thomas the Tank paper plate containing a package wrapped in silver foil.

I nod in agreement and listen to the jazz music which pipes out from speakers wonkily perched on our little apple tree. To me, it is more enchanting here than in the Big Apple. I unwrap the food to find a scrumptious-looking row of char-grilled king prawns. They're skewered on a sprig of rosemary and oozing with garlic oil.

'Do you like my Albert Ferrari dress?' Nat spins around. 'Phoebe lent it to me from the fashion wardrobe at Flair Magazine. She's sooo my N.B.F. I got her number from your phone. You don't mind do you?'

My Phoebe has lent Nat a designer Alberta Ferretti dress. My sense of outrage remains temporarily un-voiced as I bite into the prawns. My mouth explodes with a delicious burst of flavour.

'And get this down you, Deb.' Pete thrusts a cocktail into my hand. 'It's my special homegrown cucumber basil Martini!'

'Actually, Nat,' I swallow the prawn whole and blurt out, 'I know it's your birthday, but it is a bit naughty of you. And it's an Alberta Ferretti dress, not a sports car …'

'No need to get your knickers in a twist, Deb.' Nat shrugs her sequined shoulders.

'I wouldn't say that!' Our heated conversation is interrupted by Toby, who walks up to us. 'I rather like the sound of Deborah's twisted knickers! Evening ladies,' he winks at me and turns round to face Nat. He hands her a package. 'Here's a little birthday gift for you.'

Nat speedily unwraps the (recycled Daily Telegraph) wrapping paper, to find a pretty wooden bracelet.

#NTS: Birthday bangle. How come she gets the pretty pressie, and I … a packet of carrot seeds. I'm struck by two more thoughts: What knickers am I actually wearing? Oh god no, it's the joke Mickey Mouse ones that Stu put in my Xmas stocking last year. And also … surely Toby doesn't read the "Daily Torygraph?"

'Hope you like it. Grace chose it for you.' He slides the bangle onto her wrist.

'Talking of Grace, is she not here tonight?'

'Yoo hoo, Tobes.' My hopeful enquiry is cut short by Hen, who skips up to us dressed in a tiny denim skirt and green chiffon top. It's as transparent as the cocktail I take a large swig from.

'I love your outfit.' Nat stares at Hen's strawberry frilly bra, which is clearly on display through said top.

'Well, as everyone in gardening circles knows, sheers are important!' Hen throws back her mane of hair, laughs, and grabs Toby's hand. 'Come and have a dance Tobes! By the way Deborah, you might want to check your teeth!'

Watching them skip off together, I take another swig of my drink and grit my teeth to retrieve the errant piece of basil once floating in the cocktail. It's now lodged between my molars.

'In the navy ...' I walk on as the music changes.

I pass Bernie - Are they leather trousers he's wearing? - in full Village People dancing mode. Next to him, Mr Prakeesh, owner of the local newsagent, flails his arms around like a wind turbine as he dances with Delia. Poor little Sammi's parents (who I've not yet had the pleasure of meeting) continue smooching; their tongues and body parts glued to each other like the orange spots on our pear trees.

I take another swig of my drink as I pass Ben-G who is seemingly in deep conversation with a frog. Next to him, Jarvis, dressed head to toe in yellow is rummaging through the compost bin. I crane my neck around looking for Toby and Hen. They seemed to have vanished.

'Whenever my mum and dad yuckily kiss like that, it's followed by them playing petting games in their bedroom and making animal noises!' says poor little Sammi emerging from the canopy of rainforest that is our wildly overgrown Jack 'n the beanstalk runner bean bed. 'Dora the explorer, I'm coming back in.' He lifts a clump of mud, wipes the camouflage over his face and disappears back into the wild.

I walk on, pausing besides a group of people standing by the cob oven. It's filled with a mouthwatering selection of char-grilled meat and pizza and flickers of golden light which are spitting out onto the ...

'Bledy fire hazard, this party,' says Dougie, as he tries to move several teenage gatecrashers who are smoking whilst perched on the bales of hay. 'Begger off you chives.'

I pause beside our potting table which has now been turned into a buffet table. It's filled with a rainbow of salads, Chez Lottie. I dip a piece of pitta into an aubergine dip. It's the one item of food which is perhaps a little too spicy for a drooling Tikka 'n Marsala, who are also perched on the table mouths coated with residual …

'Happy loaf mass, Deborah.' I am joined by DG, who like Jarvis is dressed head to toe in yellow.

'Loaf what?'

'Happy Lammas.' She places her palms together in a prayer position. 'Today, the first of August, is the festival of Lammas when it is traditional to present a loaf of bread made from new corn.'

I sneak a look over to our corn bed, relieved to see that the speedily growing (now eighteen-inch-high stalks) remain un-plundered.

'Lammas is halfway between the Summer Solstice and Autumnal Equinox.' She lifts a loaf of Hovis out of her bag. 'At this time we become conscious of the sacrifice the Sun God is preparing to make. We experience a sense of abundance at the same time as beginning to feel an urgency to prepare for the death of Winter.'

'The only dying to be done at my party is for a drink!' declares sequined-sun-goddess Nat, her spirits (several martinis behind her) riding as high as the hemline on her dress. She skips up to us and tops up my empty cocktail glass.

DG continues, 'Lammas Day used to be a time for foretelling marriages and trying out new partners. Two people would agree to a trial marriage to see whether they were suited for wedlock. At the end of the day, if they didn't get on, the couple could part.'

Trial marriages, trying out new partners I hear? Happy, happy Lammas day indeed. I look around for Toby. Just where has he gone?

'Anyway, poor Jarvis is a bit down in the dumps.' DG smiles as Jarvis walks up to us. 'His TV programme, like its name, has been dumped,' she sighs.

'Dumped like opera singer in flat no.17,' adds Nat. 'I've invited her here tonight. Wonder who she could cop off with? By the way, love your two matching yellow outfits.'

'They're saffron,' says Jarvis, frowning.

'Personally, I like older, large women,' says Ben-G, who has joined us. 'I'd get off with her.'

'Talking of all things large and crusty … pizza's up!' Pete comes up to us holding two delicious-looking plates filled with slices of pizza.

'So tell me, Ben-G, are you actually a Rastafarian?' Jarvis places three slices on top of each other and takes a large bite.

'And you a Trustafarian?' Ben-G bites into a battered courgette flower atop a pizza slice.

'Actually, I'm a sun god,' Jarvis sighs as a trickle of cheese drips down his top to form a confluence of yellows. He lifts a silk hankie out of his pocket and dabs away at the stain.

I walk on into the green room. A mirror ball is rotating slowly on a pole attached to the ceiling. I can't believe it but Toby is there alone, sitting on a tree stump.

'Ah, here you are Deborah, I've been looking for you.' He hands me a flower. 'This is for you.'

A flower pour moi. I clutch the beautiful little pink bell-shaped flower, my heart beating louder than the techno music which starts to reverberate around.

'Go on, suck it.' He looks into my eyes, lifts the stem of the flower and snaps it off at its base. 'It won't harm you.'

'Suck it,' I hear. Is Toby really expecting me to suck a flower? I think not …

I feel the quivering stem placed in my mouth. I close my eyes. My lips part slowly, I rest the little perfumed tube upon my tongue and take a cautious lick. The merest hint of nectar escapes into my mouth. A little moan escapes my mouth as I suck more greedily, releasing more honey, more sweetness, experiencing that fleeting moment, that glimpse of life inside a flower. For I am that bee, that pollinator, the honeybird …

I open my eyes to see harlequins of light dancing around the green room, to see Toby smile as the music outside, as if on cue, slows down and Marvin Gaye starts to hear it through our grapevine. I smile back. Feel myself start to swoon (bit like our un-watered pak choi.) This is it … I take in a deep breath. It's the moment I've been waiting for all year. Toby leans towards me and …

'Oy, Deb! Are you really eating a flower?' calls out Nat as she bursts into the green room. 'Call me old fashioned but I think I'll stick to a good ol' banger?' She roars with laughter. 'What do you call a guy who is the life and soul of the party? A fungi! Get it? fungi as in the mushroom … not fun guy!' She grabs Toby's hand. 'C'mon, it's karaoke time!'

She drags him out into Lottie.

I reluctantly follow them to find that the empty garlic and onion bulb-shaped bed has been transformed into a makeshift karaoke stage. Planks of wood wonkily laid over it.

A wobbly Delia and DG are clutching microphones whilst trying to read song lyrics which are quickly scrolling down on Pete's laptop.

'Sisters are doing it for themselves,' they wail. 'Yes we are.'

'I didn't know they were sisters,' says poor little Sammi, his face smeared in a mix of Summer pudding and mud pie.

'I like a bit of girlie action.' Ben-G takes another puff of his er … cigarette.

I place several yummy-looking skewers of grilled strawberries sprinkled with balsamic and sugar on a plate and sit down to watch their surprisingly good performance.

Around me, the sky turns from navy to cobalt blue as night draws its shapes in. The frilly kales are tinged with silver. Towers of sweetcorn stand majestic and aloft. Sunflowers smile brightly in the darkness, illuminating Bernie who is laying on the ground snogging a woman whose hair is a deeper shade of purple than our cabbages which they roll onto. Delia, who is dancing with Dougie, waves at me, whilst James, who stands amid a group of his friends, blushes shyly at a pretty girl.

'You smell nice, young man.' Dora sits down next to Ben-G. Her hair is covered in twigs. 'I do like a man with a nice aftershave.' She sniffs the air. 'It's sort of Oakey and musky.'

'Deb, have you met Di?' Nat introduces me to a petite woman with short spiky brown hair and an elfin-like frame. 'She's an opera singer.'

'How wonderful!' I shake Di's hand. 'I love opera. Particularly La Scala, where ...'

'La scala,' agrees Nat, 'I love their pesto sauce. Talking of sauces Di, you must try our homemade tomato...'

'Darling, what a charming little party, tres rustique ...'

Moving from one diva to another, I turn round to find Phoebe standing beside me. 'Phoebes, what a lovely, er, surprise. What are you doing here?' I ask.

'I invited her, to thank her for the Ferrari,' says Nat, straightening out the creases in the dress which is now bunched around her *cuisse*. 'Feebee's gonna write a piece on the new range of herbal beauty products you and I are launching,' she races on.

'Must say, you are a sly one, Debo.' Phoebe kisses me extravagantly on both cheeks.

'Where's Princess Daisy?' Poor little Sammi rushes up to us and starts sobbing.

'I didn't know you had royalty coming tonight.' Phoebe's smile widens.

'And rock royalty. That Bob Plant didn't turn up,' Nat sighs. 'Rude git!'

'Seriously, guys, we can't find Princess Daisy anywhere,' says Pete brandishing a twenty-foot fruit-picking pole.

'Well, I hope she hasn't been eaten by a fox.' Bernie joins us. His lips are smeared in a mix of purple lipstick and lumpy homemade tomato sauce. 'Only last month I saw a headless chicken with its gizzards hanging out and ...'

'If ever I saw blessing in the air, I see it now in this still early day, where lemon-green the vaporous morning drips wet sunlight on the powder of my eye.'

All attention is turned towards Hen, who has turned the karaoke machine off and stands on the stage, mid-stanza.

'Friends and countrymen,' Nat grabs the microphone from her. 'Your country needs you. Princess Daisy ... Sammi's guinea pig has gone missing. Let us form a search party and find her. Let us leave no lettuce leaf un-parted, no cabbage leave unopened. Let us leave no stone unturned ...'

'There will always be an England ...' A beautiful voice, at first no more than a whisper, resonates through the garden. 'While there's a country lane,' Opera singer, Di, continues to sing out loud. Her small build belies the most incredible, powerful voice. 'Wherever there's a cottage small, beside a field of grain …'

'There'll always be an England,' Nat links my arm as everyone around Lottie starts to sing along. Everyone except Dougie, who with one hand is trying to orchestrate a rendition of "O Flower of Scotland," and with the other, have a good feel of my bottom.

As we form a line and begin the search, all patriotic singing is drowned out by the sound of a loud crashing, followed by a strange animal squeal.

The fairy lights go out, plunging Lottie into darkness.

I topple over and feel a searing in my palm, a dagger-like incision as my hand is impaled into a bamboo cane. 'It's far from the getting caned I'd planned for the party,' I hear Nat add.

Lottie spins round. All goes black.

Chapter 45
Not so good ol' blighty

It's an overcast Sunday afternoon. The weather is as grey as my hand.

The good news … Princess Daisy has been found in the chives bed and is fine. The bad news … that's more than can be said for my hand. It's swollen due to an allergic reaction from the large splinter, has a deep gash from the bamboo cane, and is now accessorised with a bandage care of a visit to the Royal Free Hospital A&E department late last night.

'You'll be all right Deb.' Nat slaps me on the shoulder, causing a ripple of pain to surge down my arm. 'Surely you know the saying, old gardeners never die, they just spade away!' She laughs and continues thinning out the chives, which she claims are as woody as her head.

DG strolls up to us with her arm slung around a grinning Bernie. 'Talking of pain relief, we stayed up all night making you a batch of chilli plasters.' They giggle as their hands brush against each other. She lifts a mound of dressing pads which are covered with red and green bits and coated with a tar-coloured liquid.

'These are made from an old recipe mixing crushed chillies with mustard powder, coconut oil and beeswax.' Bernie casts his eyes lingeringly down DG's Punjabi suit.

'We slowly simmered the ingredients together and steeped the alchemical potion in dressing pads. We then brought them straight here to you.' DG smiles coyly back at Bernie. 'Shall I remove your bandage now, Deborah, and apply it to the wound?'

I feel a wave of nausea wash over me, as much from the prospect of chilli plasters, as from DG and Bernie's idea of foreplay.

'The force certainly isn't with you,' calls out Bernie from the chippie bed. 'Your wound is not the only blight around here.' He caresses a tomato plant. 'Just look at the yellow leaves on these toms. These dark blotches will be followed by wilting foliage and stems.'

'Sounds like Pete after last night,' Nat chuckles. 'Great craic wasn't it!'

'Your feckin' party kept the whole street up all night,' comes an angry yell from over the fence. 'I've complained to the council's neighbourhood noise protection committee.'

'Miserable sod!' Nat ignores Mr Parkeeper's complaint and turns round to wink at DG. 'Talking of which, where's lover boy, Jarvis?'

'He ... er, had to be in Sussex early this morning for a family brunch, so he left last night,' says DG, stroking

Bernie's hand as he tugs off yellow leaves from the tomato plants.

'And I found this feckin' bottle in my rose bed.' Mr Parkeeper leans over the fence and frantically waves an empty bottle of tequila. 'It's squashed one of my prize roses. You's feckers are going pay for it.'

'Bit of a slammer then, eh!' Nat nudges me in the ribs. I wince in pain.

'I hope that bollix blight kills the lot of your poncey, organic crops.' Mr Parkeeper lobs the bottle back over the fence. 'I'd drown the lot of you in the strongest bottle of Bordeaux …'

I'm struck by two thoughts: 1. A drink problem would certainly explain Mr Parkeeper's less-than-salubrious disposition. 2. Bordeaux? I'd better lock up …

'And before you add more worry lines to your face, Deb, spraying crops with Bordeaux does not involve me breaking into Stu's wine cellar!' Nat quickly adds.

'Bordeaux is a copper-based fungicide spray that contains nasty unsexy chemicals.' Bernie pops a little green tomato into DG's mouth and licks his lips.

'But talking of Stu's stuff, I hope he won't mind that I've borrowed this …' Nat walks up to our overflowing potluck maypole and lifts Stu's hat from it. The bespoke hat he bought last month in the Cote D'Azur has now been re-planted with parsley.

'But that's Stu's new planters hat,' I protest.

'Well, he's got the right name for it!' Nat roars with laughter. 'I found it when I was clearing up last night whilst you were at the hospital!

'And you've got feckin' aphids.' Mr Parkeeper shoves his fist up at us and disappears into his garden shed.

'Did you know that aphids excrete a sugary substance which sticks to leaves causing a sooty mould?' Bernie lifts a cold leftover sausage from the bird feeder table.

'Bet this would be delicious with a sprig of parsley!' He grabs a clump out of Stu's hat and pops it into his mouth.

I snatch the hat from Nat. My indignation burning as deeply as my wound.

'Mr Parkeeper's right.' Bernie walks over to the brassiere bed. 'You have a mass of aphids on the underside of these cabbage leaves. Did you know that one aphid can asexually produce a hundred babies a month, and these babies can each reproduce within fifteen days of birth? They're called virginoparae ...'

'Talking of which,' says Nat, cradling a giant courgette, 'opera singer, Di, told me she's thirty-three and still a ...'

'Any other gossip from last night?' I change the subject.

'Yes, you'll be pleased to hear this, Deb.' Nat winks at me. 'I hear all's not well in camp Toby and St Grace.'

Hold on a mo … I place all thoughts of nymphomaniac aphids, virtuous divas, and bulging marrows to one side to ingest Nat's last comment. Toby and Grace *problèmes dans l'amour*. Surely not? But then, where was St Grace last night?

Shafts of sunlight suddenly break through the grey clouds. It promises to be a lovely day.

'C'mon Deborah,' DG grabs my hand, 'we mustn't forget to apply the chilli plasters to your poor hand. Shall we do it now?'

Chapter 46
Carmen Kohlarabanda

Kohlrabi is an orange-sized green and purple spiky cabbage with tentacles growing out of it. It looks like an alien and is popular in Germany. It has a swollen globe-shaped stem and resembles a turnip growing on a cabbage root. Its stems can be white, purple, or green, and is topped with a rosette of long blueish leaves. Kohlrabi, which is milder and sweeter than cabbage or turnip, can be sown in August ready for early Autumn harvest as it enjoys an Autumn frost, and is a cool weather crop.

Raw, it tastes a cross between an apple and celery, a sort of celeriac alternative. Sadly, I wasn't able to attend DG's Kohlrabi sowing and sauerkraut picklin' workshop today (using our freshly harvested red caulies) due to appointment at doctor to remove my bandage.

Little purple book

Talking of all things sour and purple ... Stu has returned from the US. He's furious that he had to attend a board meeting with the CEOs of several big banks wearing a pink shirt.

It appears that I'd neglected to rinse out the washing machine to prevent the beetroot dye I'd been experimenting with from staining his shirts.

He didn't laugh at my attempt to humour him by saying that: 'I would dye for him ...'

Chapter 47
Autumn collection

They say it takes *all sorts,* but isn't this going a little too far?

I take a closer look at the headline in my American Vogue Magazine: 'Designers take inspiration from Bassetts Liquorice allsorts. Strawberry chequered, flecked chocolate 'n orange. This Autumn's to-die-for clothing collections reference blocks of candy colour ...'

I take a large swig of my vodka and homemade elderflower and ponder on how the fashion world has gone to seed since transferring my attention from haute, to hort-couture. I flip over the page, safe in the knowledge that I can enjoy another undisturbed afternoon hour of Vogue and Grazia-gazing. Nat, poor little Sammi, and DG have gone away on a bushcraft course. I sadly was unable to attend due to throbbing wound.

Ouch! On the page in front of me, shock ... more like frock horror. There's an image of S.J.P. strolling through the streets of New York wearing a hessian toga dress. Never mind 'Sex in the City,' her look is more, 'Sacks in the City!' I sink back into my deckchair to ogle a picture of Giselle Bundchen at the Serpentine Summer party wearing a new young designer's must-have horse blanket wrap.'

A slip of paper has been wedged in between the parties and trends. It's a note from Nat. It reads:

Oy Deb, forget these collections, it's *our* must-have Autumn collection that counts. Late Summer sowing is a time overlooked by many new gardeners but not us! Put this magazine down now and go online to order the following seeds. Will cost you fifteen pounds, the cost of two copies of this mag. P.S. you would look fat in that coat opposite. Luv Nat xxx

I should be angry, but can't help at smile at Nat's audacity, and how well she knows me even though we are relatively new friends. I lift my drink, swig back the contents in one gulp, and begrudgingly scan my eyes down the first few items on Nat's list.

Hessian Sack Dress

Nat's natty Summer sowing – 'Autumn collection' list

1. Broad beans. Aquadulce Longpods. To be sowed outside September/October for a crop next May.

2. (JJ) Kales. Nero de Toscana. To be sowed early Autumn in green room for tender baby leaves throughout the Winter.

3. Lettuce. Winter Marvel. Sow late summer for an Autumn harvest. We'll continue to sow in the green room right up till November.

Winter marvel indeed! I stare at a pic in the mag of Kate Moss sporting a pair of Prada galoshes walking arm in arm into Claridges with Ronnie Wood. What was that someone once said about a rolling stone gathering no …

4. Sanguina beetroot. Ideal for sowing in green room in August for pulling as tender baby beet in Autumn.

Whilst we are on the subject of pulling …

5. Quick-headed calabrese … Sounds like Madonna's gorgeous new Sicilian boyfriend. I turn the page to see a pic of Maddy and NBF snogging. Just how old is he?

6. Peas. 'Serpette Guilloteau' is to be sown Oct in the green room for an early Spring crop and then from January.

7. Spring Cabbage. Precoce de Louviers. Sow in September for early Spring cabbage.

8. Hardy oriental greens. Ideal to keep veg going from late summer to Winter. Santoh Quick Yellow Pak Choi. Has pale green rounded leaves that can be harvested as soon as just one month after sowing. Mizuna, sow from September in the green room.

Talking about green boy, I put the list down and sigh. Where is Toby? I haven't seen him since the party and have had no news, either way, about him and St G.

I look up into the early evening sky as the sun appears for the first time today. The buttercup summer sun is now tinged with a copper hue. I zip up James' hoodie. Around me, Lottie is chocka full of produce; runner beans, courgettes. Marrows … and more marrows, a giant sunflower has even popped up in the middle of our paving!

I breathe in a peppery scent of rocket topped with yellow flowers (the rocket having gone to seed) A potent aroma of lavender and mint. Un-ripe green tomatoes with their citrus-like smell. A tart imagined sweetness of thickset, thorny blackberries which (despite our constant pruning), have snaked their way into Lottie.

'Summer's lease doth indeed have too short a date,' I think, as I feel a change in the air; a pause, sweet mustiness. A woody aroma from soil as rich as chocolate.

I lift my basket. It's time to wander around and pick from our abundant crop. Am going to make a delish summer minestrone for supper tonight.

In front of me, a robin lands on my Grazia mag. His tiny claws tread upon Chanel's catwalk promise of red scarlet. I smile, my old mate robin redbreast, back in town, ready to start on his Autumn collection.

AUTUMN

'Autumn is a second spring when every leaf
is a flower.' —Albert Camus

September
*My Autumn collection
...far from poultry...*

Chapter 48
Lord preserve us

'I hope you'll enjoy reading Albert Camus, Deborah,' says Hen, de-stoning our freshly harvested plums. 'It's going to be a great first novel to discuss at my philosophy group which Nat tells me you want to join.' She lifts a book out from her satchel and hands it to me.

'The Myth of Sisyphus.' Mischief maker Nat looks at the book and winks. 'Sounds more like an STD, than a book!'

'STD? I'm afraid I'm not up to date with modern literature,' says RHS Delia, as she continues to grate lemons. She wipes her citrusy hands down the front of the apron Nat has lent her. She's seemingly oblivious to the image of a naked male torso covering the front of it.

'Anyway ladies, I'm pleased to welcome you into my kitchen for our preserve-making workshop.' I cast my eyes along the bucolic kitchen table overflowing with plums, lemons, blackberries, crab apples, and er … marrows.

'Absurdism. The movement of which Camus was founding member, as I'm sure you'll be keen to discover, Deborah, is a philosophical school of thought which refers to the conflict between the human tendency to seek inherent meaning in life and the human inability to find any,' says Hen, lifting up a crab apple. 'Let's now turn our attention to pectin.'

'Who was he?' asks Nat, as she opens a bag of preserving sugar.

'Pectin is a natural gelling agent found in ripe fruit,' Hen replies in a voice more crabby than the apple she starts to core. 'By adding pectin to the mix, it will help set our jam. Toby and I foraged for them early this morn.' She stares wistfully at the crab apples and sighs. 'It's so sad the amount of fruit that goes unpicked each autumn. By the way, what do you make with the huge pear tree outside your house, Deborah?'

#NTS: Pear tree. What pear tree? The only pears I've seen are the adverts for the 'au' ones … in the back of Tatler.

'Yeah, my Pete makes wicked pear crumbles from your tree every year,' says Nat nudging me in the ribs.

I look down at the recipe, pleased that no one can see my cheeks - they're as red as hedgerow jam recipe in front of me. I start to weigh the quantities of sugar needed for the jam but can't read the small print without my glasses. It's a fact I'm certainly not going to admit to Hen. I lift up the bag of sugar and empty the whole of its contents into the mixing bowl.

'Yes, Toby and I are going harvesting for beloved, windfall fruit from the streets around us.' Hen places a handful of chopped apples into my new Le Creuset pan. 'Did you know we import ninety-five percent of our fruit into this country?' She sighs. 'Toby and I are going to design a fruit tree map of area. It's a project we are both passionate about.'

#NTS: Toby: A project I'm wickedly passionate about.

'Talking of Toby, I haven't seen him in a few weeks, how is he?' The smile I share with Hen is as sickly sweet as the jam mix I start to stir.

'He's been v. busy with council stuff but is going to come to next week's "Introduction to chicken keeping," lecture.'

#NTS: Chickens. Wonder if I can persuade Nat to keep some?

'Yes, we're going to organise a foraging on Hampstead Heath,' Hen continues.

'Foraging? I thought that's what those queer blokes got up to?' Dora comes hobbling into the kitchen.

'No dear,' Nat sits Dora down, 'that's cottage ...'

'As we enter Sept, it makes me soo reflective.' Hen slides her hand down her hair which is a shade more autumn russet.

The door bursts open, and in poor little Sammi races in. He scoops up a handful of blackberries and shoves them into his mouth. He then wipes his stained hands all over my new Liberties tablecloth.

Henna Hen lifts a giant marrow. 'As well as making plum and blackberry jam today, we are going to make marrow and ginger jam. I also thought about making confiture aux fleurs de pissenlits -'

'There's no need for that kind of language,' laughs Nat.

Lord preserve us! I take the giant marrow that Hen hands me to chop. It was going to be a long afternoon ...

LITTLE GREEN BOOK OF JAMMY DODGERS!

9 pm: Scrubbing best Le Creuset pan totally stained with dried jam.

9:30 pm: Still scrubbing best Le Creuset pan still stained with dried jam - super-glued with preserving sugar.

10:30 pm: Have binned best ruined-Le-Creuset-pan-stained-with-dried-jam – superglued-with-preserving-sugar-permabonded-with-pectin.

10:32 pm: Reading first page of Hen's Camus book whilst eating sickly sweet marrow jam. Don't know which is more absurd. Forced to open bottle of Hen's elderflower champagne to sluice away cloying taste.

10:33 pm Online, have found great site; 'Things your grandmother knew.'

Apparently, to clean a badly burnt pan simply fill it with cold water, float an onion in it, simmer, allow to cool, and burnt matter will float to the surface. Bet Henna Hen doesn't know this one. Have retrieved best soon-to-be-good-as-new Le Creuset pan from bin.

10:34 pm Can't find any onions. No choice but to open second bottle of Hen's elderflower champagne.

11:35 pm Have put on Jamie's parka and beanie hat. Out in street searching for pear tree. Hope Nat's not looking …

Absurd Marrow & ginger jam recipe

Makes about 4 lbs (2 kg) of jam.

Ingredients:
3 lb (1.5 kg) marrow
1 lb (500 g) crab apples
2 oz (50 g) root ginger
Juice of 2 lemons (or 4 tablespoons of bottled Lemon Juice)
3 lb (1.5 kg) jam sugar

Method:
Peel the marrow, discard the seeds and cut into cubes.Peel and core the apples and cut into cubes.

Steam until tender and then mash.

Add lemon juice.

Bruise the root ginger and wrap in a piece of muslin and place in the pan.

*Add the **right** amount of sugar, simmer and stir until dissolved.*

Bring to the boil for about thirty minutes, stirring occasionally as the pulp thickens and setting point is reached.

Pot into sterilised re-cycled jars and cover.

To test for setting point: Put a saucer into the freezer well before you start boiling. Spoon a little jam onto the saucer. Once cool, push it with your finger. If the jam wrinkles, it's ready.

To sterilise jars: wash thoroughly in hot soapy water. Switch oven onto 150% and place jars in oven for 15 minutes ...

***Confiture aux fleurs de pissenlits**. Dandelion Flower Jam to you 'n me ...*

Ingredients:
250 g. dandelion flower buds

1.5 l. water

750 g. preserving sugar for each litre juice obtained after boiling

Juice of 1 lemon

2 oranges

Rinse oranges and cut into small pieces without peeling.

Rinse dandelion flower buds and dry.

Boil both ingredients together in the water for 1 hour, then drain them through a sieve.

Measure the juice left, add lemon juice plus the correct amount of sugar. Boil for another hour. Cool the juice before storing it in sterilised jars.

Chapter 49.
Transexual plants & bio-sexual eggs

'Jarvis is bi-sexual,' DG bursts into tears.

'Oh don't worry dear, my Harold swung both ways too,' replies Lady Olivia, in a loud theatrical voice. She strokes a gilt-framed picture on the wall displaying an image of her collecting a BAFTA for her portrayal of Blanche Du Bois in the 1970's production of: 'A Streetcar named Desire'. She continues, 'My mother used to say it doesn't matter what you do in the bedroom as long as you don't do it in the street and frighten the horses!'

Taking DG's hand, Lady Olivia leads us through the hallway in her grand Primrose Hill house. We pass maroon walls covered with more pictures: Lady Olivia sitting on Larry Olivier's lap. Another one of her sharing a joke with the Redgraves in St. Trop. There's even a note from dear old Dickie thanking Olly for …

Sweeping open the double balcony doors, she ushers us out into a huge, manicured garden. In the middle, there's a six-foot, oval-shaped, timber-framed, chicken house. A long red carpet leads up to a little hatch, above which a sign reads: 'The Globe.'

It's her thespian chicken coop!

'It's so kind of you to invite us here today, Lady Olivia,' I add, as she sashays up the red carpet, and opens up the hatch.

'We're all smallholders here together girls. Do call me Olly,' she says as she cradles a huge chicken in her arms. 'Meet Hennessee,' she strokes the bird's long dark red feathers. She traces her hand along the chicken's long orange neck. 'Williams is resting, you'll meet him later,' she gazes into the chicken's bulbous red eyes, 'Hennessee is a Derbyshire Redcap. The first thing you need to consider when selecting chickens is that it all comes down to good breeding ...'

'Doesn't everything in life.' Nat nods in agreement. 'Dunno about this m'lady rubbish,' Nat whispers in my ear. 'I've seen Ladyship Olly down the Monarch drinking five pints of Stella, singing her heart out in a broad east-end accent.'

'Personally, I'm more of a show bird myself.' Lady Olly shakes her bob of copper-permed hair. It's more ablaze than Hennessee's plumage. She straightens out her emerald green boiler suit.

'You can say that again,' says Nat, none too quietly.

'The first thing you must remember when choosing chicks,' Lady Olly places Hennessee on the grass, 'is that one must be a rooster, or a hen will give up trying to lay eggs, and start pretending that 'she' is a 'he.' She slides her arms around DG's waist. 'How do you know your chap is bi?'

Nat butts in, 'She found him in bed with a freegan bloke called ...'

'There's never any need for that kind of language, dear. One must remember that nature is a bi-sexual beast.' Lady Olly tenderly stroke DG's cheeks. 'Some plants have flowers with both male and female reproductive parts. This hermaphrodite rose, for example, is bi-sexual. But tell me, does it smell any less sweet?' She walks DG towards a deep red rose and pushes her nose down onto it.

DG sneezes and lets out a loud sob. She rushes off to the end of the garden, disappearing under a beautiful wrought iron gazebo.

'Some plants also undergo sex-switching,' Lady Olly sighs, 'reminds me of my dear friend, the late great actor, Kenneth ...'

'Back to our feathered friends, Lady Olly, What do we have to consider next?' I ask.

'Well, you want to look out for good laying ability.'

#NTS: Good laying ability. Just where is Toby? I thought he was meant to be here today.

Lady Olly continues, 'After selecting your chicks, you need to think about building a chicken coop. Healthy chickens do need a good run around.' She leads us to a long wire tunnel attached to one side of The Globe. 'The run needs to be secure, keeping foxes out, and darling chicks in.' She points to a section of wire. 'I've dug this wire netting twenty centimetres into the ground to stop predators from getting under the fence.'

Nat chuckles. 'I read this grizzly story about three hens and a cockerel named Duke. A fox had broken into their hen house one night, so they henpecked it to death! Murder most fowl, eh!'

#NTS Kentucky fried chicken. Have gone right off the idea of paying for James and his mates to get a takeout tonight.

'So, er, how many eggs can a chicken lay a year?' I ask.

'Well, Hennessee only laid one hundred and fifty eggs last year, but my dear friend Dame Maggie laid three hundred … Yoo hoo Williams,' coos Lady Olly, as a large black rooster comes strutting down the red carpet. 'Come and meet mama's new friends.'

'Yoo hoo, Olly darling!' I turn round to watch Hen come flouncing into the garden. 'So sorry, darling, for being so late. I got a last-minute call from the Donmar last night for a fab role in Sam's new play …' She rushes up, throws her arms around Olly's neck.

'But Jarvey, you don't understand, it's not as simple as that,' DG re-appears, shouting into her phone.

Strange birds indeed, I think, as DG sobs into her phone, Nat chases a bewildered-looking Hennessee and Williams up the red carpet, and Hen continues to offer … what must be termed as more than a polite kiss hello … to Lady Olly!

LITTLE GREEN BOOK

Why did the chicken cross the road?

Albert Camus:

It doesn't matter, the chicken's actions have no meaning except to him.

Nat:

Because Colonel Sanders missed one!

Darwin:

Chicken evolution has been naturally hatched over the centuries to generate a predisposition to crossroads

Deborah:

Why didn't Toby cross my road today?

Olly:

To get to the Hen party …

I carry on dipping my soldiers into one of the eggs from the box which Lady Olly gave us to take home. Must admit, the eggs are so creamy with huge yellow yolks. Did I really see Hen snogging Olly today?

Chapter 50
Cornucopia

'This is the story of the Welsh God, Mabon, Son of Light, who was stolen three days after his birth.'

Mabon's sorrowful disappearance into the womb of the world sent the sun into hiding, tilting the Earth towards a time of darkness … a time known as the Autumn Equinox. We are celebrating it today.' DG sobs as she pauses her story.

'I'd hardly call this celebrating, you haven't stopped crying for the last hour!' Nat hands DG a large glass of wine. DG hands it straight back to her.

'Don't worry, love, it's only a corny old tale!' Pete slaps DG on the back. 'You can have the first one of these!' He leans forward to stoke the barbie which is sizzling with our freshly harvested corn on the cobs. Their golden kernels are turning a gorgeous shade of caramel. The must-have colour of this season.

'So carry on.' Nat drizzles knobs of butter over the corn. 'What happened to Baby M?'

'Mabon was rescued by a blackbird, a stag, and an owl, and was reborn at Yule … the Winter Solstice,' says DG, flicking an insect off one of the growing cobs of corn. She twists the corn and pulls it free. 'According to myth, by weaving a corn stalk into a wicker woman and dressing it in fine clothes, the sun spirit trapped in the corn would be set free, and the following year's harvest guaranteed.' DG places the would-be designer corn dolly on the table. Its yellow silken threads are encased in a husk and surrounded by glossy green leaves.

'Mabon is a time for us all to recognise our personal harvest.' DG wraps her arms around her tummy and sways.

'What did the baby corn say to the mumma corn?' asks Nat.

'Where's popcorn!' Pete chuckles. 'Good one, Gire, isn't it?'

'No, it's bloody not,' DG shouts. 'I'm pregnant.' She bursts into tears.

'Jesus, d'hear that babe, she's banged up.' Nat nudges Pete.

'Er, congratulations.' I walk over and kiss DG. The streaks of purple eyeliner running down her face smear over mine.

'How far gone are you?' asks Nat.

'Five weeks.'

Now maths was never my strong point, but mid-September minus five weeks leads to the night of the summer barbie. The *Bernie* Barbie. I take a large swig of my wine and try to block out the picture of a bald baby with a little red plait.

'So it's no longer bye-bye, bi-Jarvis, is it then?' Nat reasons. 'Get the pun … bye as in saying "good-bye", and "bi" as in sexual …'

'He may be bi, but he clearly doesn't shoot blanks.' Pete nods in agreement with Nat.

'Can you both just shut up,' bawls DG. 'I'm not sure whose baby it is.' She jumps up and runs out of Lottie.

'Whose baby is it then?' Pete and Nat confer. They've both clearly got a foggier memory of the night of the barbie than I do.

'I'll ask the girl who lives at no.22. She works at the Doc's surgery,' Nat offers. 'She always knows everything.'

A strange silence pervades Lottie as DG disappears indoors. Pete picks a couple of courgettes. He slices them lengthways, sprinkles them with freshly picked herbs, and pops them on the barbie. Nat strolls over to view our Xmas spuds. They've already grown two feet tall. I busy myself in the green room sowing lettuce, beetroot, kale, and spring cabbage seeds from our autumn collection order.

'Corn's up girls!' I walk out of the green room as Pete serves the corn. 'I've put you a few aside for Stuart and

James,' he considerately adds, 'and several for Gire as she's eating for two.'

'Thanks, Pete, but Stu is in America, *again*.' I sigh.

'Who'd have thought Gire would be the one playing the field.' Nat bites into the corn. 'Jesus, this is so sweet.'

'Yep, I can't believe we grew this!' I smile.

My comment is received with nods of agreement: Words no longer able to express our pleasure. I look around Lottie and grin. Even though we are now in September, we are still eating runner beans, rocket, courgettes, carrots, and red cabbage (a couple of which have popped up in the strangest places along our pathways!) Our chives have even started to grow new green shoots. Large, frilly Cavolo nero leaves sway in the gentle breeze, whilst the brightly coloured Swiss chard shines brightly in the dim early evening September light.

'Hey, you'll never guess who I just bumped into today,' Nat places an ear of finished corn down, and bites into a second one, 'Robert Plant!'

'Not Robert Plant the rock star?' I look up.

'Yep. Bob was walking down the street holding several corns on the cobs. I stopped him and we talked corn. Amazing isn't it, with all his dosh, he could eat in the finest restaurants anywhere in the world, yet this very night he's eating his own homegrown corn. The same as us. Says he might pop over sometime to have a look at ours.'

#NTS Robert Plant Chez Lottie. Must tell Stu during our Whatsapp call tonight. Led Zeppelin has always been Stu's fave band.

'Anyway, Designer-Deb, how are you gonna dress this corn dolly?' Nat lifts the corn cob which DG picked. 'You could wrap this around her.' She hands me a scarf.

'But this is a Hermes scarf.' I look down at the luxurious red and black silk scarf with its hand-stitched edges, and its unique Hermes motif. 'Where on earth did you get this?'

Nat shrugs her shoulders. 'It must've fallen into my pocket after our day at Ladyship Olly's house last week.' She lifts a pair of scissors and before I can shout, vintage-Hermes-prob-worth-hundreds, she cuts the scarf in two and wraps one half around the corn dolly's waist.

Somehow, me-thinks, Nat has never heard the Innuit saying about never thrusting your sickle into another's corn.

LITTLE GREEN BOOK

"Hermes Scarf,
Vegetable Print"

Sewed in green room:
'Winter Wonder' lettuce seeds.
'Sanguina' beetroot.
'Calabrese.'
'Precocce de Louvrier,' spring
cabbage.
(JJ) Kales. 'Nero de Toscana.'

Sewed on corn dolly:
Little Hermes ball gown with
matching bag and fabric shoes …

Not sew excited: Stu didn't
WhatsApp me. Haven't spoken to
him for a week.

Sew excited:
Just had a call from Toby inviting me to go wassailing
with him next week! Didn't like to mention that I'm not
much of a water sports fan but if it means finally seeing
Toby, am sure I can find my sea legs. Must find my
Breton blue/cream striped top.

Chapter 51
A nautical adventure?

'Wassailing, which usually takes place on Old Twelfth Night, January 17th, is a custom originating from the Anglo-Saxon 'wes hal,' to be in good health. It's a fest of singing and dancing to protect trees from evil spirits.'

I cast my eyes around the nighttime, torch-lit wassailing gathering in Finsbury Park. It's an event, far removed from the daytime sailing regatta of my expectation. Not only is Toby, or anyone I know here, but I'm surrounded by strange characters who are cavorting around a tree dressed in robes made from torn pieces of fabric.

As the speaker pauses to bang loudly on a rusty pan, I try for the umpteenth time to check the text Toby sent me with the meet-up details. I'm unable to see anything in the dim bonfire light.

'Spirit of the wildwood, of all that runs wild and free, be with us here in our sacred grove,' chants a man in a hooded white robe standing next to me. He throws out his arms with such force that he knocks my mobile out of my hand. He kneels down in front of an apple tree and empties a cask of cider over its roots. 'I, the Lord of Misrule, am Guardian of this orchard ...'

I, too, kneel down to frantically start searching for my phone. It's now buried deep in the canopy of the wildwood, soggy twigs, and misrule man's scrumpy mulched leaves. I feel a hand pinch my derriere. 'Toby?' I call out and jump up.

'Health to thee, goddess of the apple tree,' says a man covered head to toe in ivy. 'Well to bear, pocket-fulls, hat-fulls, peck-fulls.' He grabs his crotch. 'Hi there, sexy, I'm Colin. D'ya fancy bit of one-to-one wassailing?'

The joke … 'why did the apple go out with the fig? Because its date didn't turn up,' does not come to mind as I quickly move away from crotch-grabbing Colin. I scurry over to the next tree, desperately looking for my phone. Several characters are hanging pieces of toast soaked in cider on the branches of the trees.

'Love and joy come to you and to your wassail too,' they cry out as they start to bang on pots and pans.
#NTS Le Creuset. Soo pleased my best pan is safely tucked away at home.

They continue beating the tree with sticks. It's a custom to awaken the sleeping trees and encourage a bountiful crop for the following year. I don't know about waking the sleeping trees but am certain any folk living within a ten-mile radius will not be getting any sleep.

A haunting melody starts to resonate through the toasty trees. The tree beating stops, torches are raised, and everyone falls silent as a beautiful young man playing the saxophone appears through the trees. The silver light from his sax reflects on his pale blonde hair. He looks and sounds like an angel; a veritable Raphael. Lifting his sax to his lips, he plays a series of mellifluous notes, serenading, er … I can't believe it … St Grace. She walks alongside him, her arm thrown tightly round his waist. 'Lo sweeten'd with the Summer light, the full juiced apple waxing over-mellow drops in the silent night.' St Grace pauses from her poetry, to kiss sax-angel on the neck. He stops playing and turns around to give her a breathless kiss on the lips.

#NTS Sax-Sex-with-the-St? She's obvs not quite such a saint! What is going on? Where's Toby? Have they split up? I feel myself overcome by a moment of pure poetry.

She looks lovingly into his eyes, 'there's sweet music here that softer falls on …' Their musings are interrupted by the sound of loud tango musak. I realise with horror that my mobile is ringing. 'So sorry, I think it's mine. I dropped it somewhere on the …'

'Oh, it's you, Deborah. I might have known,' tuts St Grace. 'What are *you* doing here?'

I might ask the same of you, I refrain from replying, as sax angel slowly slides his hand down her back and up her (doubtless) cashmere jumper.

'Have you met Alexandre?' She slides her hand across his torso. 'Alex is from Paris. He can't speak English, but hey, who needs language?' She giggles.

The moment of calm broken, the apple folk resume their chanting and beating the bark out of the tree.

Ex-St G and Alex disappear into the orchard of clearly not-so-forbidden fruit, whilst the Lord of Misrule and Apple tree man, on-looked by a cheering crowd, dunk their heads into barrels of water floating with apples.

'Do you know there's a special wassailing custom which states that by twisting the stalk of an apple, and counting the letter you get up to before the stalk breaks off, will reveal the name of your next lover?' Crotch-grabbing Colin comes up to me and hands me an apple. Why does 'T' have to be such a long way down the alphabet? I ponder, as I try to twist the stalk as gently as possible …

A, B – Jesus, I watch the stalk come off at the blasted letter 'C.'

'I've got a 'D.' Colin looks up expectantly up at me. 'What's your name?'

'Er … Pixie,' I reply.

'Pixie, like the apple variety. Very juicy and aromatic. A reliable heavy cropper.' He casts his eyes down my ill-advised skimpy Breton top, various parts of my anatomy, unfortunately, reacting to the cold. I zip up my yachting jacket, wrap my arms around my body.
'Can be a bit frosty though!' he laughs. 'Anyway, this'll soon warm you up. Get some of this down you, Pix.' He shoves a bottle filled with suspicious liquid and slices of apples into my hand. 'It's my homemade, Apple Colins!'

Lifting the bottle to take a reluctant sip, my mouth fills with a lovely, pungent, fizzy sweetness. I take another long swig.

'Fancy trying out the apple bobbing?' He uncurls a length of ivy, and before I can cry … 'I'm more ivy league, than …' he twists it round my waist and leads me towards the barrels of fun.

LITTLE GREEN BOOK

10:30 pm. Managed to finally extricate myself from crotch-grabbing Colin and his cocktails and found my phone nestling amongst several fallen apples.
10:58 pm. Dashed into Lidl two minutes before store closing. Plan to re-attempt apple stalk twisting wassailing custom. What I can't find are any loose, local apples. What I do find are bagged apples from the USA. Thought this was meant to be the harvest season in Europe. Why do supermarkets import apples from the US? Can't believe I am thinking about apple provenance. What's happened to me !? And why is my hair sopping wet?

Apple (Crotch-)Colin's cocktail recipe:
2 parts gin
2 parts puree of locally foraged apples generous squeeze of lemon juice
2 tablespoons of maple syrup in a shaker half-filled with ice cubes, combine the gin, lemon juice, and puree. Shake well. Strain into a glass filled with ice cubes. Drizzle over the maple syrup. Add the apple slice and enjoy …

OCTOBER
Hort-couture

Chapter 52.
Conkering heroes

Have politely declined Nat's invitation to join her, Pete, and Princess Daisy the guinea pig, on a mini break to watch poor little Sammi try and win the 'King Conker,' annual Conker Championships in Oundle, Northamptonshire.

Said championship apparently attracts an International crowd with 'Wllheim the Conkerer' … a German competitor claiming the runner up position last year.

This year's faves include, 'The Minge Petals' and 'The Nut crackers.'

Chapter 53
Hips 'n whores

'Grace is a whore,' sobs Toby, as he leans against an oak tree. 'A fucking whore.' I double-check the time. Yup, it's only 10 am and Toby is drunk.

'Er, why don't you sit down, have a sip of my espresso and tell me all about it,' I suggest as I unscrew my new brown flask and pour him a shot of coffee.

He flops down besides the tree, tears running down his cheeks. His wrongly buttoned-up linen shirt rises to reveal his oh … so muscular … pecs. I try to overt my eyes. Now is the time to offer the hand of friendship … not thoughts of my wandering hands.

I concentrate on looking around the thickly wooded cluster of trees on Hampstead Heath. We are the first to arrive for a foraging walk. It's a long-awaited outing with Toby which I almost had to cancel after catching a nasty, post wassailing cold.

Toby moans. 'She's moved to Paris with a musician …' Mais oui. Sex-sax angel Alexandre. I recall a little disloyally as I wrap my organic wool pashmina around my neck.

'Maybe it's for the best.' He wipes his eyes, and slowly rifles his hand through his disheveled hair, down his face, across that stubble …

Oh, to be those little bristles. I lift a fallen acorn from the ground and stare at the little hard green shell.

'But maybe I'm like this steadfast Oak.' He traces his hand across the bark of the tree. 'King of the forest, and she is the fallen leaf.' He looks at me. 'As we both know, there are many more acorns on this tree.' He hands me a tiny acorn, his hazel eyes staring deeply into mine. He outstretches his arm to grab my hand, and pull me down. I, wanna-be-wood-nymphet, push all thoughts of husbondage, (yet again in the USA) to one side; I close my eyes and imagine the arms of the mighty oak curling around me. Branches entwining, thickening in girth. The October wind covering us in a bed of falling leaves. Seeds dispersing ...'You know, Deborah, you're the one I find really ...'

'Here's my Tobey wobey.' I flip open my eyes to find Hen standing in front of us. 'What are you doing down there, Deborah?' She laughs. 'You've got a twig stuck up your nose.'

'I was just pouring Toby some coffee.' I jump up. 'It's, er, freshly ground.'

'Come to Mother Hen.' She wraps the velvet folds of her purple cape around Toby, helps him up, and they disappear off.

'Shit, double shit, what was I thinking?' I jump up and wipe off my nose accessory. I step back, only to trip over my flask which has camouflaged itself amongst the woodland flora. I fall backwards onto the ground, daggers of pain shoot up my leg. I burst into tears.

'Are you alright there?' A burly man with a mop of long dark curly hair, dressed in a chunky Aran jumper and jeans looks at me with concern. 'Can you walk?' he asks in a soft Irish brogue.

'I think so.' I nod gratefully and stand up, trying not to place the weight of my body on my injured ankle until the pain subsides.

'I'm Cathal, here today to lead the foraging walk. Are you one of my group?'

I nod, unable to speak.

'Here, let me help you.' He places his arm around my waist and helps me along. 'It's a grand day for it isn't it?'

Leaning on Cathal, whose strangely calm presence seems to make me forget I only met him twenty seconds ago, I sniffle and hobble on. I look around at what admittedly (the pain of my ankle/Toby/my stupidity, aside) is a typically beautiful Autumnal day.

'You're going to have a bit of a shiner, there!' Cathal looks down at my ankle. 'Hope he's worth it! He smiles at me through his kind, dark brown eyes. 'Ah … here's the rest of our group.'

We pause besides a clearing in the trees where four other foragers await.

'We're here to collect mag … er … mushrooms,' a boy (not much older than my James) eagerly tells Cathal as introductions are made.

'It's for our geography GCSE,' his friend reassures us.

'I'm just here to have some fun,' laughs a plump lady with ruddy cheeks, her hair piled up in a cottage-loaf-styled bun. 'Good to meet you folks, I'm Harry!' She lifts up an old-fashioned wicker basket.

A man in a green raincoat wags his finger. 'The name's Dixon. I'm here to make sure there is no over-picking. The rise of commercial foraging is threatening wildlife and causing huge environmental damage.'

'I can assure you, sir, that my foraging is completely sustainable.' Cathal smiles disarmingly at Dixon (of dock leaf green!) 'I hold Hampstead Heath and all its life force, both the seen and unseen in complete reverence. See that grand old Oak over there.' Cathal points to my Toby fantasising tree. 'Did you know that in the Celtic world, we recognise the Oak tree, Crann Bethadh, as a gateway between two worlds?'

Toby, I sigh. I lift out the tiny acorn Toby gave me from my pocket, and place it back down on the ground.

'Anyway, according to my list, we are two people short.'
Cathal unscrambles a piece of paper. 'Ah well, they'll
surely catch us up. Now, young lady.' He turns round to
grin at me. 'I'm going to call you my Sheehogue ... tree
faerie. Are you sure you're able to walk?'

'Funnily enough, my pain has completely gone,' I, shee-
something-or-other, smile back at him, and walk on.

'Sloes, the fruit of the blackthorn are ripening nicely now.'
Cathal pauses besides a spiky bush and picks a tiny
purple plum. 'These will turn a beautiful dusty-blue
colour.' He hands it to me. I raise it towards my mouth. 'I
wouldn't do that if I were you.' He places his strong,
weathered hand over mine. 'Sloes taste bitter and furry
when eaten raw. No, they're better turned into hedgerow
jam, sloe gin, or have you ever tried Slyder?'

Slyder. The last thing I wanted to be reminded of. I cough
as I remember crotch-grabbing Colin's cocktails ... one of
which was a supposed non-alcoholic Slyder. Talking of
Colin, I can hardly forget him. He's already texted me
fifteen times this week! He must have got my number
from my phone.

'And here's a hawthorn. It's one of the most abundant
berries. Often referred to as 'haws.' Cathal picks a
handful of beautiful dark red berries and places them in
Harry's basket. 'In the Spring, I make a great haw
pudding by covering layers of young haw leaves and
rashers of bacon with a light suet pastry, rolled up and
steaming ...'

'Grace, the steaming whore would like that.' All attention is turned towards Toby, who staggers up to us. 'You must be Cattle, the forager?' He attempts to shake Cathal's hand.

'The name's Cathal, spelt Kaarthahl.' Cathal grabs Toby as he swerves, threatening to fall. 'And as I was saying, in April you can eat young haw leaves straight from tree.'

'Grace is a fuckin' ...'

'Is this man drunk?' Mr. Dixon objects, much to the amusement of Harry and the boys.

'He's just, er, had bad news.' I walk over to link Toby's arm.

'She's my wood nympho ...' Toby leans forward to kiss me.

'There you are, Tobes.' Hen comes dashing up to us. 'He's quite alright with me, thank you very much, Deborah.' She unlinks his arm and leads Toby off.

'I was just, er ...' My face flushes a deeper shade of crimson than the haws as I start to cough. A purge of phlegm, greener than the youngest of Spring haw leaves, comes out from my nose. I lift a hankie from my pocket.

'That's a nasty cough you've got there.' Cathal places his hand upon my shoulder. 'We'll have to do something about it. Have you ever tried homemade elderberry cough medicine?' He points to a large tree filled with dark purple berries.

'Ah, Sambucus nigra.' Hen re-joins the group having lain Toby down for a nap. She throws open her arms. 'Faith be with red berries blasting, blooming in all lands. Did you know that …'

'What I do know, Miss, is that your friend here has a nasty cough.' Cathal disregards Hen's theatrics. 'But whilst on the subject of elders,' he turns round to face me, his eyes glistening as warmly as the berries on the tree, 'Have you ever tried a lovely claret Pontack sauce made with elderberries?'

'Bet that'd be delish served with wild duck.' I lick my lips.

'Or a rich sausage casserole,' he suggests.

'Served with red cabbage and …'

'Lashings of mash,' Cathal finishes my sentence.

'Are you a cook?' I ask.

'Love it!' he replies.

'Do you mind having a little respect for the vegetarians amongst us!' sighs Hen.

'Oh look, here's an Angus beefsteak,' call out the boys, who are huddled over a small patch of ground.

'And look at these blackberries.' Hen raises a plump blackberry to her mouth, teases it around her lips and smiles at Cathal. 'Do you know, whilst I'm an actor, I'm also considering taking a course in Batology.'

'Well, it's the right time of year for it with Halloween just round the corner!' I laugh.

'No, Deborah, surely you know that Batology is the study of brambles?' Hen raises her eyebrows.

'Wow, is this a dead man's finger?' the boys call out as they stare at a clump of mushrooms. They're overlooked by Mr. Dixon, who has started to write notes on everything being picked.

'Talking of the seasons, don't you love it when the leaves turn?' Hen pauses beside a tree with fantastic red leaves. 'Haven't you got an Acer, Deborah?'

'I've been advised that they don't pay much interest,' I hesitantly reply, wondering what the link is between autumn and bank accounts.

'I think, Miss, that my friend here is just being a little ironic!' Cathal smiles at me and touches a russet leaf. 'But I'll grant you this Acer maple tree is a beautiful colour. I do like a girl who appreciates the craic!'

'Isn't this a Castanea sativa?' asks Harry.

#NTS: Craics, Castaneas, Acers? Must swot up on botanical classification.

'Yes, they're more commonly found in woods in southern England and can grow up to 100ft tall,' explains Cathal.

'And they are all under the protection of the Royal Parks,' Mr. Dixon is quick to point out.

'I always say there's nothing more English than roasting sweet chestnuts on a Sunday afternoon, don't you agree?' Hen flutters her eyelashes at Cathal.

'I wouldn't know, I'm Irish,' he grimaces back at her. He turns round to grin at me. 'Don't you just love chestnuts fried with a rasher and boiled Brussels, or chestnut and parsnip soup?'

'Yum!' I lick my lips.

'Of course, environmentally, we should all be growing sweet chestnuts as an alternative economic nut crop,' Hen raises her voice. 'They're nutritionally comparable to rice and could provide a viable carbohydrate staple when the depletion of fossil fuels means we can no longer rely on imported rice.'

'Chestnut flour is also great for baking, albeit a reluctant riser!' adds Harry.

'Bit like my son, then!'

The whole group except Hen and Mr. Dixon burst out laughing at my comment. We walk on pausing besides another oak tree.

'Did you know that we used to roast acorns as a substitute for coffee during World War Two,' explains Mr Dixon. 'Now that is what I consider a totally acceptable form of foraging.'

'Grace is a little fuckin' fallen acorn,' Toby mutters from behind the other side of the tree where he is lying asleep.

'Acorns can be placed between the mattress of a lover's bed to keep him faithful,' adds Hen disappearing off doubtless to gather more fallen acorns.

As the official part of the tour comes to a close, the boys head off, laughing at the list of edible wild mushrooms given to them by Cathal. Of particular amusement is a mushroom called a Shagging Inkcap. Meanwhile, Harry, closely scrutinised by Mr. Dixon, continues filling her basket with rose hips, haws, and rowan berries for an Autumn pudding.

As for moi … talking further about dark, luscious, newly harvestable autumnal fruit, I retire with Cathal to a café down to the road. It's time to share a bacon bap and further explore the potential of this season's unexpected new hawticultural delight …

LITTLE whore-ticultural recipe BOOK

'Packed full of Vitamin C (containing 50% more by comparative weight than oranges) rosehips help keep colds at bay, and help build one's immune system ...' I turn the page of my Foragers handbook, and sneeze. 'Diluted with five parts cold water, hips make great kids cordial.' Hey, never mind a kids' drink ... how about a hip cocktail - rosehip syrup mixed with blackberries in a glass of champagne!

Maybe it's time to return Mutant Collin's twentieth missed call!

Rosehip Syrup
Ingredients:
1kg rosehips, washed and chopped
1kg caster sugar
Muslin/clean cotton cloth and big sieve.
Boil 2 litres of water in a large pan. Throw in chopped rosehips with stalks removed, boil, remove from the heat, cover, and leave to infuse for 30 minutes.

-Strain the mixture through a cloth placed over sieve/ colander. Tip in the rosehip mixture, and leave suspended over the bowl.

-Set the strained juice aside and transfer the rosehip pulp back to the saucepan, along with another litre of boiling water.

-Bring to a boil, remove from the heat, infuse for another half an hour, and strain as before.

-Discard the pulp and combine the two lots of strained juice.

-Bring to a boil and simmer until the volume has reduced by half. -Remove from the heat. Add the sugar and stir until dissolved. Return to the stove, bring to a boil and boil hard for 5 minutes. Pour into warmed, sterilised jars or bottles and seal.

Harry's Autumn pudding
A delish pudding recipe made by replacing bright red summer fruits with dark autumnal ones.
Ingredients:

Serves 6
200g sloes/damsons stoned and chopped
200g crab apples, peeled, cored, and chopped
250g blackberries
4 tbsp caster sugar
¼ tsp ground cinnamon
1 whole star anise
8-10 thin slices of white bread, preferably a day old, crusts removed

- Place fruit in a saucepan. Add sugar, cinnamon, and 100ml water. Bring to a simmer, place the star anise on top, then cover and cook for 5-10 minutes until the

apples have turned to pulp, fruit is soft and swimming in juice.

- Remove star anise. Strain off juice. Cut the bread into enough rectangles and triangles to line the base and sides of a one-litre pudding basin. Keep a couple of bits to make a lid.
- Dip both sides of each piece into the bowl of juice. Fit into the basin, overlapping the bread at the seams.
- Keeping back some of the juice, tip the fruit into the bread-lined mould.
- Cover the top with more dipped bread, then fold over the sides and press down to seal.
- Find a plate that fits into the top of the pudding basin, and weigh it down with a heavy tin. Allow to cool, then place in the fridge overnight.
- To turn out, carefully run a palette knife around the outside and invert it onto a serving plate. Pour over the extra juice, making sure you cover any bits that haven't been stained a deep red. Serve in slices with lashings of cream.

Pontack sauce

A traditional hunter/gatherer's recipe. Happy hunting …

I close my eyes and imagine a foggy early morn in a deserted moorland. I'm strolling hand in hand with burly hunter/gatherer. Brace of pheasants (braces are soo this season) slung over the shoulder of his chunky Aran jumper. The basket of berries I'm carrying matches the colour of my herringbone Norfolk jacket and plus-fours …

God no! This daydream must stop. Right now. I cannot do plus fours!

Ingredients:
1-pint claret
1-pint elderberries
1 teaspoon salt
Handful of peppercorns
12 cloves
I onion finely chopped
Half teaspoon ginger

-Pour Claret over elderberries in a dish, cover, and allow to stand overnight in oven at very low heat
-Next day pour off liquid put in saucepan with rest of ingredients
-Boil for ten minutes and serve with dish of your choice.

Chapter 54
Crop rotation

Does not refer to dress hemlines, but a system whereby crops are grown in different beds each year to help prevent pest and disease build-up.

'Different crops take different levels of nutrients from the soil,' Dougie continues to drawl on. His words are as grey as the mid-October late afternoon. 'That's why we bed swop.'

#NTS: Bed swopping. Not the kind I find my mind wandering to after last week's delicious foraging trip

'I would suggest you follow the four-year crop rotation system as invented by Jethro Tull.'

'What's a 1970's prog rock band got to do with crop rotation?' asks Nat. She turns round to face me. 'I bet you were more of a Bay City rollers fan, eh Deb!'

'Did you know that swedes are brassicas even though they look like a root crop?' I quickly change the subject to avoid Nat drawing me into any age-admitting-pop-crush. 'Also, that the potato family includes tomatoes and aubergines?'

'Blimey, there's more inter-breeding than our royal family!' Nat bursts out laughing. I can't help but join in.

Dougie shoots us a look sourer than the unripe green tomatoes we are picking for our chutney-making session. 'You should both read Jethro Tull, the famous 18th-century agriculturalist's book on horse hoeing husbandry.'

I smile sweetly at him. 'Also, according to the Great Tit, carrots don't like to be soil enriched or they develop new growing points which results in something called fanging!'

'Talking about fanging,' Nat races on, 'Deb and I are hosting a fancy dress Halloween party next week, Dougie. Wanna come? We're gonna carve pumpkins into weird shapes.' She points to our pumpkins, which have grown unbelievably large.

#Halloween hoo-ha? That's the first I've heard of it.

I put down the wheelbarrow filled with the spent runner bean plants which I'm about to cart to the compost area. 'Nat, there's absolutely no way I am getting involved in any ...'

'You'll make a great old hag, Deb!' Nat punches me in the ribs. 'You know how you love to dress up! You could design a great costume.'

'And don't be in too much of a hurry to clear the garden of rotting plants, as they will provide shelter during late Autumn for wildlife.' Dougie ignores Nat's invite and walks over to our decaying courgettes. 'Perhaps now we could turn our attention to successful overwintering ...'

#NTS - St. Barts. My idea of successful overwintering.

I re-lift the wheelbarrow and can't help but smile as I wheel it along Lottie. I pass orange nasturtium flowers which are luminescent in the dying afternoon light. The peppery aroma of self-seeded rocket pungent in the damp, autumnal air. And tiny baubles of Brussel sprouts, clinging to thickset green stems.

I stop the wheelbarrow beside a newly flowering pretty white anemone. White, eh? Perhaps I could make a Halloween white Witch of Narnia dress. Accessorise with white wig and long white nails … Aagh, I look down at my hands. My manicured nails of a year ago are now replaced by short black, soil enriched stumpy ones.

'Talking about over-wintering,' squeals Nat, as she dashes out from the green room. 'Our perpetual spinach, swede, and lettuce seeds have germinated. Hurrah! Anyway, Deb,' she continues, 'we need to start making plans for our party. You'll be pleased to hear that Toby is defo coming. I've been through all your phone contacts and even texted that bloke you met at wassailing and some cattle forager …'

LITTLE GREEN BOOK

<u>*JETHRO TULL'S ROCKIN: FOUR-YEAR CROP*</u>
<u>*ROTATION SYSTEM*</u>

YEAR 1
Potatoes. Legumes. Brassicas. Onions/*roots

YEAR 2
Legumes. Bay City Rollers. Onion/*roots. Potatoes

YEAR 3
Brassicas. Onions/*roots. Potatoes. Legumes

YEAR 4
Onions/*roots. Potatoes. Legumes. Brassicas.

* to be followed by manure

HAPPY FAMILIES

Includes: Brassicas family - cabbages, caulies, kale, broccoli, calabrese, suedes, turnips, and radishes.

Legumes - beans and peas, anything with bean in its name!

Know your onions – garlic, leek, and chives.
Potatoes - tomatoes and aubergines.

What's the marrow you? Cucumbers, marrows, courgettes, melons, and pumpkins. Can be planted around JT's crop rotation, as can sweetcorn and salad

Happy families does not include:
-Me and Nat. I can't believe she phoned all my contacts and has managed to inveigle me into another party …
Just where are my black fishnets …?

Other jobs we did today:
Minted - Dug up a clump of mint from the Pimms patch. Placed in pot inside the kitchen on window ledge. Hopefully will have mint sauce throughout the winter.

Chives - Carefully dug up clump of chives, cut foilage to 2" above roots, potted, and placed inside green room.

Potatoes - Moved our Xmas spuds (now with 18-inch high greenery!!) into the green room.

Green manure – Broadcast Hungarian Grazing across empty brassica and legume beds to add organic matter to the soil, improve texture, and fix nitrogen.

Leaf moulds – Collected falling leaves and placed inside old hessian sack found by Nat. Placed sack behind compost area. Will apparently rot down to make a great soil improver in a year.

Cleaning tools – Sadly, had no choice but to offer Ben-G bard a tenner to scrub and oil my share of tools as had v. important meeting to go to at Saatchi gallery wine bar.

Chapter 55
Dark side o' the moon

It's all hallows eve: Halloween. A night filled with dread and horror. In particular, my anticipation of being involved in another of Nat's parties, which is now to be combined with a wake, as we have had a bereavement in the community.

Dressed in black thigh boots, a pencil skirt, and a parka jacket, I flick back my mane of long purple hair and saunter outside.

Lottie has been dimly lit with hollowed-out turnips filled with tea lights perched on wonky bamboo canes. There are carved pumpkins scattered around the beds. A circle of masked characters dressed in black are surrounding a giant frog. On closer inspection, I discover it's Bernie dressed in a frog costume. He's straddling a garden fork, dancing the Monster Mash, which is piping out through a PA system perched atop a plank of wood above the water butt. I'm told it's an 'intervention' to placate the evil spirits.

Talking about evil spirits, I walk up to Pete, who has set up a makeshift bar on our potting table. It's laden with jugs of iridescent cocktails.

'Try this Bayou slime, Deb.' He hands me a green cocktail. 'Or should I call you Cruella?'

My efforts to assure him I'm Morticia Addams are interrupted by DG, who climbs atop the table.

'Tonight, the Feast of Samhain celebrates the Lord of Death who leads all departed souls.' Her words are interrupted by a loud howling that echoes across the garden. She continues, 'In this night, O Sun King, I mark your passing through sunset into the Land of the Young of all who have gone before.' She pauses to wipe away her stream of tears. 'Teach us to know that in the time of the greatest darkness, there is the greatest light.'

Tikka the dog, bounds up to her, his tail thrashing against the table, howling in distress.

'I can't believe he's gone,' sobs Nat, dressed in a witches costume, pointy hat and surprisingly realistically looking blacked out front tooth. 'Poor Marsala.' She bends down to stroke Tikka.

'Trick or treat?' It's Fliff. She walks up to us. 'Why is everyone crying?' She greets me with an extravagant air kiss. 'I thought this meant to be a jolly eco-Halloween party?'

'Our pal, Marsala, has passed into the great unknown. So it's a wake too,' sniffs Nat.

'Is the doggy awake now?' asks Dora, her face covered in mud. 'I thought the dog was dead.'

'Er, lovely to see you.' I pour Fliff a large glass of blackberry and vodka, Dracula's kiss cocktail. I link her arm. 'Let's go and get something to eat?' I lead her towards the barbie, which smolders with what Pete is advertising as, 'breadcrumbed body parts.'

'So, where's Stu?' enquires Fliff.

'Er ... he's at a work dinner,' I reply.

'You poor darling, you must feel a bit neglected,' she shares a fake sorrowful smile, 'he never seems to take you anywhere ...'

'Deb, do you fancy coming with me next week to see the film, "From squeals to meals?"' asks Amphibian Bernie, leaping up to us. His face and plait might be painted green, his body clad in a green fake fur costume, but I've never been more pleased to see him. 'It's a must-see film about the pig industry,' he explains. 'You'll never eat pork again. Bring your friend if you like.' He casts his bulging frog-like eyes down Fliff's clinging grey silk shirt.

'Er, love your top, Fliff.' I take a bite out of my bread-crumbed chicken thigh.

'It's made of soy silk, which I'm sure you know is an eco-fibre,' she grimaces at Bernie. 'It's manufactured by liquefying and extruding soy protein into long fibres that ...'

'It feels like cashmere to me.' Bernie reaches out his breadcrumbed, slippery arm to touch the shirt. I leave them to talk about the joys of tofu waste and walk on. The potluck maypole is heaving under the weight of strange containers. Our designer-clad corn dolly is perched like an angel at its tip. Crouched down at its base, DG sits, her arms curled around a little ginger cat.

'Come and meet Tom Cat Soya, my new baby kitten,' DG bursts into tears and takes a large swig out of her blue cocktail.

I bend down to stroke the cute little tabby kit. 'Gaia, should you be drinking alcohol?'

'Go on, get another down you woman.' Bernie comes up holding a tray of cocktails. He hands her a red one.

'I, er … really don't think she should be drinking that,' I grab the cocktail from DG.

'Why ever not?' asks Bernie.

'Oh, pass me that bloody devil's handshake.' DG grabs the cocktail and drinks it down in one swig.

'Our house cat at Green Ending Funerals has just had a silver female tabby. Maybe they could mate and produce a litter.' Bernie hands DG another drink. DG lets out a loud sob. Bernie says, 'If you don't like that killer zombie, I can always get you a …'

'She's bleedin' well preggers.' Nat walks up to us holding her pointy witche's hat. It's now planted with a garlic bulb. 'The baby is yours, Bernie boy.'

'Who's pregnant?' Bernie shrugs his shoulders. 'The cat or Gaia?'

'There are more things in heaven and earth, Horatio, than are dreamt of in your philosophy,' Ben G bard hands round a joint. 'Have I missed anything?'

'Anyone for a severed finger dipped into blood sauce?' Pete holds a tray of chips smeared in tomato sauce.

'Gire is pregnant, Bernie, with your baby,' shouts Nat throwing open her arms with such force that she dislodges the plank of wood holding up the PA system, which she is standing next to. The PA crashes down into the water butt, lets out a strange fizzing noise, and goes silent.

'You mean I'm going to be a …' says Bernie, his face glowing with delight. He turns round to face DG, whose face has turned a shade of green, to match his costume.

Rushing back indoors, DG is followed by Bernie, who looks like the cat who had got the cream.

'Oh well, pleased we got that out in the open.' Nat, having cast her spell, picks up her twig broom. 'Ah here's my besom.'

'She's got a large besom.' Poor little Sammi runs up to us, pointing at Fliff. 'Grandad Petey told me to always go for girls with large besoms.'

'Love is a smoke made with the fumes of sighs. A fire sparkling in a lover's eyes.' Ben G hands Fliff the joint. 'I think that Romeo knew what he was on about.'

'Talking about lovers,' Nat continues, 'they say that if you gaze into water at Halloween, you'll see the face of a future lover stare back at you.'

What silly Halloween nonsense, I think, walking over to the wildlife tank. It's now filled with all manner of oxygenating and marginal plants, with twig bridges and stick walkway systems. It's a veritable water-world cornucopia. Leaning over it, I jump back as a frog leaps out at me.

'Hi sexy, what are you up to?' Toby's reflection stares back at me.

'Oh, hi … er, Toby, I, was just …' The frog dives back into the pond causing the water to ripple. When it settles, a different reflection is revealed. It's Cathal from the foraging walk. The frog magically transformed into not one, but two handsome princes.

#NTS: Not such a Grimm tale!

'Your friend Nat invited me here tonight. I hope you don't mind.' He smiles.

'Ah, here's my apple queen!' My Bridget Jones moment is shattered as I feel a pinch on my bottom. I turn around to find Crotch-grabbing, Colin, standing in between Toby and Cathal.

'Attention everyone, it's time for the toasts,' yells Nat clinking on her glass, calling everyone to attention. 'Please all raise your glasses to toast the life of our canine pal, Marsala, who will be missed by us all.'

'Marsala.!' everyone toasts as glasses are clinked.

'And how about toasting our wonderful allotment … Lottie,' adds Nat, 'I can't bloody well believe how much we've managed to grow and eat! And how pretty the garden looks.' Nat walks up and throws her arms around me. 'You know it's our first anniversary next week, Deb? So this is our birthday party, too!'

'To Lottie,' everyone cries out.

'And I'd like to add a toast.' I look over at Toby and smile. 'It's all thanks to you, Toby. I can't believe that it was a year ago that you knocked on my door and changed my life… for the better. Thank you.'

'Here's to Toby.' Everyone knocks back their drinks.

'And here's to communities coming together and to new friends.' Toby clinks glasses with Cathal and winks at me.

'And to fun,' adds Dora, as she and poor little Sammi charge off.

'Talking of which, it's time for the seed-spitting competition,' Pete laughs. 'Frogs welcome to join in!'

I retire to a corner of the garden, sit down on a tree stump and look around.

The night sky abounds with streaks of violet and rose, charcoal and cornflower blue. There are peals of laughter as the pumpkin pip spitting contest begins. Toby, Cathal, Pete, and Crotch-Collin, are all competing for the title of King Spit.

Out of the corner of my eye, I spot Ben-G handing a rather dubious-looking lumpy chocolate brownie 'Soul Cake' to Fliff. Poor little Sammi and Dora continue searching for Dora's false teeth, which have disappeared somewhere under the earth. Brings a whole new meaning to the term: root treatment.

I look over at Nat and Tikka, who have embarked upon a spot of night-time garlic and spring onion sowing, whilst DG and Bernie lead the rest of the party in some kind of devotional dance, the music miraculously having sprung back to life.

I imagine beneath the rich, fertile earth, all manner of scampering creatures, perhaps having their own Halloween party. The microbial monster mash.

Above me, a new crescent moon appears from behind the clouds to shine resplendent above. I tilt my head to one side, making the moon look like an incomplete question mark. To the other side, it looks like a sickle; but mostly, a smile.

I take in a deep breath as I realise that the moon ... as indeed all life, in all its phases can be anything I want it to be.

What a simply wondrous world.

Frog Beanie (Hat!)

Chapter 56
Much to relish?

To celebrate Lottie's first anniversary, Nat and I are spending the day in my kitchen, creating herb-flavoured oils. According to Nat, they will make great Xmas pressies.

The recipe in front of us suggests placing sprigs of sage, rosemary, and tarragon into sterilised recycled bottles, filling them with oil, adding chillies, garlic, and sealing. What it doesn't state is having a large swig of red wine in between every step. It's only 11 am, and we are well and truly oiled.

'I love you, Deb.' Tears roll down Nat's face as she turns her attention to chopping onions for our green tomato chutney. 'You might be a bit spoilt, and posh, but you're still my BF.'

'You're my best chum, too,' I reply, ladling sultanas into a pan. And, as I lift my glass of red to clink hers, I release that she is. Despite her *Nattery's* and er ... candidness, Nat is the kindest, most supportive, and definitely the most fun woman I've ever met.

'So next year, I'm thinking we should grow and launch a range of wild edible foods,' says Nat, turning up the temperature in the oven where we are cooking a pumpkin to make soup. 'We could sell dandelion fritters, nettle porridge, burdock salsas, comfrey samosas, herb shampoos, and bath bombs?' She lifts the wine bottle and takes a large swig from it. 'We could turn your fancy dining room into an extended kitchen. You never use it as your Stu's always away, and you and James always eat dins in front of the telly.'

#NTS: Buy new window blinds. Wonder what time Selfridges closes today?

'We could launch our own range of herbal teas,' suggests Nat. 'Gire also wants to grow soya beans. Told me that soya means 'meat of the field,' in Chinese. And talking of meat, your Stu agrees that we should all spend Xmas together. We'll roast a whole lamb on a spit. Plant showstopper onions on Boxing day ...'

#NTS: Air miles. Must cash them in to purchase Barbados Xmas flights.

Nat empties the bucket of green toms we harvested last week into the boiling pan and opens the oven door. I grab the bottle of red from her and gulp it down.

'And guess what?' Nat's breathless enthusiasm remains as unabated as the temperature in the kitchen. 'I've got a great name for the food co-op we're gonna set up ... 'The WAG's: We Are Green. Get it?'

I'd rather not, I think as I burst out laughing.

'Seriously, Deb,' Nat wipes her tears of onions and merriment from her face, 'I think we should help encourage other people to live more sustainably. You and me could make a great team. We could run a small holding... even though we live in the centre of the city ... We could call it: 'High-Heels and Small Holding.'

I smile at what is really quite a funny name.

Nat races on. I'm thinking green roofs and solar panels. We'll generate our own energy, and make our own biofuel. Pete and me will sell our car and share Stu's BMW. We could even keep bees on our green roof ...

#NTS: Must hide the spare car keys.

'... And going even further, we'll become environmental activists. We'll stand up to all those nasty chemical companies. Explode the myths on those genetically modified orgasms ...'

Nat's talk of explosive activism is suddenly replaced by a real-life explosion as a torrent of pumpkin seeds blast out from the oven. The overheated seeds in the centre of the pumpkin have caused the fruit to explode and a bombardment of pumpkin chunks detonate all over us. As I'm standing directly in the firing line, I jump away to avoid being hit by the scalding hot seeds, accidentally knocking one of the bottles of oil off the table.

As if in slow motion, I watch the bottle, like a domino effect, come crashing to the ground. Seeds and sharp fragments of glass fly everywhere. Oil drips, slides, chutney gurgles ...

Much to relish? I don't think so!

'Nataaalieeeeee -'

LITTLE GREEN BOOK

RECIPE FOR GREEN TOMATO CHUTNEY

Makes about 3 kg. 8 jars. Prep 25 mins. Cook 1 hour 15 mins.
Ingredients:
Sober chef!
2.5 kg green tomatoes
500 g onions
500 g sultanas
500 g foraged apples
500 g brown sugar
1.14 litre pickling vinegar

Method:
Slice the tomatoes. Chop the onions. Layer both in a bowl.

Chop the sultanas, peel, core and chop apples/pears. Put the sugar and vinegar into a large pan and bring to the boil, stirring to dissolve the sugar. Add the sultanas and apples and simmer for 10 mins.

Tip the toms and onions into the pan and return to the boil.

Simmer for 1 hr, stirring occasionally until the mixture is thick and pulpy.

Transfer to sterilised jars. Seal with lids.

EPI-LOG
(Forestry Commission approved)

Nov 14th. It's a year to the day, since our first dig. Our total spend. £800. £200 left in the kitty (not to be spent on repairing oven door)

On reflection, if we had built a cold frame, bought compost from our local waste authority, and swopped seeds, the cost could have been reduced to a few hundred pounds.

Next year, we will procure 'well-rotted' manure from the local city farm, fruit bushes and plant from the many free resources out there. We will contact local allotmenteers to see what they can share ... there it is ... the 'a' word I've refused to use all year!

I can't believe it was only a year ago when I held an umbrella whilst diggin' to shield myself from the rain. A year ago that I confused permaculture with a hairstyle!

So, what has been my best memory of the year, and worst?

My worst memory has to be shovelling Stan's shit ... all forty wheel-barrels of them. Although in retrospect, was it really the worst or simply the funniest?
My favourite memories ... where to start? I've sucked flowers and eaten them. I've felt the fur-lined husks of

imperceptibly growing corn on the cob. I've mixed with cabinet makers (or is it members) and drunk nettle beer.

I now find myself in shops ogling at the colours and textures of squash and fennel with same lustful eyes I used to reserve for fabrics. My cravings are not for Monmouth St. coffee beans, but broad ones. My late-night intimate gasps are oft to be heard whilst perusing the pages of a gardening book. I even secretly watch Gardeners World.

What I've learnt most is that by sowing seeds and getting your hands dirty you are relating to the soil; to soil life. You are connecting with the seasons, water, weather - the real production of food. You are connecting with life itself.

Simply clear a piece of ground, dig it over, throw in some seeds and watch the magic start to happen.

For as our garden grows and changes... perhaps, so do we.

Thats Shallot!!

POTATOB

Nov 14th - 11 am

Dear Santa,

Please could I have a good quality pair of secateurs, some shears, a pruning saw, books on the principles of bio-dynamic gardening, compost making, running a smallholding, edible perennials, and preserve making.

Talking about condiments, I won't be needing any jars of Fortnum and Mason's chutney this year, as have made fifty of my own. But whilst on the subject of F&M, please could you throw in a few jars of their gentleman's relish … and whilst talking of relishing gentlemen, please could I have …

Actually, Santa, what I want most of all is simply another year of digging and growmance …

Love, The High-Heeled gardener.

ps. If I'm not being too greedy (as have been extremely good girl this year … despite trying much to the contrary!) could you also squeeze into my stocking a pair of Jimmy Choos with little red bows and …

Acknowledgments

Thanks for your patient support to my eco-lover, Wooly... You know who are!

And my son, Lu.

Deborah Jackson-Brown, thanks for the hilarious and gorgeous illustrations.

Eli Giordana, such a cute cover. Thank you.

Respect to all you novice High-Heeled Gardeners. May your stilettos not get stuck in the mud.

A big heartfelt thanks and love to all you climate and social justice activists out there. Keep on going!

To Dickie, my publisher ... congrats on Malchik Media. *Salut.*

Debbie Bourne
Think&Do Activator
Thinkanddocamden.org.uk
@ThinkDoCamden
@tkentishtown
@HeeledGardener

About the Author

Debbie Bourne, author of the Eco-Romance series, lives in Camden, London, UK, with her hubbie and son.

A few years ago, there was a knock on her door ... that changed her life forever. You'll have to read the first book in the series, *The High-Heeled Gardener,* to find out about her big "growmance."

It could happen to you!

Debbie also co-runs Think&Do, an environmental and social action organisation based in Camden, London.

For Debbie, homemade sloe gin and elderflower bubbly are her cocktails of choice.

She can now appreciate the difference between a hedgerow and a hedge fund. And green is very much the new black!

@tkentishtown
@ThinkDoCamden
@HeeledGardener

For USA and UK book enquires:
richard@richardlynttonbooks.com
www.richardlynttonbooks.com

Pro-log
Let there be light ...

'Welcome to your second home, Deb.'

'Second home? What are you talking about?' I ask Nat as the smudged outline of an old Gothic church appears through the misty September morning.

I look up along the crumbling stone walls and up the spire. While I must have walked past this church in the middle of Kentish Town Road hundreds of times, I realise I've never stopped to look at the rather ornate, rundown building.

'This deconsecrated church was meant to be turned into a posh block of flats,' says Nat. 'But I've met with the Bishop of Edmonton and he's agreed to lease it to us.'

'Bishop of who?' I laugh. 'The only bishop you know is Bishop's Stortford, where your mum was born!'

'Oh ye of little faith,' Nat says, pointing up at the cross above the entrance. 'All I had to do was contact the Diocese of London and point out to the bishop that this empty church would make a great base for a climate action group, like ours.

Amen. The bishop agreed to lease it to us free of charge for a year!'

'What climate action group? I look at the cross, several loose nails clearly responsible for its unfortunate flexure. 'And more importantly, what on earth would we want to do with it?'

'Exactly, Deb!' Nat thumps me on the back. 'It's all about the Earth and saving it. 'This church is going to be the base for our inspiring new community eco project. The bishop loved our idea!'

Our eco project? *Our* idea? The only idea I have is to end this outing, get out of the damp, and retreat to Cafe Espresso for a steaming cup of hazelnut latte.

Probably best to pause here and explain something about us two. While Nat is my new best friend, we come from completely different backgrounds. I'm a fashion designer who for many years worked for top international fashion brands, although if I'm honest, I haven't had a job for a couple of years. But this was hopefully about to change. Nat is a dab hand at power machinery and works part time at Charles Wilson tool hire down the road. The tools of my trade are chiffon and lace; for Nat, it's grinders and planers. We met three years ago, when we turned a disused patch of land that surrounded my house and Nat's flat into a thriving community garden—a garden that now grows more than 50 varieties of fruit and veg, and even supplies produce to a local veg box scheme.

'I know it's probably just some tax avoidance scam to prove that the diocese are doing their bit for the environment and not just selling off properties,' says Nat, grabbing my hand and pulling me along the uneven cobbled path to the front door. 'But as the guv here once said, knock and the door will be opened. So, I just knocked, and, hey presto, this church is ours, gratis, with phones and internet all thrown in until

September next year. If it's a success, maybe we'll get it for good.'

I stare at the front door, it's once-intricate wooden panels now inlaid with wood lice and beetle grubs. Instead of the door being opened to us, it's more like the door is just about hanging on from rusty hinges. Above the door, my eyes fix on a rather grotesque looking gargoyle, its menacing features adorned with lichen.

'A God life soon to be turned into our very own Good Life! Just add a vowel – another "o." Get it?' Nat, the would-be grammarian, bursts out laughing. 'Remember that telly series from the seventies? I'll be Margot and you can be Barbara!'

My mind flashes back to the TV show, 'The Good Life.' Margot, wasn't she the posh one?

'But instead of one family's go at self-sufficiency,' Nat interrupts my musing on social status, 'our narrative will be all about creating community climate action, and co-efficiency.'

Climate action? Co-efficiency? I listen to Nat spout out her newly swotted-up, bishop-impressing eco terms, while my only narrative remains to go to the café. Never mind adding or dropping an "o," I want to pick up an "a" — for almond croissant.

'The Good Life! That's what we will call our project!' Nat excitedly races on. 'It's going to be all about supporting the environment, creating enterprise, and helping our community flourish from this church. Our very own Good Life hub.'

'No, I'm sorry Nat, creating a community garden was one thing, but a community eco hub is a complete other thing. And not one I have any interest in pursuing.' I turn and start to walk away.

'Deb!' Nat calls out. 'Can't you just picture a hub full of handsome conservationists and environmental do-gooders? All doing good here. We'll cook local food, develop projects to protect nature, generate our own energy. It's all about sharing …'

Sharing handsome conservationists? I'm suddenly thinking Ben Fogle… not such a bad premise. And Bear Gryll's recent TV series had an eco-slant to it. Maybe I could just take a quick peek inside the church…

Nat lifts a large antique key from her carrier bag and inserts it in the lock. With a creak, just like in a horror movie, the door opens.

In front of us, a cavernous room stretches into the dim distance. A nasty dank smell pervades the air. Fumbling in my purple leather Chloe bag, with its well-ordered compartments, I locate my mobile in the pitch black and manage to switch on the phone's torch. I shine it up onto the pointed arches and wooden beams that hold up vaulted ceiling. A balcony overlooks the rows of askew pews. I look around what once must have been a very grand room, its walls stuccoed and painted in a curious shade of peach. Several huge stone arches loom above diamond paned windows decorated with richly coloured stained glass. Although I'm not religious in the slightest, I'm struck by the display of skill in the architecture, the tarnished grandeur.

'But we don't know anything about climate, er…action, Nat.' I take a deep breath. 'We are just two local mums who set up a community veg patch.'

I refrain from adding that I couldn't even spell the word environmentalism at a pub quiz last week. Or mention the alarming chat I had on the phone last night with my husbondage Stu, who is on yet another business trip in the

US. Stu told me about a potential job offer that would mean him leaving the Bank of England, where he is a micro—or macro economist, for a prestigious teaching post at Yale University in Connecticut. I may not be the brainiest of people—more at home with a needle, than a pen—but even I've heard of Yale.

Stu didn't laugh when I told him I didn't see myself as a Stepford wife.

I sigh, take a deep breath, and share the one bit of info Nat does know about. 'Anyhow, I'm really hoping that I'm going to be offered a styling job at Selfridges. I know it's a bit vacuous and all about encouraging people to buy more clothes—the opposite of what you're talking about creating here, but...'

'Well, you can style this church now!' Nat chuckles. 'Look, I agree with you, perhaps we don't know much yet about environmental campaigning, but we will soon learn. After all, as you are always saying, we've all got to do our bit to help combat global warming.'

Yes, but I'd meant more along the lines of buying a scarf made of recycled cashmere. But I keep this less than altruistic thought to myself.

'Anyway,' Nat persists, 'we are going to invite an assortment of worthy causes to come and help us get down and dirty sprucing up this space, at the same time trying to convince us why we should give them free desk space and shared comms.'

As I look around the room, a ray of daylight steals in through a window, illuminating layers of thick dust and cobwebs. Could this sad, damp space really be returned into a thriving hub of community? My eyes alight on a beautiful stained-glass window of a man with his indigo cloak wrapped around a baby, his arm pointing along the panels of browns and ochre. Perhaps symbols of a desert. I look at the next panel and its now neglected story of struggle and hope. My musings are interrupted as I feel something unpleasant suddenly brush past my ankles. I shine my phone torch down to see a rat scamper its way through the aisles. As I let out a shriek, my phone and bag fall to the floor, plunging the room back into near darkness.

'Hello, is everything OK?' A voice of concern pierces the gloom. 'Hold on a mo, I'll turn on the lights.'

I hear the flick of a switch, and the church is flooded with light. A gorgeous man is standing there. Let there be light indeed!

'Allow me to introduce myself. I'm Father Guy Mowbray. So sorry you didn't realise the electricity was still turned on. I do hate to hear a damsel in distress.' He rifles his hand through waves of golden hair.

Hold on a mo, indeed. Did this guy say Father Guy Mowbray? Mowbray as in the pork pie and Father as in...'

'You must be Deborah?' He hurries up to me.

And you must be ... a vicar? I look at his low-slung jeans, his T-shirt hugging his muscled arms in just the right places. Surely it wasn't possible?

He crouches down to help me pick up the scattered contents of my bag. Close enough that I can almost feel the silken hairs on his bare arm brush against my own arm right through my double-down parka jacket.

'I see you like Doritos, too!' He scoops up a handful of chips—my other guilty pleasure. 'So tell me, Dorito-Deborah, are you a zesty salsa or chilli heatwave girl?' He smiles at me through eyes as intensely blue as the Indian Ocean I swam in only last month.

@NTS: strike all non-eco-friendly similes from mind

'Deb's favourite flavour is sour cream. I'm the flamin' hot lover.' Nat butts in, brushing past me. 'And of course, Deb's OK. It was just a brush with one of God's little creatures who have made this fine building their home over the past year! Good to see you again, Father Guy.' She shakes his hand as he stands up.

'Ah yes, this little problem of the rodent infestation has been bought to my attention, but I gather you have plans to deal with it straightaway. Anyway, good to meet you Dorito...er, Deborah. I've heard so much about you.' Father Guy takes my hand and holds it. I feel my body flood with warmth (spiritual warmth, of course) while an unpleasant chill settles over my brain at the mention of rats. The biggest rat being Natalie, with her latest less than consulted upon eco shenanigans— whatever the flavour.

'I believe everyone was terribly upset when the diocese decided to deconsecrate this church, only to have it remain unused, and unloved for a year while plans for its future were finalised.' Father Guy shakes his head. 'Terrible how quickly deterioration sets in.' He pauses to wipe a layer of thick dust off one of the pews. 'You must be pleased that the bishop has decided to assign a short-term lease to you ladies. I'm newly appointed to run the parish in this area, but the Bishop has asked me to oversee this project alongside my other church, St Margarets. Quite frankly, while I'm not sure this place can ever be made good, we will need to be in close contact.' He smiles at me. 'Natalie has told me that you are interested in holding unofficial multi-faith services here. Are you practising, Deborah?'

Practising what? My eyes run down his body.

'She's Jewish,' Nat interjects, 'but has always been very interested in learning more about the New Testament. After all, as she is always telling me, it is the most famous book in the history of the world!'

My protestations remain unvoiced as Nat's steel-tipped boot nudges my ankle.

'How wonderful,' says Father Guy. 'That is certainly something we can explore together. Anyway, talking about exploring, do let me give you a tour of the church. Our new shared home. For now. And do call me Guy.'

Gorgeous Guy—GG—it is, I decide, as we follow him back towards what he tells me was the vestibule at the church entrance.

'This church was built in the style of Gothic Revival in the second half of the 19th century,' GG explains. 'At this time England saw an unprecedented expansion in the number of churches being erected in response to a growing population. I do find it ironic that the so-called "enlightened" Industrial Revolution has led us to a point in history where anthropogenic climate change is now of grave threat to us all. Don't you agree, Deborah?'

'Jesus, just look at this!' Nat's outburst prevents me from having to answer GG.

@NTS: Anthro what?

'It's disgusting,' Nat says. 'This is the first thing we are gonna clean up.' She stares into a large white marble font. The assorted invertebrates laying prostrate in it are clearly not there to be baptised.

GG nods in agreement and leads on to the nave, the main area of the church. I look up at the cornice work decorated with ribbon motifs. All the walls, in fact the whole church, look quite frankly in need of a jolly good coat of paint—and not peach.

GG pauses besides a rather grand wooden dais, a small winding staircase leading up to a booth with badly chipped gilt paint.

'And here is the pulpit—the sacred desk!' As GG starts to ascend the stairs, I can't help but notice the way his taut buttocks press against his jeans. This guy totally works out.

Nat whispers: 'Bet you are praying Father Guy will be up there delivering his sermon on the mount. Like mount me!'

'Be quiet Natalie,' I hiss. 'As you well know, I am a … happily married woman.'

I imagine husbondage Stu and me at our lovely home, roaring fire illuminating our Farrow & Ball-painted walls, Stu sipping claret and sampling the cheese plate while reading his FT. Me, well into the latest edition of 'Grazia.' Mind you, Stu has been away rather a lot recently with work. Best replace that vignette with me on my own tucking into a cheese and pickle sarnie.

'Wow, look at this!' Nat dives into an ornately carved wooden cubicle and pulls the curtain behind her. 'This must have been the confession box,' says her muffled voice from inside.

I touch what must have once been a wonderful velvet curtain in a deep shade of carmine. It's now just a mouldering piece of fabric. This certainly could do with a good dry-clean. I stare at the intricate carved lattice work, a *fleur de lis* carved into the confessional window, which casts a shadow on the facing wall.

'And through here, ladies, is the vestry,' GG leads on.

We follow him into a small room at the back of the church. 'This will be my office.' Nat says. Then her voice rises. 'Wait a minute, what's going on? There's a bed in here!'

It's actually a blow-up plastic mattress laid on the floor. But I must admit it does look rather cosy with its Thomas the Tank Engine duvet cover, pillows and a pink floral bedside lamp complete with tassels. There's also a bedside book, 'The Moneyless Manifesto.' It's laying open at a chapter headed: 'How I started to live without money and thrive with the local gift economy.'

'Hmm, I'm sure there's a very simple explanation,' GG murmurs as we follow him back into the church. 'But I'm sure it will be the first of many challenges that might make this place untenable.'

'Just imagine this fantastic space filled with desks, people brimming with energy and ideas.' Nat, ever the optimist, ignores GG's gloomy comment and turns round and grins. 'The pews can be used to create seating around tables made from pallets, and recycled wood could be sourced for our cafe.'

Nat has a questionable concept of recycling. I remember that when we were creating our community garden all sorts of suspiciously new pieces of furniture started appearing, including a bathtub in which Nat grew herbs—a bath from a very expensive bathroom boutique in Primrose Hill that apparently had just been left outside the shop in the street.'

'This space is a wonderful canvas, Deb.' Nat throws her arm around me. 'You are a designer, so design this.'

'I gather you may set up a microbrewery in the crypt?' GG adds.

'You want to brew beer in a church?' I blurt out.

'We certainly do, Deb,' says Nat. 'And we will grow the hops ourselves. We could call it: "Land of Hop and Glory!"'

We all burst out laughing.

'What I don't understand, Father, er, Guy, is how come we been given this space?' My unplanned question pops out.

'To be frank, the Bishop has been approached by a developer who's keen to turn this church into a block of flats.' GG coughs to clear his throat. 'But the diocese, in conjunction with the council, have decided to take time some time to consider what's best for, er… the whole parish. Increasingly cash-strapped ecclesiastical bodies are having to sell off more and more churches.'

'But if it's all about financial turnover, how on earth could anything we do compete with a block of flats?'

GG sighs. 'I believe a successful parish project is one that benefits, and pays homage to, the history of the community. The Bishop and I are therefore keen to hear your plan, which Natalie told him you have both been working very hard on.'

'Er, plenty of time for that, Father Guy. Why don't we go and look outside?' Nat grabs my hand, and charges towards the door at the back of the church.

'Deb was very interested to take a look at the flying buttresses.'

We go outside into the back garden. In front of us, the trunks of apple trees, from what would have once been a wonderful orchard, lean over despondently; their gnarled branches look like they hadn't been pruned since the Creation. A garden of Eden, *pas exactment.* I look around at the compacted clay soil, the only evidence of life being a profusion of bindweed and brambles now covering everything.

'Jesus never promised us a rose garden, but he'll go through the thorns with us,' Nat adds her spiritual offering as she starts to pull the weeds out.

I walk on along the rather uneven cobbled path and let out a yelp as I stub my toe on something hard. I bend down and brush aside weeds to uncover the start of a lovely old brick wall.

'I wonder if this garden is a vegetable potager based on the four-bed cross design?' I ask GG. Who says watching 'Pointless' on daytime TV has no benefits?

'Well, wouldn't that be wonderful.' GG smiles at me. 'I have visited many monastic gardens and always find it marvellous to look out from a window and see the garden in the shape of a cross. I look forward to uncovering the secrets of this garden with you…and more, Dorito-Deborah. As it is said: "I am the vine, you are the branches; he who abides in Me and I in him, will bear much fruit."

I look away as my face flushes a ripe shade of blackberry to match the bramble clawing against my parka.

'I want to get down and dirty and build a cob pizza oven here.' Nat gives a wry smile. 'It's the only down and dirty coming my way in the foreseeable future,' she pauses, 'seeing that my old man left me last night.'

'What? Pete's left you?' I blurt out. Talk about jaw hitting floor…

'Yeah, he's run off with Di, the opera singer who lives in our block. They've gone on a classical tour of Italy.'

Pete? Nat's meek hubby who wouldn't say boo to a goose? A man whose idea of culture is a karaoke night at the Bull and Gate pub? Running off with an opera singer and touring coliseums?

'I'm soo sorry, Nat. I don't know what to say.' I wrap my arm around her.

She smiles sadly. 'Well, we need all the time we can get to concentrate on this project, don't we Deb? Then there's the launch of my political career to think of.'

Political career? The nearest political sentiment Nat has ever expressed was when the council tried to close her beloved Lidl, next door to this church, over an infestation of rats.

All thoughts of politics, Nat's sad news about absconding Pete, plus her *fait accompli* statement about us needing time to concentrate on a project that two hours ago didn't exist, are lost when we hear a rustling in a tree at the far end of the garden. We all turn to see a squirrel dart down the tree trunk and disappear over the fence to the Lidl car park. A head—a human one—appears through the branches.

'Hi down there! I'm just doing a bit of scrumping. This is the one tree that seems to have borne any fruit this year. I blame the wet spring.' A man in his early forties climbs down from the tree, carefully balancing a circle of apples in a battered, upturned fedora hat. He's wearing khaki shirt and trousers and I can't help but chuckle at what looks like a botanical

Indiana Jones: no whip but an apple picker, and no gun in his holster but a rusty pair of secateurs.

'My name is Richard. My friends call me Rich.' He has a broad Geordie accent. 'I'm picking fruit and apples that would have gone to waste. Are you the ladies starting up the project here?' He walks up to us. 'I'm embarking on a project where I'm going to live for one year without any money. I'm going to teach folk to rethink their reliance on money's divisive power and show them how to escape its grip.'

'Is that your bed in the vestry?' Nat snaps.

'I'm here to introduce you to the sharing and gift economy. With the challenges of the climate emergency and global inequality, we've got to find new ways to live successful lives. Resource depletion is rife.' Rich sighs. 'And yes, that is my bed,' he says blushing, as he tries not to stare at her body. Nat may be petite in height, but she is generously built-in other departments. And not even her works jacket with its Charles Wilson Tool-Hire branding, can hide this fact.

'Well, I'm not having you depleting our resources.' Nat says, voice rising.

'Nice duvet cover on your bed, Richard,' I change the subject. 'Did you get it from IKEA? I love popping in there, everything is so cheap.'

'IKEA?' Richard snaps. 'That's a typical example of a corporation that has used the economies-of-scale model to create the problems that the world faces today.' Well, that's telling us…

'Ah! There you are Father Guy,' a much calmer voice interrupts. It belongs to a very smartly dressed man who has just walked into the garden. 'So sorry for being a little early.'

'Ladies, this is Thomas Montjoy. He runs a company called Greener Properties,' GG mumbles in an embarrassed tone. 'I, er …wasn't expecting to meet you here, Thomas.'

'Greener *what*? Nat directs her less than placatory tone to Thomas Montjoy.

I stare at his Savile Row suit and highly polished shoes, which are outshone by an even more polished smile.

'Father Guy, I just wanted to give you a sneak preview of the brochure before it goes to print.' Montjoy scrolls down on his phone to show Father Guy various pictures. 'You can see the flats will have off-street parking here and …'

I push aside a bramble and walk over to Montjoy. I peer over GG's shoulder to see the picture of a gleaming new boutique apartment block—one that is to be built on the site of this church.

'Of course, I understand it's entirely speculative right now,' Montjoy laughs. 'Look, I've got a driver parked outside who can whisk us off to the new gastropub down the road. I can fill you in on the details there.'

'Yoo-hoo!' There's another new voice. We turn to see a woman come strolling into the garden. Wondering how this day could get any stranger, I stare at the woman's tweed braid-trimmed Chanel jacket. An Alice band holds back a bob of perfectly groomed blonde hair. 'I'm Sacha,' she says in a very plummy voice. 'I had a tweet saying you are inviting folk to be involved in a new eco project. My pitch is this: does anyone fancy a cricket burger? After all, edible insects are going to play a big part in the future of our food security.'

The stunned silence that follows is broken only by the sound of another apple falling to the ground. Did we hear her right? Cricket burger?

'Anyway, Father Guy, shall we go?' Montjoy points to the door.

'Some lovely apples you could eat right here,' Rich picks one up and offers it to GG. 'And they're free.'

GG looks at the green apple, which, like his face, is flushed with crimson. He runs his hand along its lovely waxy skin.

'I mean, I'm not offering you a cricket burger right away,' Sacha says hopefully. 'It's more like…'

GG pops the apple into his hoodie pocket and turns to follow Montjoy out of the garden.

I wave at GG who gives me a slightly flustered look and waves back, I hear a crunch—and not of the apple kind. I bend down to see that the heel of my new Jimmy Choo has snapped on a cobble stone.

'Well I think that went brilliantly!' says Nat ignoring the fact that I'm now holding a broken designer shoe, and am about to refer to GG's boss in a less than devotional manner.

'Apart from that Thomas Montjoy.'

Nat takes the apple that Rich hands her and bites into it. She links my arm, 'Look around Deb. Imagine chickens and bees, wildflowers and communal meals.' She points to my shoe. 'It's our new story of High Heels to Small Holdings: our very own good life.'